"Why are you doing this?" Alex asked.

"Because I want you in my life."

She looked out the window where a plane taxied away from the gate. "I'm in your life as much as I can be, Chase."

He tugged her around until she faced him and then he locked his gaze with hers. "I don't want us to just be friends, Alex. I want to share my life with you. The way we did before. Don't you remember how it was? You were my best friend. We told each other everything. I know you and you know me in a way no one else does. Tell me you don't miss that and I'll leave you alone."

She closed her eyes. Why did he have to do this now, when she was feeling more vulnerable than ever?

Dear Reader,

Thanks for checking out my second release with Harlequin Superromance! Whether you have a traditional or not so traditional family, my guess is you've had both moments of challenge and triumph with your family. My goal in *A Family Reunited* was to show that no matter how crazy life can get, our families can be a source of strength.

Maybe you can relate to Alexandra Peterson's desire to cut a wide path around her father and siblings. Their attitudes and behavior are a mystery to her and she has little patience to try to decipher them, but when her brother falls victim to cancer and her father calls on her for help, Alex's response is to return home, not only to assist with her brother's care, but to also reconcile the broken relationships of her past.

She's ill prepared to include ex-boyfriend, Chase Carrolton, in those reconciliations, though. However, when Chase proves to be a vital link in her plan to find her brother a stem-cell donor, she has little choice but to confront her unresolved feelings for her high school sweetheart. How can Alex hope to stay focused on her family when Chase announces his plan to win back her heart?

I hope you enjoy Alex and Chase's story. I'm in the process of creating my new website. It should be completed by the time you read this, so stop by and say hi at www.doriegraham.com. I'd love to hear from you.

Enjoy!

Dorie Graham

A Family Reunited

DORIE GRAHAM

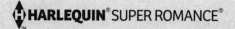

HARLEQUIN®SUPER ROMANCE®

ISBN-13: 978-0-373-71851-1

A FAMILY REUNITED

HARLEQUIN®
™ www.Harlequin.com

Printed in U.S.A.

ABOUT THE AUTHOR

Dorie was initially struck by the writing muse at the tender age of nine, when she stayed up past her bedtime for the first time ever to finish a short story. That attempt resulted in her teacher reading her work aloud to the class, then submitting her story to *Highlights* magazine. Unfortunately, Dorie took the magazine's request to shorten the story as a flat rejection.

Over the years she followed the muse from time to time, but didn't get serious about writing until after the birth of her third child. Even then it took about five years of juggling husband, children, nonprofit work and her writing before she finally mastered the art of rejection and landed her first sale in September 2001. Currently, she resides in Roswell, Georgia, a suburb of metro-Atlanta, with her two supportive daughters. A full-time working, single mom, she spends her free time hanging with her daughters and friends, watching movies, running and of course, writing. You can stop by and visit her at www.doriegraham.com.

Books by Dorie Graham

Other titles by this author available in ebook format.

I've made dedications to my parents and my sisters in previous books, but I'd be remiss if I dedicated this book to anyone other than my birth family. Theresa and Raymond Buckley, Marion Buckley Shoults, David Buckley, Carol Anderson, Maureen McRorie, Cliff Buckley and Cathleen Breed, thank you all for sharing with me so many ups and downs and especially for standing by me during the worst of the downs. I love you all.

One of my favorite parts of writing this book came from researching Chase's profession as a university museum curator. I had the wonderful fortune to meet Julia Brock, curator at a local university and her good friend, A., both of whom supplied me with invaluable information and brainstorming fodder for the scenes involving Chase's work environment.

Ladies, I couldn't have done it without you! A., look for your special thank-you at the end of the book.

Also, much appreciation to Jamie Latrice Allen, social service case manager/post foster care at Chatham County Department of Family and Children Services for helping me iron out all the details relating to foster care and custody proceedings.

I hope I managed to ask all the right questions in these areas and apply the answers accurately. Any errors I've made are a result of my misinterpretation of the excellent information provided and in no means a reflection on these wonderfully helpful sources.

CHAPTER ONE

ALEXANDRA PETERSON PULLED the pillow from her face and squinted at the digital display of the clock on her nightstand. 5:57 a.m.? How had she managed to wake before her alarm after sleeping less than four hours? With a groan, she rolled to sitting. No sense in trying to go back to sleep. She was awake and she might as well get to the office to prepare for her meeting with her boss, the senior vice president of finance, Pete Andrews, and the CFO, Darren Roberts.

A quick half an hour later, thanks to having laid out her clothes and leaving her computer bag packed and ready by the door the previous night, she sped along I-95 toward her office in midtown Baltimore. At least traffic was still fairly clear at this hour. A record twenty minutes later she counted off the floors as the elevator carried her to six. Thankfully, the management had updated the elevators in the old brick building.

Subdued lighting greeted her as she swiped into the quiet reception area. Only one or two of her coworkers ever arrived this early and they were at the other end of the floor, closer to the executive suites. She enjoyed arriving at her office before the crowd and the rush.

Quiet blanketed her as she docked her laptop in the privacy of her office. While the computer whirred to life, she let her gaze drift out her window, over the parking lot of the old church next door. She might not have the best

view, but she'd worked hard for the promotion that had
snagged her the tiny back office.

Not that she'd minded the long hours and extra work.
She'd loved her job as a senior finance manager for Mana
Health Care, a company specializing in managing long-
term-care facilities. Now as vice president of finance, she
finally had the SVP of finance's, as well as the CFO's,
ear and could help implement some of the changes she
saw as necessary for making them a more efficient and
profitable corporation. That is, efficient now and hopefully profitable down the road.

Sighing, she settled into her chair. She had to put some
finishing touches on the presentation she planned to share
with her boss and his boss at their 10:00 a.m. meeting.
Confidence filled her. She took pride in always showing
up prepared.

Two hours later she blinked, trying to drum up some
moisture to soothe the grit from her eyes. Her head
pounded, the result of too little sleep. She grabbed her
coffee cup, only to find she'd already sucked down the
contents.

"Well, that won't do," she said as she slipped out of her
office and headed toward the break room, cup in hand.

The consultant, who worked in clinical, whose name
she could never remember, headed in her direction. Alex
worked her mouth into what she hoped was a smile and
nodded at the woman. The consultant frowned, passing
her without comment.

Alex shrugged. Maybe the woman was having an off
morning. She could certainly relate to that. The scent of
strong coffee filled the air as Alex approached the cof-
feemaker.

Stifling a yawn, she wavered over the baskets filled
with the little liquid creamers before grabbing a handful

of French vanilla containers. Only the good stuff would do this morning.

Whispering sounded over her shoulder. She turned to find a couple of the junior financial analysts standing behind her. They straightened as she smiled.

"Good morning," she said. "Sorry, let me get out of your way. I'm moving a little slowly today. Late night."

The older guy, George, arched his eyebrows. "Working hard to get all of your reporting turned in, no doubt."

"Actually, yes," she said, satisfaction filling her.

Staying up until the wee hours completing her efficiency savings report for her boss had been worth it. She'd finished the summary and emailed it to him along with the detailed report before crashing for those few hours of sleep. He'd obviously given her work his seal of approval, since he'd copied her on his forward to the CFO early that morning.

"Yes, we all know," the younger analyst said, anger evident in his tone.

"Oh." She cradled her full coffee mug in her hands as she began to feel uneasy. Surely word hadn't gotten out yet about her suggested pay cuts. "Have a good day," she said, before turning to leave.

Two more coworkers passed Alex without comment or acknowledgement of her greetings. Dismay filled her as she slipped back into her office. They must have heard about her suggestion. Why else would she be getting the cold shoulder? Did that mean the company was planning to move forward with her plan?

Shaking off her nerves, she opened the report she'd poured so much of her heart into. The neat rows of numbers and totals at the bottom soothed her. Here in the cells and formulas everything made sense. She might not understand the people around her, especially not this morning, but numbers always spoke to her.

The printer hummed as it printed the summary spreadsheet. She pulled the page from the output tray and smiled as she reviewed the neat columns, the bold totals that all lined up and told the financial story of Mana Health Care in succinct detail. How satisfying. Darren would be very pleased to see her plan to reduce their spending and eventually increase their profit margin. With her suggestions in place they'd break even for the next quarter or two, then be back in the black by year's end—quite a feat considering the current state of the economy.

The long hours over the past week and missed weekends had been worth it. Alex had drilled down into every area of their business, shaving off the extra expenses at each opportunity. Frowning now, she reviewed the savings they would gain from the small across-the-board pay cut. She'd hated to include it, but it meant keeping jobs they'd otherwise have to eliminate.

Yawning, she glanced at the time display on her monitor. She'd be meeting with them in less than twenty minutes. Surely this was the icing on the cake she needed, just in time for bonus incentive reviews, where she'd recommended only a slight reduction.

They didn't want to destroy employee morale, after all.

The chirp of an incoming instant message drew her attention again to the screen. Anticipation filled her. A little balloon with Darren's name displayed the incoming message. Reviewed report. Please stop by to discuss.

Now? she replied, glancing at her calendar and their 10:00 a.m. meeting entry.

Yes.

What about her boss, Pete? Had he also been called

in early? Surely, he'd want to be present in any review of the report.

Her heart thudded as she typed, On my way.

The scent of overheated coffee wafted over her as she passed the employee break room and headed toward the CFO's office at the far end of the floor, three fresh copies of her presentation in hand. She padded along the carpet, pacing herself so as not to arrive too soon while remaining prompt. She didn't want to give the impression she was overly anxious.

Instant messages offered little insight into the sender's mood. Had Darren been pleased with all her hard work? Did he want her to find more savings opportunities in any of the departments? Did he agree with her assessment on where they could trim the fat from their company?

She stopped outside the CFO's closed door and turned questioningly to his executive assistant, who was stationed at a desk across the aisle. Alex said, "He asked me to drop by."

The young woman continued typing without looking up, saying, "Stevens is in with him."

Alex nodded, though the woman remained focused on her typing. Mark Stevens was head of procurement, and that department had played heavily in her report. She'd identified some serious savings opportunities in both their capital expenditures and daily operational expenses. Was Darren discussing her findings with Mark?

"Did he call Pete in, as well?"

Again without looking up, the woman shook her head. "I believe he's taking the morning off."

"Oh," Alex said, surprised. Maybe Pete would call in for their meeting.

She faced the closed door and squared her shoulders.

The CFO had summoned her. She tapped lightly, then pushed the door open far enough to duck her head in.

Darren glanced at her and held up his index finger. "Give us a minute, Alex."

"Sure," she said. She withdrew and quietly closed the door, stifling her impatience. Why had he asked for her if he wasn't ready? The efficiency report was only the beginning. She had a pile of spreadsheets waiting for her to review, a conference call and committee meetings to prepare for.

She hovered outside Darren's office as muffled laughter sounded from inside. She frowned. They couldn't be discussing her report. Her recommendations hadn't included anything laughable.

She glanced at the two upholstered chairs in the nook between the CFO's and CEO's offices. Should she take a seat to wait? She glanced again at the CFO's executive assistant. The woman continued her intent typing.

Alex settled into the closest chair, folding her hands over her notebook and presentations. Too bad she'd left her smartphone in her office. She could at least have been tackling some of her email.

Anticipation filled her as the moments ticked by and more laughter sounded through the door. Obviously, Darren was in a good mood. Could his good spirits be a result of her report? She'd presented a solid plan for putting them in the black by year's end. Certainly this was reason to celebrate.

Five minutes later the CFO's door opened. Darren stood in the doorway, shaking Mark Stevens's hand. "I'm glad we're on the same page in this, Mark," Darren said. "We've got to hit the ground running with this new initiative. I knew I could count on you."

New initiative? She'd suggested a very specific action

plan to go along with her report. Could that be this new initiative? Alex straightened all five feet four inches of herself, still feeling small next to Mark's six plus feet of bulk. All smiles, the man seemed to be taking the cuts to his department in stride. Plastering on a smile, she waited patiently while the men exchanged pleasantries.

At last, Mark headed down the hall and Darren turned to her, gesturing toward his open door. "After you."

With a nod she stepped into the lush inner sanctum of the CFO's office. Mahogany gleamed among the splashes of potted plants strategically placed throughout the space. She perched in one of the chairs at the conference table dominating the area near the floor-to-ceiling windows. Where her view reflected the gray of the worn parking lot next door, his view took in the leafy green trails of the park below.

"Good morning, Alex," Darren said as he took the seat across from her, his hands steepled before him.

"Good morning, Darren," she said, gripping her pen. "Mark seemed to be in a good mood."

Her boss nodded. "His son is headed for regionals."

"That's great," Alex said, though she had no idea what regionals were, or that Mark even had a son, for that matter.

"It is, actually. My daughter was into competitive swimming at that age. She made it to state."

Again, Alex was at a loss, so she smiled and nodded. "Is Pete calling in?"

He frowned. "Pete has personal business he's attending to this morning."

"Oh. I guess I can follow up with him later." She slid a copy of the presentation over to him. "I put together this slide presentation to show how we can implement the new strategies we'll need to execute some of the savings in my report."

He flattened his hand on the presentation without looking at it. "How's your family, Alex?"

"My family?" she asked, again tamping down her impatience.

The company's current spending trends were slowly bleeding away any chance of stability. If they didn't take quick action, even her plan wouldn't be able to help them. They needed to act and they needed to act now.

"Yes," he said, his gray eyes intent on her. "I know you don't have a husband or kids, but surely you have a significant other, or at least parents, siblings…"

The mention of her family sent the familiar unease skittering through her. Her family was the epitome of dysfunctional, and as far as a significant other, she couldn't remember the last time she'd even missed having one.

What did any of this matter?

"I don't… They're fine," she said. She hated to admit that beyond her younger brother and sister she had little idea how the rest of her family was doing.

"Good." He nodded. "Family is important, don't you think?"

She shifted in her seat. "I suppose, though…it really depends on the family."

His eyebrows arched. "I guess you're right. For me, my family comes first." He stopped, his gray gaze again piercing her.

She nodded, saying, "That's great."

"I think it's important we're all on the same page here, Alex."

"Sure," she said, her discomfort intensifying. What was he talking about? Why weren't they discussing her report? "It's important we're all team players."

"Yes, we should all want what's best for the greater good of all," he said.

She exhaled. "Yes, and I think my findings support that. I know an across-the-board wage cut might not be met with the greatest enthusiasm, but when everyone understands it's for the greater good, we shouldn't have too much trouble implementing it. Surely it's better than the massive layoffs we'd need instead."

He picked up her presentation, but rather than flip through the pages, he rolled it into a tight tube. "You did good work on that report. I want you to know I appreciate your efforts. We can rest assured we looked at all alternatives before moving forward with the new company initiative."

"Yes, I heard you mention something about that to Mark. Do you mean an initiative based on the cost-effective measures in my email and supported by my report?" She gestured toward the tube in his hand. "I've detailed an action plan—"

"We're going with the layoffs."

Surprise filled her. She blinked. "What?"

"You did good work. Your report summarized in clear detail how far off our profitability mark we are. Unfortunately, your findings indicate we're not in a position to play around with this." He dropped the rolled presentation. "We need drastic action."

"No, wait. I think maybe you misinterpreted the data. The across-the-board cut would eliminate the need for layoffs."

He shook his head. "The board won't go for it. They held an emergency conference call early this morning. They're taking an aggressive stance. At this point it wouldn't be enough. They're banking on a profit this quarter. Break even isn't going to do it."

Her stomach knotted. "But you're talking about people's livelihoods."

His lips tightened into a thin line. "We're talking about the greater good of all, or of the majority in this instance. I was hoping we'd be in agreement on this."

Confusion filled her. "I don't understand how the board can do this. It really isn't necessary to lay people off."

"It's done, Alex. I forwarded them your findings as soon as I reviewed them. They're all appreciative of the work you've done. We're all happy to give you glowing recommendations."

"What?"

He nodded toward his closed door. "My assistant is already drafting my letter of reference."

"What?" she asked again. How could this be happening? "Are you saying I'm fired?"

"It's a layoff, Alex. These things happen. Don't take it personally. It's business. While the board appreciated your efforts, the members feel your position is extraneous."

Her mind whirled. *She* was being laid off? And because she'd killed herself to give them the report that had helped them decide this was their best move? She stared at him, speechless.

Darren had the decency not to be able to make eye contact. "Again, you've done an impeccable job. HR will be contacting you this morning regarding your severance package. Actually, they were supposed to be in on this meeting with you, but they're tied up with the rest of the layoffs. I assured them you'd be okay with a separate debrief. Pete really felt I should wait for him to discuss this with you, as well, but I also assured him you'd understand."

She slowly rose, leaving her copies of the presentation on his conference table. Her reflection stared back at her from the polished mahogany. A mixture of anger, disbelief and despair rose in her.

Without another word, she turned toward the door.

"Alex," Darren said, "this isn't easy for any of us. These are the times we all draw on the strength of our families."

She merely shook her head as she pushed through his door. There was no strength in her family. For as long as she could remember, her father had owned a hardware store. Duct tape was his magic fix for just about everything. One day her aunt had borrowed their vacuum cleaner, only to find it held together with the silvery tape. She'd jokingly dubbed them the Broken Family and the name had stuck.

The knot in Alex's stomach tightened. Her senior year in high school her mother had caught her father cheating on her. They'd gone through an embittered divorce that truly left their family broken in the worst way.

No, Alex didn't have family to support her through this, nor did she want one.

She straightened. She was a strong, independent woman. She'd find a way through this mess and she'd do it on her own. If Darren thought believing in family meant they were on the same page, it was just as well she was leaving. That was one page she didn't care to decipher.

CHAPTER TWO

THE REST OF THE MORNING passed in a surreal haze. Alex tied up the few projects she felt compelled to hand off to one or two of the remaining financial analysts. She couldn't bring herself to give anything to Mark Stevens, though. Darren's pronouncement that the board felt her position was extraneous was a bending of the truth. Mark was evidently taking over her job and one of his managers was taking over his role as vice president of procurement. That manager's position was being eliminated.

So, what Darren had actually meant was that Alex, herself, was extraneous.

George, the older analyst from the break room that morning, leaned against her desk as she handed him the manila folder of data she'd put together on the company's purchase card usage.

"Darren had this on a back burner, but we...*you* can realize at least a twenty percent savings by following up on noncompliant usage and instituting blocks on key accounts." She wiggled her fingers over the file. "It's all in the email I sent you with the electronic copies."

George shrugged and said, "I'll see what I can do to get someone excited about it. If I can get Mark to buy into it, he'll get Darren on board."

She nodded and dumped another file in her to-be-shredded pile. "Thanks, that's probably a good strategy."

"It isn't your fault, you know."

She glanced at him, her eyebrows raised.

"You know," he said. "This morning in the break room and all the talk flying around today. You were just doing your job with your efficiencies report."

She sank into her chair. "I gave them all the ammunition they needed, didn't I?"

"If it makes you feel any better, most people think your layoff isn't justified. Kind of cold of them, actually," he said as he flipped through the contents of the file. He looked up and held her gaze. "You do good work."

"Thanks," she said, though her confidence had bottomed out. How was she supposed to find a new job in this economy? Why had she been so diligent in pulling together that report?

George straightened. "I should get back to work. Well…thanks and good luck."

She merely nodded as he left. HR had given her the option of leaving right away and cashing in vacation time or staying to finish the week. She couldn't imagine sticking around where she wasn't wanted.

Her cell phone vibrated as she packed up the last of her personal belongings. She shook her head as her boss's name scrolled across the screen. How could Pete have abandoned her this morning? Surely, he'd been informed of the board's decision.

She pressed Accept, but before she could utter a word, Pete said, "Alex, I'm so sorry."

"I'm stunned. I never saw this coming."

"I don't know what to say. I was very upset when Darren called me."

"Well, you're safe, aren't you?" she asked.

A short silence hummed across the connection. "I opted for an early retirement. I thought it might spare you, but it didn't make a difference in the end."

"I'm so sorry."

"It's okay. I couldn't stay with a company that doesn't value its employees more than that. How are you?"

"I'll survive."

"I'll put out some feelers for you. We'll get you another position. Darren's a fool to let you slip away."

"Thanks, Pete, I appreciate that."

"I'm just so sorry things turned out this way, Alex. Keep in touch."

"I will," she said before disconnecting.

An hour later she walked into the quiet of her apartment. She clicked on her music to dispel the stillness. Adele's smoky tones filled the air. Alex set down her box of personal items and closed her eyes, fighting back the panic threatening to consume her.

What if she couldn't find another financial position? How could Darren have let the board vote against her? How could they have gone with tampering with people's livelihoods when a wage cut had been a perfectly viable solution? There was right and wrong and these layoffs were wrong.

A sick feeling swirled in her stomach. It was just as well she'd gotten the boot. She was responsible for all those other people losing their jobs. At least the guilt was somehow more tolerable knowing she was in the same boat.

She should have never let herself feel secure in that job. She'd been ignorantly blissful since her promotion. How foolish of her. All good things came to an end. It was inevitable.

With a shake of her head, she moved into her kitchen. Maybe a beer would dull the sting of her layoff. She paused with her hand on her refrigerator. The light on her answering machine blinked from the desk tucked into the nook by the laundry room door.

She had no idea why she kept the old relic. She'd been meaning to cancel her house landline. Everyone who mattered called her on her cell. The calls on her landline were mostly solicitors, except for her younger sister, Becky, who sometimes called on that number.

Though Becky, always a daddy's girl, had remained sympathetic to their father postdivorce, she tried in vain to bring peace to their family. Year after year, she'd attempted to get everyone together for the holidays. The only time Alex paid her calls any attention, though, was when her sister called with updates on their mother.

She pressed the message button and headed back to the refrigerator. She'd just located a lone bottle of dark ale tucked away at the back behind an old container of rice from Chinese takeout when a familiar voice played from the old machine.

"Um, hello, Alexandra, this is your father. I know we haven't talked in a long time and I know you've never forgiven me for what happened, but I really need you to call me. Please. It's important."

He left his number. The machine cut off the recording to auto-rewind. She opened the ale and took a long swallow as the tape whirred to a stop. Shaking her head she sat at her desk and turned on her computer.

She stared at the answering machine. No way was she calling her father. Nothing he had to say would change the fact he'd destroyed his marriage and their family with his selfishness. She had better things to do with her time, like find a new job. As her desktop booted up, she pressed the delete button on her answering machine and took another long swallow as a beep announced the successful deletion of the message.

A THICK COAT of green pollen coated the worn wooden steps of Chase Carrolton's front porch as he hefted his suitcase across the old planks. Telltale footprints marked the passage of an earlier visitor. He sighed, weariness filling him as he jiggled his key into the front lock. The door opened without him having to turn the key, though.

He shook his head, glancing again at the footprints. His young stepsister, Kara, had evidently crashed here while he'd been out of town and once again she'd neglected to lock the door.

The scent of roasted chicken filled the air as he rolled his bag into the front room. He fought the smile tugging at his lips. Whatever trouble the girl had gotten herself into this time, it was nice to enter his house and for it to have the semblance of home. He'd grown weary of returning from these exhibition setup trips to the emptiness.

"Chase?" Kara Anders headed toward him from the kitchen, drying her hands on a dish towel. Her long blond hair was tied back in a ponytail and pink tinged her cheeks. "I was guessing you'd be back tonight. Dinner's almost ready."

"Kara, does Pansy know you're here?" he asked. Pansy was his stepsister's third foster mother this year.

Kara did an about-face and headed back toward the kitchen. "I'm sautéing Brussels sprouts, just the way you like. I even found some of the sun-dried tomatoes from last time in your pantry."

With a shake of his head he discarded his bag at the foot of the staircase and followed her into the kitchen. "So, let me guess, she doesn't get you, wants to control you and won't see reason. And where did you get the Brussels sprouts and chicken, by the way? Please tell me you didn't pilfer them from your foster parents."

She cast him a scathing glance as she pulled the

chicken from the oven. "I have a job, remember? I work at the ice cream shop." Stirring the Brussels sprouts with a wooden spoon, she said, "These would come out so much better if you'd get an iron skillet."

"Of course, an iron skillet. It's on my list. What's going on? Did you get into another fight? I can't take the cops showing up here accusing me of harboring a runaway again."

"Fine." She threw the wooden spoon into the sink. "If you want me to go back to that hellhole, I will."

He steeled himself against the hurt in her dark eyes. He always let himself get taken in by that look and he always lived to regret it. It wasn't his fault she'd ended up in foster care.

He'd been only twenty and still in school when his father had gotten arrested for driving under the influence. Since Kara's mother had long since fled and no other relative stepped forward, the girl had been declared abandoned. It had broken Chase's heart, and he'd kept in close touch. It was the best he could do, but Kara had a tendency toward trouble. She'd already had one stint in juvie court because of her temper.

"When are you going to start making the best of your situation?" he asked. "You can't rock the boat."

"I don't. I try to get along."

"I've lived with you. I know how you are. This is your third foster home in, what, five months? And it's never your fault? You're such a peach to get along with?"

Kara grabbed her book bag from one of the kitchen chairs and hoisted it over her shoulder. "Okay, I'm out of here. But you have no idea what it's like."

Regret filled him. "Wait." He gestured toward the food. "Thank you for the wonderful dinner. Please stay and share it with me."

She glared at him for a moment before easing her book bag back onto the chair. "I know your mom ran off first and then mine left us, so it's been kind of crappy for you, but at least you've always had your dad."

He opened his mouth, but she stayed him with her hand. "I know he has his issues, but at least he's *your* dad and he's not bad when he's sober. Look, you've never been in foster care, shuffled from house to house, living with people who just see you as a meal ticket. It's not like they really want kids. It sucks, Chase. I hate it there."

He pulled out a carving knife and busied himself with the chicken while she spoke. It was always like this with Kara. She'd come to blow off steam. Like it or not, besides his father, she was the only family he had. And she was right. He'd never been in her shoes, so how could he judge her?

After serving up the food, he settled across from her at the table. "I know it's no picnic, Kara, but you have to admit trouble seems to follow you. I can't handle any more run-ins with the cops. You've got to straighten up."

She stabbed at the chicken on her plate. "I don't look for trouble. I've been trying, honestly. It just isn't easy."

"How's school?" he asked.

Again, she scowled at him, then just shook her head. "Trig?"

"It's Greek to me. I try, but I'm so lost I don't know what questions to ask to try to figure it out. I wanted to go in early to see my teacher before school, but the freaking bus takes forever to get there from the boons where we live." She brightened and turned to him. "I'll bet if I could catch the bus from here I'd get there in plenty of time to get help before school."

"You mean like a one-time spend the night, just so you

can make it in early?" he asked. "I could just drop you off on my way to the museum."

"You would do that?"

"Of course. Why not? I'd have to clear your spending the night with Pansy, of course."

Kara's smile faded. "She'll say no."

"Why would she say no?"

"You don't get it. She hates me. If she thinks I'll benefit in any way, she'll be totally against it."

"Come on," he said. "She has no reason to be disagreeable. I'll talk to her."

"Forget it." She dropped her napkin on the table and rose. "I'd better get back. She'll be pitching a fit that I wasn't there last night to do my chores."

Disappointment filled him as he rose to face her. "You stayed here last night and didn't tell her where you were, didn't you? Why do you do things like that? No wonder she's upset with you. I'm surprised the cops haven't been by yet, looking for you again. You can't keep going MIA like that."

"She doesn't care. She doesn't notice most of the time. It's only when she needs something from me that it's a problem."

"Is it really that bad?"

"Yes," she said. Her gaze slipped away. "Like I said, you have no idea."

"I'll talk to Pansy and we'll find a day this week for you to spend the night and get help the next morning. Maybe I can find a tutor who lives out your way."

"Forget it," she repeated as she again hoisted her book bag to her shoulder. "It won't work out. It doesn't matter."

She headed toward the front door and he strode after her. "I'll drive you."

"No," she said and faced him with her hands up to

stop him. "The shit's going to fly as is and it'll be worse if you're there. I'll take the bus."

"No, Kara, it's late. I'll drive you. I'll just drop you off. I won't stay if you don't want me to. I don't even have to come in. She never has to see me."

"She sees everything and then she'll be pissed at you, too, and she won't let me spend the night. I promise you, it's better this way. Really."

The determination in her gaze halted him. "I don't want to cause you any trouble," he said. "I just need to know you're safe."

Her dark gaze softened. "I know that." She hugged him—a quick but fierce hug. "Maybe she'll let me come stay. You can try asking her. I'll text you when I'm there. I'll be fine."

"Promise?"

"Yes." She blew him a kiss then headed out the door.

He followed her, stopping on the porch as she hurried down the steps. "I'm driving over there if I don't get your text," he said.

She waved in response and hurried up the street toward the bus stop. He glanced at the sun low on the horizon. She'd be late getting home. He should have made her call her foster mom to tell her she was on the way. He'd have to get the woman's number. Surely, he could intervene on Kara's behalf and help make peace between the two.

He stayed out on the porch long after the sun had set. He should check in with his father, make sure he'd eaten and paid his bills, and check his usual hiding places for stashed bottles. They'd all been clear the last couple of visits and his old man had been attending his AA meetings regularly. Hopefully, he was still on the wagon.

Family. He had no choice but to love them. After all, they were all he had. Laughter drifted to him from somewhere up the block. It was a pleasant sound, reminiscent of happier times in his childhood, back when family had a whole different meaning for him. He shook his head as the emptiness of his life settled over him again. There had to be something more out there for him.

CHAPTER THREE

Music floated over the speakers of the grocery store as Chase pushed his cart along the frozen-food aisle. He'd opted for the minicart, which still looked pitifully empty, even after he'd made the rounds of half the store. Buying for one didn't stock up to much. He really needed to start eating healthier, the way he had when he'd lived with his father and Kara.

Even as a young girl, Kara had always insisted on healthier eating. No chicken nuggets for her, like the other four-year-olds. She liked home-cooked meals, and unfortunately, that meant Chase had to do the cooking. He stared at the selection of frozen dinners and pizza. Somehow the single-serving frozen meals seemed a little pathetic.

Sighing, he shoved the lonely boxes back onto the refrigerated shelves. He'd start with the produce section and get some fresh vegetables, then some meat. Surely he could make some simple meals for himself. He could always take extras to his father. The man never ate a decent meal.

Chase had helped himself to a hearty assortment of carrots, broccoli and lettuce, satisfied with the way the vegetables filled his basket, when a man standing by the apples caught his attention. Chase turned toward the man, recognition dawning over him. Could that be Jacob Peterson, Robert and Alex's father?

Alex Peterson. At least it didn't still hurt to think about her. How long had it been since he'd thought of her and her family? At one time they'd been like a second family to him. A real family, with a mother as well as a father and five adoring kids. At least they'd been adoring before the divorce that turned them into an everyday-dysfunctional kind of family.

Yes, that kind of family Chase knew all too well.

He circled around past the oranges to the assorted apples, stopping just short of where the man stood staring blankly at the fruit. It had been a while, but it looked like Alex's father. *Alex.* He hadn't thought about her in forever, not since he'd gotten over her dropping him like a hot coal.

"Mr. Peterson?" Chase asked.

Still the man who'd been the father of his best friend and the first girl to claim his heart stood lost in thought.

Chase cleared his throat. "Jacob?"

Jacob Peterson startled. His gaze sharpened, zeroing in on Chase. Finally, he gestured toward Chase, saying, "I know you. You're my boy Robert's friend. You dated my daughter Alexandra."

"Yes, Mr. Peterson, I'm Chase Carrolton."

"That's it," Jacob said and shook Chase's hand. "Chase, yes, I knew that. It's good to see you. You were always at our house. Look at you, all grown up. How long has it been?"

"Too long," Chase said. "Something like ten years? How are you? How are Robert and Alex?"

Jacob's expression fell. He shook his head. "You haven't been in touch with Robert?"

Guilt filled Chase. "We kept up with each other for a long time, but we've lost touch over the past couple of years. I've had so much going on. I think the last time I talked to Robert he was headed to Seattle for a doctoral program."

"Oh, that was a few years back," Jacob said. "Robert was doing very well for a while. He was an associate professor at Antioch."

"Good for him," Chase said. "Is he still there? I should get in touch with him."

"Actually, he's come back here now. He's staying at the house. He's on leave from the university."

"Oh," Chase said, curiosity filling him. "What kind of leave?"

Jacob frowned. "He's on medical leave."

"Medical leave? What's going on? Is he okay?" Concern replaced his guilt.

Jacob's gaze found his. The man's eyes, so much like Alex's, were as clear a blue as Chase remembered, though troubled in a way they hadn't been even back during what Chase thought of as the Dark Days at the Petersons'. Jacob shook his head, his eyebrows furrowed in concern. He said, "He's been better. He was diagnosed nearly a year ago with Hodgkin's lymphoma."

"Cancer?" Chase asked, stunned. Robert had always been active and healthy. How could this be?

Jacob nodded. "He had several rounds of chemo and it looked like it was working. The tumors shrank, but then they grew with a vengeance, increasing in size and number, even during treatment. Then his oncologist had him go through a stem cell transplant."

"Stem cell?"

"It's like a bone marrow transplant." Jacob's shoulders heaved. "They used his own blood stem cells to re-grow his immune system after they destroyed it trying to kill the cancer. It very nearly killed him, but the damn swelling started again in his neck within a week of the transplant."

His gaze met Chase's. "It's not good. He's weak. But his oncologist is recommending a second transplant. He'll need a donor this time. They want to type family first to see if one of his siblings is a match. They'll type me, too, but parents are only a fifty percent match. They're hoping for higher."

"So does that mean maybe Alex, Steven, Becky or Megan will be a full match?" Chase asked. "At least he has a lot of possibilities in his siblings."

"That's the hope. He's got a one in four shot at finding a donor among them, if we can get them all to agree to be typed and possibly be a donor," Jacob said.

Chase straightened. "Surely, none of them would say no."

Jacob's shoulders shifted in a shrug. A weary sigh escaped him. "I've been trying to round them all up. Most of them have either done the typing or agreed to. Becky's still here. She's married and helps manage the hardware store. They're expecting their first child. Megan will come, of course, but she won't be able to stick around. She has her daughter to care for. Steven is getting his blood typed, but he can't leave his job now. He's in Mobile."

He sighed. "There's no need for him to come if he isn't a match, so we'll see how that goes. I left Alex a message, but haven't heard back from her. Maybe she has a new number?" He looked at Chase questioningly.

Chase shook his head. "I'm sorry, I wouldn't know. I haven't talked to Alex since she left Atlanta."

Jacob squeezed Chase's shoulder. "Don't worry, Becky will track her down if need be."

"I'm sure if Alex knew what was going on, she'd drop everything to come help."

"I hope so." Jacob grabbed a bag of apples and dropped them in his cart. "They can all do their blood typing in their respective cities. The real issue is getting one of them to come help. Once we find a donor, Robert is going to need care 24/7 for a number of months while he recuperates. I can't do it on my own. I did it this last round with Becky's help when she could get away from the store, but she's been pretty much managing it for me since all of this started, and she's running herself ragged. She can't keep it up. I'm going to have to get back there on a regular basis."

"Look, I travel a lot for work, but I'd like to help when I can. Do you think Robert would mind if I stopped by to see him?"

"I don't know how he'll feel about it, but I'll take whatever help I can get. You boys always got along great. No reason why that can't continue."

"Thanks," Chase said. "You're still at the same address?"

Jacob smiled briefly. "Oh, yes, we're still at the old house." He frowned again. "I moved back after Ruth... Well, she's in a home now. She has early-onset Alzheimer's."

Chase frowned. "I'm so sorry, Jacob. I didn't know. Your family has certainly seen its share of hard times."

"We have, but so have so many others. We'll get through this." He shook Chase's hand. "It was good running into you, Chase. I'll let Robert know you'll be stopping by sometime."

"Yes," Chase said. "Please do."

"ONCE UPON A TIME there was a house by the sea, with a bountiful garden and a man and a woman who loved each other with all their hearts. The house was a place of beauty and light and the couple filled it with the laughter of their children."

Alex's sister Megan Baxter brushed a strand of hair from her four-year-old daughter's cheek and smiled at Alex.

Alex shifted as she leaned against the doorjamb. After all this time, Megan still viewed the world through rose-colored glasses. It often proved a point of contention between the sisters, especially with Megan's perpetual insistence on trying to get their family back together.

"Go on, Momma, finish it," Carly, Megan's daughter, insisted.

"Give me a hug good-night first," Alex said as she moved into the room. After her day she didn't have the stomach for fairy tales. She'd only come for dinner at Carly's urging. If not for her niece, Alex would be hard-pressed to spend time with her sister.

Carly wrapped her arms around Alex's neck and planted a wet kiss on her cheek. She said, "Next time *you* can tell me a bedtime story, Aunt Alex."

"No way," Megan said. "She'll tell you horror stories and give you nightmares."

"I'm not that bad," Alex said. "I wouldn't scare the kid." Although giving her a dose of reality might not be a bad idea.

"It's okay," Carly said. "I like spooky ghost stories."

"Alex, stick around. I want to talk to you. I'll finish up here then we can have a glass of wine," Megan said.

Alex nodded, though the last thing she wanted was another lecture from her sister on why she should reconcile with her father and older brother so they could plan the next holiday gathering. She headed to Megan's kitchen, passing the den, where her brother-in-law Brad was engrossed in a crime drama.

Brad was a good guy, who worked hard as an investment broker. When Megan, a corporate attorney, had been offered a job with a Fortune 500 company in Baltimore, Brad had started his own firm from scratch to follow her there. Alex gave him kudos for that.

She poured Megan a glass of red wine and a sparkling water for herself. The ale she'd had earlier was enough to tide her over for a while.

She took a sip of the water as her sister entered the kitchen. Alex held up her hand before Megan could say anything. "I've had a really rough day. I can't take any family lectures tonight."

Megan nodded as she slipped into the seat across from Alex. "I know, Alex, you still haven't forgiven and forgotten."

Alex groaned. She didn't want to rehash the past again with her sister. This was exactly why she'd been frustrated when Megan had taken that job and set up house a mere ten-minute drive from her. Sometimes she thought her sister had deliberately targeted Baltimore to be close enough to pester her.

She tossed back her water, then set down the glass. "I got laid off today."

Megan's blue eyes rounded. "Oh, my, I'm so sorry, Alex."

"You and me both."

"Actually, it may be a blessing in disguise."

Alex ran her fingers through her hair. "Hon, I don't know if I can take your overly optimistic view right now."

"I'm sorry. It's just that… Did you talk to Dad? He said he called and left you a message."

Ugh. Here it comes, family lecture time. "I had a lousy day. The last thing I wanted was to talk to Dad."

"It's Robert," Megan said.

"I've been meaning to call him," Alex said, guilt swamping her.

Megan had kept her apprised of their brother's battle with Hodgkin's. He and Alex hadn't gotten along since their parents split and Robert had taken their father's side. It still made her blood boil to think about it. Again, there was right and wrong and their father's cheating on their mother was wrong.

How could Robert support that?

Still, Alex had meant to check on him numerous times over the past few months. It was always too late at night to call, though, or she just got caught up in work. Once, she had actually called and left a message, but he hadn't called her back.

She shook her head and asked, "How is he?"

"Not good," Megan said. "The autologous stem cell transplant failed."

"What does that mean? Can't they try other chemo?"

Megan bit her lip, her eyes troubled. "It means he relapsed. The tumors started growing again. Dad says the oncologist wants him to have a second stem cell transplant, this one with a donor."

"*Another* stem cell transplant?" Alex asked. "Wasn't the last one risky enough?"

"Well, yes, and the high dose chemo they hit him with apparently *didn't* kill the cancer." Her gaze fell. "It had a lot of bad side effects, too, like it destroyed his immune system, wiped out his blood cells. He's like a newborn now. He can't be exposed to anything. Dad doesn't let him go anywhere but the clinic. And he's lost all kinds of weight.

"And who knows what else? I did some research. Dad doesn't always ask everything he should and Robert, well, he needs someone there as a backup. What I've found,

though, is that the one they want to do now is an alloge-
neic transplant and there's the risk of his body rejecting
the cells. His prognosis isn't good."

Concern filled Alex. "Surely there's another alternative. Maybe we should look at holistic treatments."

"Dr. Braden, his oncologist, feels this is his best chance
at beating this."

"It just sounds like more of the same brutality," Alex
said. "Can his body withstand all that chemo?"

"They want to type all of us to see if we can be donors.
That's why Dad was calling. Robert needs every chance
to find a match he can get. His siblings are his best bet."

That sick feeling stirred again in Alex's stomach. "How
can this be happening?"

Megan grabbed her hand. "He needs us, Alex."

"Of course. I'll get tested or typed or whatever it is.
Just because I don't agree with Robert doesn't mean I
wish him any harm."

Megan relaxed in her chair. "Good, then you'll call
Dad?"

"Yes." Alex nodded, already dreading the conversation with her father. "I'll call him."

"There's more, Alex."

"What?" This was bad enough. How could there be
more?

"Dad said the clinic wants him to sign a new document that Robert will have someone caring for him 24/7
for about a week before to one hundred days following
the transplant. Dad can't cover the entire time. He's already frazzled from this past time. Becky's been trying
to run the store on her own, but she's having some dif-
ficulty with it. She's getting closer to her due date. She
needs him at the store. He needs help."

Alex stared at her sister as the sick feeling swelled

through her. "He needs someone to come stay with them to help him with Robert?"

"Yes," Megan said. "See? A blessing in disguise."

"Megan, I'm an accountant, a financial analyst, a VP of finance. At least I was. But I'm not a caregiver."

"You could be all those things and still be a caregiver. Who else among us can pick up from our lives and transplant back to Atlanta?" Megan asked.

Good question. Alex blew out a breath. It did appear her new circumstances made her a prime candidate for the job. Heaven help her brother.

Sighing, she pulled out her phone and opened a new contact. "Okay, give me Dad's number. I deleted it."

CHAPTER FOUR

THE CHIRPING OF Chase's phone sounded over the NPR broadcaster's piece in their series on meat eating in the United States. He checked the display and exhaled in relief when he saw it was Kara. Mrs. Dixon, one of the museum's benefactors, had already called twice since he'd been back, but he wasn't yet ready to face her and her requests for the collection.

He turned down his radio and answered. "What's up, Kara?"

"Hey, Chase, are you working?"

"I'm on my way to see an old friend."

"Cool. So, did you call Pansy?" Kara asked. "About me spending the night? I texted you her number."

"I left her a voice mail."

"She's not going to call you back," she said. "You'll just have to keep calling her until she answers."

He frowned. "I left her a message and told her who I was."

"She doesn't listen to her messages."

"Fine. I'll just stop to see her, then."

"You'd come all the way out here?"

"It's important you go in early, right?" he asked.

"Yes."

"Okay. I won't have a chance today, but I promise I'll stop by before I leave town again. If she doesn't want you spending the night, I'll come get you early one morning."

"Thanks, Chase, I really appreciate it. I want to spend the night, though. I'll do your laundry or something while I'm there."

"No problem, Kara. We'll get you taken care of."

He disconnected as he turned down a familiar Brookhaven street. He hadn't been in this part of Atlanta in years. A memory of walking along the old sidewalk hand in hand with Alex swept over him.

Alex. How was she? The thought of her possible return sent anticipation shimmering through him.

The area held some good memories. Slowing, he passed what used to be the Caryns' place. He and Robert had hung out with Matt Caryn until he'd moved junior year. The house had gotten run-down after the family had left, but it looked like it had been renovated at some point. He counted two more driveways, then pulled up in front of the Petersons' house. The house appeared much as it had the last time he'd seen it, maybe a little more worn, but neat, with trimmed bushes and fresh paint on the mailbox, if not on the shutters.

How had he lost touch with Robert? Guilt filled him as he walked up the brick-lined steps, then along the flagstone walk. He and Robert had helped lay the stones for that walk. They'd been barely big enough to carry them one at a time, but Robert's dad had been very patient. The man was twice the father his had ever been. It was a shame Alex had never gotten over her parents' breakup.

He pressed the doorbell and waited, glancing along the railed porch. The old swing he and Alex had spent many a summer evening in still hung at the far end.

The door creaked open and her dad smiled as he stepped back and gestured him in. "Chase, I was hoping that might be you."

He shook the man's hand. "Mr. Peterson, it's so good to see you again."

Robert's father waved his hand. "We're all adults here. Why don't you call me Jacob? Mr. Peterson makes me feel like my father."

"Yes, sir, Jacob it is."

"Robert is out back." He shook his head. "His doctor finally cleared him to be outdoors and he's insisting on working in the yard. Though he won't be able to keep it up for long."

Chase followed him through the familiar rooms, though the decor had changed over the years. Even though he'd seen Robert since high school, he'd only been by the house on rare occasion since Alex had moved out after her high school graduation.

They exited the house through the French doors opening onto the patio. The May sun filtered through an overhang of bright green branches, casting dappled light over the cool space below. Robert stood over a bush off to one side, wielding a pair of hedge clippers. He straightened as Chase approached, his movements stiff and slow.

Chase schooled his features. He'd braced himself, not knowing how Robert might appear. Besides the short crop of evidently newly grown hair, deep circles ringed his childhood friend's eyes, and his clothes hung on him, his frame slighter than it had been, even in high school. Fatigue etched lines in Robert's face, even as he extended his hand and pulled Chase into a hug.

"Robert," Chase said, shocked at the slight feel of his friend, his shoulder blades protruding through his T-shirt.

Yet, when he pulled back, light shone in his friend's eyes, a tired light, but a light nonetheless. Maybe the chemo and first transplant had failed, but Robert seemed to still have some fight left in him.

"Chase." Robert stepped back, shaking his head. "I'm sorry I've been out of touch, man."

"No, I got distracted myself. New job, school, all the other usual stuff. Still, I should have made more of an effort." Chase gestured to Jacob, who'd taken the clippers from Robert. "I'm so glad I ran into your dad. I can't believe you've been going through all of this and I had no idea."

Before Robert could respond, Jacob pointed toward the French doors with the clippers. "Robert, why don't you take Chase inside and get him something cold to drink?"

"Sure," Robert said as he gestured for Chase to precede him inside. "It's getting a little hot out and I could use something myself."

When they reached the kitchen, Robert lowered himself into one of the chairs and nodded toward a cabinet. "Glasses are in there. I hope water's okay. We don't have much else. I'm on a no-sugar diet and most of the good stuff is full of sugar. Ice maker is out, though. Unless you want to use the old cubed stuff in the trays."

"I think this is where the glasses were the last time I was here," Chase said as he pulled out two glasses.

"Yes, some things never change."

Chase nodded as he filled the glasses from the station on the refrigerator door. "Are you hungry?"

Robert's shoulders shifted in a heavy sigh. "I should probably eat something." He stared out the window as Chase set his water glass on the table. "I thought I'd have more of an appetite, you know, since I've been off the chemo for a few weeks. I'm doing radiation until we find a donor. I'm not sure why we're bothering, since I seem nonresponsive to everything they've thrown at me so far. But, since they think it's worth trying, I figure I might as well."

"It must be hell."

"It hasn't been a picnic, but every time I think I have it bad, I come across someone who's in a worse place." Robert shrugged. "I'm not going to complain. I have my good days and my bad. Complaining won't change anything."

"You should probably try to eat, though," Chase said. "So, any other diet restrictions?"

"I should probably limit more than I do, but I try to cut back on meat and dairy."

"What do you eat, then?"

"That's part of the problem. I'm not sure what to eat without that, but Megan sent some articles about fighting cancer with nutrition and there are charts about what to eat and not eat to raise my alkalinity." He paused. "I looked online and for every argument for it, there's one against it. It's hard to tell what's what. It's important to her, though, so I'm giving it a try. Doc says as long as I'm getting the nutrition I need it's okay. There's some whole-grain bread we could use for some veggie sandwiches. I think that would probably work. All the veggies have already been cleaned. Dad's diligent about that, since my immune system is still not back to where it should be."

"Okay." Chase gathered sandwich ingredients onto the table, so he could sit with Robert while he prepared their meal.

Robert reached for a cucumber. "I can slice this if you hand me a knife. I'm not totally useless."

"Go for it," Chase said and handed him a knife before cutting into a tomato. "Your dad said you're having a stem cell transplant. It's like a bone marrow transplant, right?"

"More or less."

"It's a tough process?" Chase asked.

"They try to kill the cancer without killing the patient. Sometimes it works."

"I'd like to come by to help, however you need me, as long as I'm in town. I travel more than I'd like for work, but I'm never gone for more than a couple of days."

"Still at the museum?"

"Yes, and these days it takes me all over the place, though I'm going to have to put my foot down on that at some point." He shook his head. Mrs. Dixon and her collection couldn't keep running his work life. "But like I said, I'm around a good bit and I can pitch in here. Do chores, figure out what it is you're supposed to be eating, make sure you get your lazy ass out and moving."

Robert shook his head. "I'm not going to be beating you in any races anytime soon."

"Ha, like you ever could."

His blue eyes glittered. "I recall a time or two."

"You'll get back to it."

The crease between Robert's eyebrows deepened. "Chase, I really appreciate you coming by, but you should know this isn't easy for me."

"I can't imagine it would be."

Robert stared again out the window, the knife still in his hand. "I don't mean the chemo and the transplants, which can be pretty damn debilitating. I mean having people over, having to deal with all this…concern. I don't… like having to put up a front that everything's okay when it isn't."

"Robert, you don't have to be like that with me—"

"Especially with you." He lowered his head. "You knew me when I was strong and healthy. And now look at me…."

"You look fine to me—besides, I don't give a damn about any of that. This is a temporary setback. You'll kick this cancer's ass and come back stronger than ever."

"I know you mean well, but I don't want you coming by here until I'm back to the old me."

"Robert—"

"Thank you for your offer of help, but I'm okay." He slowly stood, bracing himself on the table. "I'm sorry, Chase, I'm going to rest. It was good to see you."

Stunned, Chase stared at his friend as he walked stiffly out of the kitchen. Robert didn't want his help.

"He'll be all right," Jacob said from the hall entryway. "He's just proud. It can't be easy for him to see how strong and healthy you are—how he thinks he should be. He hates people seeing him like this."

"But I'd like to help."

"Actually—" Jacob waved his cell phone "—it looks like we won't be needing any extra help, after all. We've got a new recruit on the way."

"Yeah, well, I hope it isn't another able body. That might put him over the edge."

"He'll have to deal with it," Jacob said.

"So, who's the new recruit?"

Jacob's mouth curved into a smile. "Someone who will probably start some fireworks around here. Alexandra is coming home."

"Alex?" A memory of laughing with her in that very kitchen drifted through Chase's mind. "She's coming for the transplant?"

"She was going to get typed then come once we had a donor and this new transplant was a go, but I talked her into coming right away. Seems her schedule just freed up."

"When will she be here?"

"As soon as she can pack and load up her car. She's shooting for the day after tomorrow. She's breaking the drive into two days."

"That soon?" Chase asked. At least Robert and Jacob

would have some help. But the last time he'd seen Alex, she'd been pretty upset with her brother and father. "I can't believe she's coming."

Jacob sucked in a breath. "I'm a little surprised myself, but I'm glad. Maybe we can finally work things out. I know I'd like that."

"Oh, Jacob, I hope so. She was a hardheaded girl, though. I'm guessing she might still be the same."

"Yes." Jacob nodded slowly. "I'm guessing you're probably right."

ALEX STOOD ON THE PORCH of the house she'd grown up in, staring at the door. She hadn't been here since her mother had left and her father had moved back in. Why had her mother ever agreed to that? Becky swore Mom had suggested the move while she'd been of sound mind, but Alex couldn't fathom why her mother had remained on good terms with the man after he'd destroyed their marriage.

Alex certainly hadn't been as charitable toward her father.

How strange to not feel right about walking into her childhood home. A light breeze rustled the wind chimes hanging above the porch swing, the tinkling stirring memories of summers past. Alex deliberately ignored the urge to glance in that direction. Giving in to that urge would only serve to raise thoughts of Chase Carrolton. And she couldn't think about Chase right now, not when she had to face her father and brother.

Before she could knock, the door swung open. Her father stood on the threshold. Gray framed his face and filtered through the darker strands of his hair. The lines around his eyes and mouth had deepened and he seemed somehow smaller than she'd remembered.

"Alexandra," he said and stepped back, gesturing her forward. "Come inside."

She hesitated for another second, then moved inside, stopping to face him in the entryway, her arms folded tightly across her chest. "Dad."

"I'm so glad you came." He shifted his arms, not quite opening them, but not dropping them back to his sides.

"Of course I came." She inhaled and straightened. "Look, I don't want there to be any misunderstanding. I'm only here for Robert. I hope that you and I can live together in a civil manner, but nothing is forgiven or forgotten on my part."

He nodded slowly, his gaze falling. "Of course. I understand. I gathered that from our phone conversation."

She turned toward the entry table, hating having to be so blunt, but relieved to have the situation clearly addressed. Stacks of mail covered most of the entry table's surface. She cocked her head. "Is that all junk mail or are there bills in there?"

"You won't have to worry about any of that." He scooped the envelopes into one pile. "I pay everything automatically online."

"You can ask them to not send the bills."

"It's fine, honey. Where are your bags?" The crease between his eyebrows deepened. "You are staying, aren't you?"

Exhaustion rolled over her. Driving from Baltimore had taken its toll and now she had little energy to deal with her home-wrecking father. "Yes, I'm staying. I only have a few bags. I'll get them later."

He continued to frown, as though he might argue, but then he nodded. "Well, I washed the sheets on your bed and there are clean towels in the bathroom. You're in your old room that Megan moved into when you left.

Most of her stuff is still in there, though. We can sort through it and get rid of anything you don't want or put it into storage. You'll be sharing the bathroom with your brother again."

She nodded. "How is he, really?"

"He's holding his own. Has a great attitude, though I worry about him getting depressed. He gets tired more than he'd like. He's slowly building back up his strength."

"You said on the phone he needs the second transplant because the first one didn't work, but he's having radiation in the meanwhile until we find a donor."

"The radiation is tough, too, but it's just to keep the cancer at bay until the transplant."

"And what happens with the transplant? How long before all the typing is done and we have results?"

"His doctor is moving pretty quickly on it. He's having the lab expedite everything. I think everyone but you has gone in for the blood work. He's already started a search with the national donor center, just in case they find a stronger match there."

"I scheduled mine for tomorrow at the lab you gave me. Can they really find a better match than someone in his own family?" she asked.

"It's possible," her brother Robert said as he stepped into the entryway. His gaze flickered over her, but he offered no greeting. "Doc Braden is just being proactive. I appreciate that."

"Hey, Robert," she said.

Her unease intensified. Robert had never looked more frail. She hadn't known what to expect, but she hadn't been prepared for this. And to top things off, he didn't seem happy to see her.

So many bad feelings lingered between her and both

her father and her brother now. How were they ever going to manage living together again?

Silence fell over them. Alex pressed her lips together to keep from asking Robert how he was. What a stupid thing to ask someone with cancer.

"Can I make everyone lunch?" her father asked.

Robert nodded. "Sure."

"I can help," Alex offered.

"We've got some new vegan stuff we're trying out. I downloaded a new recipe," her father said.

Her gaze swung from her father to her brother. "You guys are vegan now?"

Robert's eyes narrowed. "We're pretty new to it. You can thank Megan for sending all the articles about fighting cancer on the nutritional front."

"Okay…so does that mean if I'm staying here I have to give up meat and cheese?"

"Do whatever you want," Robert said. "I'm just humoring Megan. I promised her I'd give it a try."

Dad folded his arms. "I'm in on this vegan thing as a show of solidarity for your brother."

The rumbling in Alex's stomach did little to comfort her. "Hell, I guess I'm in, too, then."

She followed Robert and her father into the kitchen. Robert filled water glasses for them while their father consulted his tablet for the recipe.

"Thanks," Alex said as she accepted the glass from her brother, though he seemed indifferent to her appreciation. "Dad, what can I do?"

"Hold on," he said as he read over the recipe.

"He kind of doesn't like people hovering while he's cooking," Robert said. "Why don't I get your bags so you can get settled in?"

"I can do it." Alex rose.

"I'll help you." Robert held her gaze, his jaw tight as though he silently dared her to argue.

"I don't have that much."

Robert crossed his arms and all but glared at her. "Look, I didn't ask for you to come, but if you're here to help, then you have to also accept help. It goes both ways."

"You should take advantage of him while you can," her father said, without looking up from the tablet. "He's pretty useless during chemo, so forget it once they get started on that again."

Five minutes later, Alex opened her trunk and frowned. She'd brought only one small suitcase and a duffel bag, which bulged with all the last-minute items that hadn't fit in the suitcase. She reached for the oversize bag, but Robert grabbed it first, shouldering it before she could protest.

As she headed up the front staircase behind him, suitcase in hand, she shook her head. Her brother might be feeling okay today, but he was moving slower than he had in the past. Still, she made no comment as he deposited the bag on the bed in her old room. He hadn't needed to mention that he hadn't asked for her to come. His attitude said it all.

But she was here and they had to make the best of it. She set down her suitcase and surveyed the room. Fleetwood Mac and Aerosmith posters covered the walls. An old computer and monitor circa the late nineties sat on the desk opposite the twin bed.

She turned to Robert. "So, Megan couldn't wait to make over my room when she moved in. She was a Fleetwood Mac fan?"

He merely shrugged. "I'll let you unpack."

"Thanks."

He turned to leave, but stopped in the doorway and was silent a moment, before saying, "We've got a good routine around here and I like it that way. I do fine on my own most of the time and I don't need a babysitter, but Dad feels better if he's here most of the time. I try to humor him, since I understand this is hard on him, too, and it makes him feel better, like he's doing something. If Becky didn't need him at the store more, we'd probably manage just fine."

"I get that you don't want me here," she said. "But Dad asked me to come and I wanted to help. I'll do my best not to step on your toes. I want you to know I didn't come for him, though, I came for you."

His eyes darkened. "Fine. I want to tell you what I told Chase, then." He cocked his head. "Did Dad tell you he ran into him?"

"Chase Carrolton?"

He nodded.

"No, he didn't mention it." Her conversation with her father had been too difficult to include small talk, not that she took news of Chase Carrolton lightly.

"When he heard about what I've been going through he stopped by to offer his help."

"I'm surprised the two of you hadn't kept up."

Chase had been so adamant about not alienating Robert during the divorce when Robert had stuck by their father, and Alex had been furious with both of them. Chase and her brother had been so close in those days. The issue had played a big part in Alex and Chase's breakup.

"We did for a while. He was pretty torn up when you left, you know," Robert said. "I mean, he didn't moan a lot about it, but I could tell he was really down for a long time after that. You really messed him up."

The old feelings of hurt stirred in her. The divorce had devastated her, and Chase's inability to emotionally support her during that time had further crushed her. "I don't want to talk about that. What did you tell him when you saw him?"

"I thanked him for his offer of help, but told him I didn't want him coming by."

"It was good of him to offer, though, Robert."

"Of course, but I hate that I even need help. I want you to know I only agreed to your coming here for Dad. It's a lot for him to take on and I appreciate that you're here to help him."

"Like I said, I'm here for *you*."

"*Dad's* here for me. He always has been. You can help him however you want, but when it comes down to it, *he's* looking after me." He again held her gaze. "I hope you understand."

"Sure, I understand," she said.

"Good. I want it clear I don't need your help, either. I'll pull my own weight and when I can't I'll make do or Dad will see to whatever I need."

"Sure," she repeated.

As he left, she sank to the bed. She'd come all this way for her brother and he wanted no part of it. What a mess this was. She stared out the window at the porch swing below.

At least Robert had sent Chase Carrolton packing and she wouldn't have to worry about having to deal with him again. That would be more than she could take.

CHAPTER FIVE

ALEX PUSHED OFF with her toe a couple of days later, gently rocking the porch swing as the chimes tinkled softly above her. She pressed her phone to her ear.

"I wish you could come down, Steven. It's not quite like being in enemy territory, but it's so uncomfortable. Last night at dinner no one said a word for the longest time. And Robert doesn't even want me here."

"I'm sure he appreciates you being there, Alex. He's always been moody like that," her younger brother said.

Of all her siblings, she and Steven got along the best, especially postdivorce. He'd been equally outraged by their father's betrayal and turned his back on him to stand by Alex in full support of their mother.

"He does appreciate it," she said. "He's just so stubborn, though. I'm not sure how all this is going to work out."

"If I could get away I'd come, but I don't have any more vacation time, and this new client is high maintenance."

A car pulled to the curb in front of the house. Alex frowned. Who could be stopping by at this hour? Like her, Steven was an early riser and his calling now hadn't been too much of a surprise, but Robert and her father were still sleeping. She'd hoped to enjoy the peace and coolness of the porch before the rest of world awoke.

A man emerged from the vehicle and Alex narrowed

her eyes. Something about the way he moved as he climbed the steps stirred a distant memory.

She frowned. "Hold on, someone's here."

"I'll just let you go, then. It's all going to work out. Just hang in there," Steven said. "I'll check on you later."

Recognition dawned over Alex as the man hit the sidewalk and strode toward her. *Chase Carrolton.* To her utter dismay, her pulse kicked up a notch.

"Okay, Steven," she said. "Have a good one."

Shoving her phone into her pocket, she rose. Why hadn't she brushed her hair this morning? Why should she even care?

Chase evidently recognized her, as well. His stride slowed as he approached. He stepped onto the porch, carrying a full grocery bag.

Her gaze skimmed the bag before settling on his face. Little of the young man she remembered remained. His shoulders and chest had filled out. His familiar gray eyes shone from a face that had lost the softness of youth. Chase was all man, and to her dissatisfaction, the woman in her responded with piqued curiosity.

"Alex," he said. "I heard you were back, or at least that you were coming back."

She nodded and stepped closer to him, though not close enough to encourage a greeting hug. Things had ended between them on too sour a note for any of that.

"Hello, Chase, Robert told me that you had stopped by."

"I did." He lifted the bag. "I was going to leave this on the porch. It's just some fruit and vegetables. I hear they've gone vegan over here and there were some good sales. I happened by a farmer's market on my way home last night."

"Oh," she said, staring at the bag. "That was very thoughtful of you."

"I didn't think anyone would be up this early. I was just going to drop it at the door." He gestured toward his car. "I'm headed to work."

"I won't keep you, then," she said.

He nodded toward the groceries. "Maybe you shouldn't mention they came from me. Robert said he didn't want me coming by. He doesn't want my...concern."

"I know. He told me. If it makes you feel any better, he basically said the same thing to me. He's very particular about just wanting Dad to look after him. I think they have their routine, though Dad's headed back to the hardware store today, so we'll see how it goes."

"Hopefully your brother will have a good day, then. Otherwise, I don't envy you."

"It'll be what it'll be," she said. "He has radiation this morning and then this afternoon I'm taking him to the clinic for an appointment with his transplant oncologist. Whether he wants me to or not, I'm driving him to both. I have a list of questions for his doctor."

Chase cringed. "I really don't envy you that. He's isn't going to like it."

"You know what?" she asked, determination filling her. "I don't care if he likes it or not. I'll do the best I can to not make him feel helpless, which won't be a problem, because he isn't, but I'm here to help and that's what I plan to do. If it were me, I'd want someone else there to decipher all the medical jargon."

"I would, too. Good for you."

"Thanks," she said.

He again nodded. "You look amazing, by the way."

"Really?" Laughing, she glanced down at her T-shirt and shorts. At least she'd changed from her boxers. "You like the rolled-out-of-bed-and-threw-on-the-nearest-clothes look?"

"I do. It's working for you," he said, his gaze warm.

Heat filled her. She straightened. "Don't."

"Don't what?"

"Don't look at me like that."

He straightened, as well, then carefully placed the bag by the door. "I apologize. It's just… I know we didn't end things on the best of terms, but we're both here because we want the best for Robert."

She nodded. "Yes, that's true."

"So, maybe we can call a truce. There's no reason we can't be friends, is there? I could probably use an inside accomplice to help me smuggle in future stashes of veggies."

"Or you could leave them by the door."

"Or that," he said, his gaze falling. "I understand. I just thought…" He gestured once more toward his car. "I should head out before traffic gets crazy."

She nodded, her arms crossed before her. A light breeze sent the wind chimes tinkling as he turned to leave.

"Chase."

He turned back to her, his eyebrows arched in question. "Truce," she said and extended her hand in an offering of peace.

He stared down at her hand, then took it and pulled her into a hug. "Thank you, Alex."

The clean scent of him wrapped around her. He held her close for a long moment, the hard line of his body pressed to hers. She closed her eyes and reminded herself how he hadn't stood by her all those years ago.

At long last he stepped back. "Will you do me a favor? Please."

For some reason she didn't want to contemplate, she bobbed her head in acquiescence.

He pulled out a business card and handed it to her. "Let me know how the doctors' appointments go. What they say about the typing results. I want to help. If I can't help Robert, then I can help you and your dad. Run errands, do chores, research…whatever you need. I want to be a support to you. You guys were always like a real family to me. I can't believe this is happening to him. He's like a brother to me, you know."

She took the card and traced her fingers over the embossed letters, surprised by the word *curator* for his title. Had her aimless ex-boyfriend made something of himself? Not that any of that mattered to her anymore.

Her throat tightened. "Thank you, Chase, I appreciate that, but it's probably better if I don't contact you. Robert might be angry if he found out and I'm walking on eggshells around here as it is."

And the last thing she needed was to get distracted by the guy who hadn't been there for her when she had really needed him.

He glanced away, pressing his lips together, then again faced her. "Okay, I understand, but you know how to reach me if you change your mind."

Again she nodded and he gave her one last, long look before he walked away. She sank slowly down onto the swing, this time perching on the edge. It was all she could do to deal with her family. Chase was another barrel of issues she couldn't handle right now.

No, it was definitely for the best that she'd sent him away.

CHASE PUSHED ASIDE thoughts of Alex that had flooded him since seeing her that morning. The woman, with her sad eyes and soft scent, had filled his mind. He needed to focus on work, though, as he picked his way past the half-plastered walls and scaffolding for the new African-art-exhibition site on the second floor of the McKinney University Art Museum in Atlanta, Georgia. He nodded to a construction worker wearing shorts and a tool belt as he measured the area where recessed shelves would display ritual masks from central Africa. He smiled. All appeared to be on schedule. Maybe he'd get out of here on time, after all.

His phone vibrated. "Hello?"

"Heads up, your favorite work buddy is on her way," Assistant Curator Donna Berry said. As far as assistant curators went, Donna was the best.

He groaned. "How does she know where to find me?"

"So sorry, she cornered me at my desk and saw I was reviewing the marketing plan for the community pro-gramming to promote the collection. And, of course, she started peppering me with questions. Then she said she needed to discuss the program with you, even though I told her it was all up to Marketing and Public Programs. I suggested she try them, but, of course, she expects you to take them all her concerns. I tried to distract her with the upcoming gala, but she wasn't having it. What were they thinking when they let her maintain control of the collection?"

Chase gritted his teeth. Paula Dixon was not only a descendant of one of the university founders, she was their biggest donor and a docent at the museum. Her late husband, Albert, had been an avid collector of African art back in the sixties and seventies and was responsible for the bulk of their West and South African collection. Back in the seventies, the collection's value had evidently merited granting the donor control in order to obtain the rare artifacts. The donation restrictions actually had given Albert control, but Paula's husband had always deferred that control to his wife.

But the woman, with her sugarcoated requests, was the bane of Chase's existence.

Chase, I don't think I can agree to any part of the collection traveling, unless you go with it and oversee every aspect of the setup. You know exactly how to best display it, from the lighting to the descriptions, even the marketing. No one else can do it like you do.

Chase, do you think we can do something about the temperature in the collection room? It's way too cold in there. People don't want to linger. We need a temperature that hints at sultry, more like Africa.

Chase, we can't keep with the same font on the collection tags. We need an update, don't you think? Something to mix it up. What do you think about Aparajita?

"I don't have time for this," he said. "I have a flight to make." And he had to stop by to see Kara's foster mother before he left.

"That's why I'm calling. Hurry and slip away before she gets there. She'll just have another ridiculous request. I wish we could turn down all her donations and not have her leading us around by the nose."

"Leading *me* around, you mean," Chase said.

The far door opened and Paula Dixon pushed inside, swathed in bright colors, her bleached hair teased high on her head. Chase groaned again. "Too late, she's found me. Give me five minutes then call me back with some emergency I need to come see to."

"Got it."

He pasted on a smile and waved at Mrs. Dixon as she approached. "Mrs. Dixon, you shouldn't be back here. Let's go grab you a cup of coffee."

Her ruby lips curved into a bright smile. "Thank you, Chase, you are always so considerate. We could do lunch, instead, my treat."

"I'm so sorry, I can't make lunch. I have a flight to catch and I have too much to do before I can leave."

"For the New Orleans exhibition?" she asked as she slipped her arm in his and he steered her away from the construction site.

"No, that's next week. I'm presenting my paper on modern African art at a conference."

"Oh," she said and waved her hand. As usual she wasn't interested in anything that didn't involve the collection her late husband had donated. She made sure Chase always understood her "requests" as far as the collection was concerned. "Did you read the new exhibition proposal? I'm surprised we haven't heard from Yale. I'm sure they would love to have it. Maybe I should write to them."

He shook his head. "If Yale were interested, we'd hear from them. You know, they do have a spectacular African art collection of their own and I'm sure they stay booked with other exhibitions well in advance."

"Yes, but I just know if you gave it the effort they'd take notice and then, of course, the collection speaks for itself."

What kind of effort was she expecting? If another university was interested in having part of the collection as an exhibition, they'd send a proposal. If Yale sent one, he'd read it, but he had plenty to do without having to court more work and in that case, since she insisted on his overseeing every installation, more travel.

They rode the elevator to the lobby, where there was an upscale coffee shop. Chase ordered an iced skinny latte and handed it to Mrs. Dixon.

She frowned at him. "You shouldn't make a lady drink alone."

"My apologies," he said. He glanced at his watch. Where was his call from Donna? "I have to preview media before I head out."

"Then let me make this quick." She headed for a bistro set, pausing while he pulled out her chair and then took the one across from her. "I have some new items from Albert's travels."

"New items?" Surprise filled him. "I thought we had the complete collection."

Albert Dixon had been meticulous in cataloging his pride and joy. Chase had pored over the list and every item was accounted for.

Her gaze darted away and then back. "It's another crate." Again her gaze diverted. "It was in storage. I'd like for you to come to the house to look it over, help me to get an idea of what the appraised value might be."

Chase glanced at her in surprise. "You want to appraise it? You don't plan to donate it to the existing collection? Are you wanting to sell it?"

She bit her lip. "Unfortunately, I've made some bad investments. Nothing irreparable, but I have an idea these few pieces would put me back on track. Besides, the museum has such a nice collection already. I'm not sure where we'd put another artifact."

"I see. I'm not certified to do any appraising, but I can give you an unofficial estimate of value."

"That would be wonderful."

"I'll look at my schedule and let you know when I can stop by."

Her smile brightened. "Excellent."

His cell phone vibrated. "Excuse me, this is Donna. I should get it."

She quirked her mouth to the side. "You can't let her proof the marketing materials next time. She did a poor job. They completely screwed it up. You'll need to see to all of that yourself going forward."

Irritation had him clenching his jaw as he unlocked his phone. He didn't have time to argue with her. "We'll have to discuss that later. I have to get this."

She patted his arm. "You go ahead, darling. I'll be expecting to hear from you when you get back. We can talk before the gala."

He bid her goodbye and then moved away to answer his cell. "Took you long enough."

"I got stuck on a call with Public Programs," Donna said. "They need to talk to you before you head out."

Shit. He'd be lucky to catch his flight at this rate. All he needed was another red-eye.

"Chase, I have something I need to talk to you about, too."

"That sounds ominous. Shoot."

She chuckled softly. "Well, you know how I always go with you to the fund-raisers, instead of you getting a real date?"

He groaned. The last time he'd gone stag to a fund-raising event, Paula Dixon had gotten drunk and hit on him. He'd sworn to never attend alone after that. "Donna, please tell me you aren't ditching me."

"You know, technically, you never asked me this time. You can't just assume I'm always going to be available. I have a boyfriend now. *He* wants to go with me."

"And what am *I* supposed to do?"

"I don't know, Chase, maybe find yourself a real girl to take."

"Like a real date?" he asked, incredulous.

"Yes, like a real date. You might even enjoy it."

"Fine," he said and disconnected. God, he hated his job.

LATE THAT AFTERNOON Chase pulled to the curb in front of the house where Kara and a number of other foster and natural children lived with her foster parents. Frustration filled him. He'd already bumped back his flight, but he still needed to hurry if he were going to make it.

Still, he'd promised Kara he'd see Pansy before he left. Hopefully the woman was home. The place stood in stark contrast to the Petersons' house. Patches of Georgia clay showed between clumps of tall weeds in the yard, and a blue tarp was draped around the base of the chimney. A bicycle lay on its side in the driveway beside a child-size plastic car, the color faded by the sun, and the garage door stood open, revealing towers of half-opened boxes and shelves of miscellaneous tools and other discarded items.

Chase had met Pansy Ashford on one other occasion, when he'd given Kara a ride home. Though the woman hadn't been overly friendly, she seemed reasonable enough. Surely, she'd be okay with his stepsister staying with him for one school night so he could drop her off early for a help session with her trig teacher.

Loud voices filtered through the open garage door as Chase approached the house. He veered in that direction and the conversation became clearer as he approached the open kitchen door off the garage. Kara, her arms filled with an overflowing laundry basket, stood with her back to him.

Pansy must have been at the stove, out of his sight, but her words rang clearly across the space. "I told you to get dinner started an hour ago. Now I have to stop what I was doing so I can do what you were supposed to do."

Chase paused. Should he interrupt?

"You told me to do the laundry first, because Lori needed her softball uniform for tonight's practice," Kara said.

"Are you back-talking me?"

"No, ma'am, I was only trying to do what you asked me to do. Besides, I was doing laundry when I was half Lori's age. Maybe she could have taken care of her own uniform."

"You think because you did laundry at her age, she should do the same?"

"It never hurt me to do my own laundry," Kara said, her voice subdued.

A harsh laugh escaped Pansy. "Why on earth would I want her to turn out anything like you? You're useless. You'll never amount to anything."

Anger simmered through Chase as he knocked on the open door. He wasn't going to stand by and let the woman belittle Kara this way.

Kara turned to him, moisture brimming in her eyes. "Chase."

"Hey," Chase said as he stepped into the kitchen. Pansy stood over a cutting board, knife in hand. He met her gaze, saying, "I hope I'm not interrupting anything."

"You are," Pansy said, "but I don't guess that's going to stop you."

"I'll make this quick, then, especially since I have a flight to catch. I'd like Kara to stay with me one night, so I can drop her off early at school to meet with her math teacher."

The woman stared hard at him for a long minute. "It won't make a difference. She's going to fail either way."

Chase stepped in front of the woman and kept his voice low. "I don't care about whatever happened to you to make you so miserable, but how you treat Kara matters to me.

I'm asking you *nicely* this time to start treating her with a little more respect."

Pansy's gaze flickered away to the celery on her cutting board. "If you want her, take her, but I'm not driving her anywhere."

"I'll ride the bus." Kara grabbed his hand and pulled him toward the door, the laundry basket balanced on her hip.

He turned to her when they reached his car. "Is she always like that?"

"Not always. She has her good days. You see now why I hate it here?"

He nodded. He'd have to talk to his father. He'd been on a good sober streak. Maybe he could take the girl in. At the very least, Kara would be a good influence on his father. "I'm going to talk to Dad."

"I don't want to live with him and he wouldn't have me, anyway. He blames me for my mom leaving, you know. He can't accept that she left both of us. Then he'd have to admit his drinking was part of what drove her away."

"He's been doing better."

"Why can't I live with you, Chase?" Kara shifted the basket. "I swear I wouldn't be any trouble."

"I don't know, Kara. I'm gone so much."

"I wouldn't mind." Her gaze held his, pleading.

He looked away. "I'll talk to Dad. He's been doing better lately. I'll help him see it would be better for both of you if you stayed with him. If DFCS will let him."

She nodded and he slipped into his car.

"Monday, next week. Will that work for me to come stay?" she asked.

"Sure, Kara."

"Okay, I'll tell my teacher I'll be in early Tuesday, then. I'll catch the bus to your house after work."

With a final nod, he pulled from the curb. He'd stop in to see his father when he returned. Whether his father took her in or not, something had to change. Kara shouldn't have to stay where she wasn't appreciated.

CHAPTER SIX

THE SMELL OF ALCOHOL emanated from the old faux-leather recliner in Chase's father's den that weekend. Chase shook his head and searched the crevice around the seat cushion, then under the chair before locating the nearly empty bottle of Jack Daniel's. He shoved the chair aside to find the stain on the carpet where the open bottle had landed, spilling part of the contents. He knelt, carpet cleaner spray bottle and rag in hand.

"You don't have to do that." His father, Roy Carrolton, leaned against the doorjamb, cradling a coffee cup in his palms.

"Is that just coffee?" Chase asked, disappointment filling him. Why had he thought his father would be ready to take on Kara?

"Yes," his father said, weariness weighing the word. "It's just coffee." He offered the cup to Chase. "See for yourself."

"When was the last time you made it to a meeting?"

"A while. I'll go today. I'm sorry, son."

Chase refused to be swayed by his father's contrite attitude. They'd had this conversation too many times before. "I'm not the one you're hurting."

"I'll do better."

Chase stood and faced his father. "Aren't you tired of doing this—of having this same conversation? It's getting old."

"I didn't ask you to come by."

"What would happen if I stopped?" Chase asked, gesturing to the chair. "Would you sit there and drink yourself into a coma?"

His father shook his head, but offered no other answer. Chase strode into the kitchen to put away the cleaner and toss the rag and whiskey bottle. He yanked open the refrigerator and stared at the empty shelves. At least they were devoid of beer.

"You need groceries. When was the last time you ate?"

His father turned from his spot to face him, without stepping any closer. "I ate yesterday. I'll get food later. If it makes you so angry, why did you come here?"

Chase slammed the refrigerator door. "I came for Kara."

His father's eyes narrowed. "That one is trouble. Why do you even bother with her?"

"She's my sister."

"Ex-stepsister. There's no blood between you."

Chase gritted his teeth to keep from saying she was all he had. His father was a burden and hadn't been a real father to him for decades, not since he'd driven away any other living relatives. Indulging in an outburst would be of no good, though.

"She doesn't have anyone else," he said instead. "She's a troubled kid, but all she needs is a little direction. I thought since you'd been doing better you might agree to let her stay here. It would be good for you to have someone around, but I see that isn't an option now."

A harsh laugh escaped his father. "That's never going to be an option. It isn't my fault she's on her own. She shouldn't have driven her mother away."

"And you had no part of that?" Chase stared hard at his father.

The man's gaze dropped. "If you're so worried about her, why don't you take her in?"

Chase straightened. Did he have a choice? "I just may do that."

"Hi, Ruth." Alex settled into the chair beside her mother. "I'm Alex."

It felt odd introducing herself to her mother, but her sister Becky had been adamant this would make things easier on their mother, especially since she hadn't remembered Alex on her last couple of visits. Sunlight streamed through the wide picture window of the sitting room of the Alzheimer's ward at Parkside Healthcare Center. Other residents dotted the room, sitting with visitors or wandering around the circular area.

"Hello," her mother, Ruth Peterson, said, glancing at her, wide-eyed. "Do I know you?"

Alex tamped down her disappointment. She saw her mother so rarely. Becky had sent a warning via Megan that their mother's lucid periods were growing shorter and less frequent. "Yes, but I haven't been to see you in a while. I've just come from Baltimore."

"Baltimore," her mother echoed.

"It's a nice place. I like it there. I moved there for work after I graduated from college."

Her mother frowned, but made no response.

Alex silently chided herself. Becky had said to keep sentences short. "It's warm outside."

"The sun is nice."

"Would you like to go for a walk?"

A smile lit her mother's face. "Yes, in the...the..." She frowned. "Where the flowers are...open."

Alex stood and offered her hand. "The flowers *are* blooming in the garden."

"I…" Her mother shook her head as she rose. "My words."

"I forget my words, too, sometimes," Alex said as she led her mother outside to the path along the garden. Becky hadn't mentioned the deterioration in her speech.

Alex's throat tightened. She missed how her mom used to comfort her whenever anything went wrong. It sucked that here she was without a job, living with her adulterous father because Robert had cancer and her mother had no idea what was happening, let alone any capacity to comfort her. It sucked that her mother was only fifty-nine, but was stricken with early-onset Alzheimer's.

"I have five children." Her mother turned her face up to the sun.

"Yes." Alex smiled. It was a small memory, but at least she remembered that.

Her mother's smile faded and she frowned. "What is this place?"

"It's Parkside. Will you tell me about your children? What are they like?" Alex asked in an effort to deflect the question.

The last time her mother had asked anything like that, Alex had tried to explain to her about her illness and why she was there. Her mother had gotten so agitated a nurse had needed to sedate her.

"I have five." Her smile returned. "Two boys and three girls."

"That's a lot of kids."

"Robert is…first, then Alex, Steven, Megan and… after…is Becky."

"Yes," Alex said and squeezed her hand, excited she'd remembered all their names.

"They all get along so nicely." Her mother pointed at a rosebush in full bloom. "Aren't the roses…"

"Beautiful," Alex finished for her. "Yes, they are." She smiled, enjoying being with her mother, even if she offered Alex little comfort.

If only Alex could travel back in time to that place her mother remembered, to the happy days when they'd all gotten along. When Chase had been a part of their family and she'd been crazy about him for as long as she could remember. This time with Robert's illness would be so much easier to handle if they were all united and strong the way they'd once been.

But there was no going back. She had only to face today with its stark realities. Thoughts of Chase plagued her, but she managed to keep them at bay...most of the time. Somehow, she'd find a way to make peace with Robert and help him in the process. Her father she'd have to take one day at a time. At least he was doing all he could for Robert. Certainly that counted for something.

"HEY, BUDDY, WHAT'S UP?" Tony Abeline, an old friend of Chase's, who practiced family law, shook Chase's hand and then gestured toward a seat.

Chase sank into the chair. Why did Tony always seem to have it all together? The man had a beautiful wife, two kids and a successful career. He had everything Chase lacked.

"I, evidently, have issues," Chase said.

Tony chuckled softly. "And you're just now figuring this out?"

"I was just at an Al-Anon meeting. I was giving my old man grief for not attending his AA meetings and I realized I hadn't been to a meeting myself in a long time."

"So the good people at Al-Anon helped you figure out all your issues?"

"The good people kindly pointed out my issues. I told

them I hate all the travel for work and, basically, they told me I need to take a stand. And even though we were talking about work, I see that isn't the only area I need to do that with. I'm usually on the fence about stuff, you know. I like to stay neutral or take my time about deciding things, but maybe that time is over and I just need to get clear—make those decisions."

"Take a stand."

"Yes, about work and other stuff, but for now about Kara."

Tony nodded. "Are you sure you want to do this? We shouldn't have to formally petition for custody. All we need to do in this case is inform your stepsister's caseworker that you want to obtain guardianship. They'll do an in-depth Relative Care Assessment, or RCA. We'll need to prove you're related through marriage. I know the girl's mother is long gone, right?"

Chase frowned. Could he prove their relationship? He was Kara's brother. He knew her better than anyone else. She'd be best off in his care. "I don't know if I can get my hands on proof, but we *are* family. We *are* related. She's my sister. They can't not let this happen on a technicality. Can they?"

Tony shrugged. "We just need to prove the relationship, show them a marriage license."

"I may be able to find that. I don't know if they ever actually divorced," Chase said. "As far as I know, Dad never saw Kara's mother or heard from her again after she split, but if they did divorce would it matter?"

"It wouldn't matter. You'd still be considered family. See if you can get a copy of the marriage license. If not, I'll dig one up in the public records."

Chase groaned inwardly. His father wasn't the most

organized, even when sober, and that marriage had been over sixteen years ago. "I'll see what I can do."

"Once you make your request for guardianship, they'll have thirty days to complete the RCA and send you written notification of the agency's decision. You can possibly get an immediate placement, though, if you have a documented history, home safety check and—" he grinned "—they check your record to make sure none of your criminal activities show up."

"I think I'm okay on that."

His friend shook his head. "Which is pretty amazing, considering some of the stunts we pulled."

Chase shrugged. "The firecrackers were your idea, as I recall, and the fire department got there in time. We remained anonymous."

"I can't believe we stuck around at all."

"I wanted to make sure the place didn't burn to the ground."

"I'm locking my boys up when they get older," Tony said. "Oh, and be prepared for a home visit. They're going to want to check out your digs to make sure it's suitable for a child." He frowned. "They're going to want to check out anyone else significant who isn't in the household. How's your father doing these days?"

Chase gritted his teeth. "He isn't a big fan of Kara's. I don't think we need to count him."

"Good. That's probably for the best."

Frustration built in Chase. He was tired of worrying about his father. "To answer your original question, yes, I want to give this guardianship thing a try. I owe Kara at least that. I should have made an effort on her behalf ten years ago when she went into foster care."

"When you were a young twentysomething, barely out of college, with no stable career or home of your own?"

Tony shook his head. "Now, that would have been a tough one. She was better off in foster care then."

"So, what are my chances now?"

His friend blew out a tired breath. "It shouldn't be difficult, but it's hard to say. It may depend on the case-worker. We'll need you to be ready for the home study. I think that should go okay, but your travel may be an issue. I wouldn't say anything about her current foster care situation, even if it's unsatisfactory. I would push your relationship as her stepbrother and that should get you all the traction you need. The preference is usually favorable where there's a family tie. If things are really as bad as you say with her foster mother, maybe the woman will be happy with a change in guardianship."

"I don't think *happy* is in Pansy's vocabulary. I know Kara can be a pain in the ass, but no one deserves to be treated the way that woman treats her. I do feel I should file a complaint, though. She has other foster kids and kids of her own. I think the agency needs to know."

"You should do it, then. You've got to do what feels right to you. I'm just saying, as the father of two, they're a handful, and mine aren't even teenagers yet, which is a whole other ball of wax. Filing the complaint might get her a better placement and then you won't have to take on the responsibility of guardianship."

Chase pressed his lips together, and then he slowly nodded. "Yeah, I'm sure I want to request guardianship."

Tony extended his hand. "Good luck to you then, my friend. Let me know if you need anything else. Oh, and if you do see Robert again, would you please give him my best?"

"Yes, I'll do that," Chase said and then turned to leave.

Maybe taking on Kara would distract him enough that he wouldn't have time to think about how Robert had banned him from the Petersons' household. Still, he wanted to help. Somehow, he'd have to find a way of doing so that would be acceptable.

In some small way he needed to make a stand with Alex's family.

SHELVES OF PLUMBING FIXTURES towered to Alex's left, and rows of caulking and tile lined the shelves to her right as she maneuvered through Three Corners Hardware. She'd been back only on rare occasions to her father's store. She'd only come today to see Becky and report on her visit with their mother and to see if her younger sister had any tips on dealing with Robert.

Becky had always been a daddy's girl, a fact that had strained her relationship with Alex long before the divorce. But her youngest sister had remained committed to maintaining a relationship with their mother, as well. She'd been Mom's main caregiver and continued to be her biggest advocate at Parkside.

Alex made her way to the counter at the far right of the store. A key-making machine took up one end, with its carousel of uncut keys. An older woman scooted in behind the counter as Alex approached, smiling widely.

"How are you today?" the woman asked.

"I'm fine, thanks. I'm looking for Becky. Is she in? I'm her sister."

The woman's eyes widened. "You're her sister? The one from Baltimore? I guess there are two of you there, though. Funny, I never would have guessed you were sisters."

"Yes, I'm Alex." She extended her hand in greeting. "I guess Becky looks more like Megan, our other sister."

The woman pumped her hand with enthusiasm. "I'm

Grace. I've heard so much about you." She frowned. "I'm so sorry about your brother being sick."

"Thank you. He's holding his own. Is Becky here?"

"Yes, of course, she's in back." She gestured toward the stockroom, where their father's office was. "She's supposed to be putting her feet up. She's been pushing herself this morning."

"Thanks."

Alex inhaled slowly as she turned the knob on the door marked Employees Only. Though Becky hadn't pushed trying to get their family together the way Megan had, she had maintained clear support of their father throughout the years. It had kept tensions between her and Alex high, and Alex had avoided her youngest sister as much as possible since she'd left home fifteen years before, keeping in touch mostly through Megan.

"Alex." Becky met her in the stockroom. She'd evidently been headed toward the front. Her belly was round with child. She rested her hand lightly on the bulge. "I thought I heard you."

"Hello, Becky."

Her relationship with Becky wasn't any better than her relationship with Robert. As long as Alex was home, though, they'd need to put aside all the hurt feelings. Hopefully, Becky would be up for that.

Thankfully, Becky embraced her without hesitation. Alex patted her sister gently, leaning across her rounded belly.

When she stepped back, she nodded toward her sister's abdomen. "How are you feeling?"

"Tired most of the time. I can't seem to catch up on my sleep." She sighed. "It's hard to get comfortable and I can't stop thinking about all the stuff that needs to get done here and, well, I worry about Robert, of course.

And Mom. You saw her?" Becky asked. "Dad said you were going."

"Yes," Alex said, not sure which of her sister's issues to address first. "We had a nice visit. She's forgetting more words, though. At least it seems like more since the last time I saw her, which was about six months ago. She didn't know me at all this time." She laughed derisively. "Kind of like the past couple of times. And she asked about where she was, but I changed the subject and that worked to distract her."

"Good. I hate when they have to sedate her."

"Yes, me, too. We had a nice time. I took her for a walk around their garden. She liked it. The roses were blooming."

"It's a blessing she doesn't understand what's happening with Robert," Becky said. She glanced down at her belly and a melancholy smile curved her lips. "It might be nice if she could appreciate this, though."

Alex nodded. "Yes, it would. If it makes a difference, Dad should be able to spend more time here, now that I can fill in for him with Robert, so that should help relieve some of your stress, help you to sleep better. Give you more time to put your feet up."

"Has Robert given you his spiel about his not wanting anyone's help but Dad's?" Becky asked.

"Yes. Has he been like that with you, too, or was that just for me?"

"I used to try to get by there more often after work." She rubbed her belly. "But it's all I can do to get through a day here, to be honest. All I want to do when I'm done is go home and crash."

Becky sighed. "Robert lets me help from a distance. I research stuff for him, send him articles. Megan does, too. But he won't let me drive him anywhere, or cook for

him, or help him when he's sick from chemo…or radiation, though I understand there isn't much to do there but
make sure he's got lots of aloe on hand, which I do." She
shook her head. "You'd better be ready for the chemo
aftereffects. He doesn't handle it well. He gets really sick
and mean as a bear. He doesn't want anyone around when
he's like that. I think he just tolerates having Dad there,
because he has to have someone. It was pretty horrible
last time. It tore him up. He couldn't swallow even his
own spit at one point. That's hospital time, of course."

"Well, he's going to have to get used to having me
around if Dad's going to be spending more time here."
Alex gestured around the stockroom. "I don't mean to be
sexist, but you shouldn't be handling all this by yourself
while you're in this condition. You should be resting."

"Grace is a huge help and we have a couple of part-
timers who come in afternoons, as well. I don't do any
lifting, but there's still so much to do besides that. I was
supposed to have inventory done weeks ago, but I'm so
behind." She laughed. "Not that sales have been breaking
any records, but we're still carrying on, and the equip-
ment rentals are stronger than ever."

"I think Dad wants to spend more time here," Alex
said.

"He definitely does, but he doesn't like to leave Robert.
He says even on days when he's feeling okay, he wants
to be there to distract him, keep him busy. Otherwise,
he gets down."

Alex nodded. Why couldn't her father have been
equally as devoted to their mother as he was to Robert?
"Becky, can I ask you something?"

"Sure."

"You're on better terms with Robert, but if you were

me, how would you get him to feel comfortable with letting me pitch in more, so Dad can be here for you?"

"I don't know, Alex, he's as stubborn as you are. You and Robert have always been alike in that way. That's probably why you two don't get along. You're both too bullheaded."

"Thanks," Alex said dryly.

"I guess I'd help him by letting him help himself. He's got so much pride. He hates having anyone do stuff for him. You know, if he's sick, place a wet washcloth where he can reach it, but don't hand it to him and whatever you do, don't wipe his brow with it or anything like that."

"I can do that. It's not like I want to baby him."

"Honestly, do you know what I think would help him the most?" Becky's blue eyes rounded.

"What?"

"Listen to him. Just be there. Let him vent. Most of the time I think all he needs is someone to talk to. He's always in such a bad mood. Maybe that would lighten him up."

"Okay," Alex said. "I'm thinking we'll just have more long, uncomfortable silences, but as long as he doesn't throw me from the room, I'll listen to him, if I can get him talking."

CHAPTER SEVEN

SILENCE GREETED CHASE as he entered his father's house for the second time that week. "Hello?"

A low light shone from the den, where his father spent most of his time when he was home, but his father wasn't asleep in his recliner and the TV sat silent in its place of honor in the room. Chase had tried to call on his way over but hadn't gotten an answer and his father hadn't returned his call.

Chase pulled out his phone and sent his father a quick text. Where r u?

While waiting for a response, he moved to the big roll-top desk sitting in the far corner. Where would his father keep his important papers? What if he didn't have a copy of the marriage license documenting his marriage to Kara's mother? At least Tony seemed confident they could get a copy from the local records office.

His phone vibrated with an incoming text. At a meeting. Ending now. Got ur message. Look in basement on metal shelves. Home soon.

Chase replied, Thanks. C u soon.

A musty odor permeated the air as Chase flipped a light switch at the bottom of the basement stairs and then entered the unfinished portion of the basement, where he found the metal shelving his father mentioned. He slid open one of the small daylight windows to let in some fresh night air.

When he tugged a cord for a bare bulb hanging in the middle of the area, light illuminated the space. Rows of boxes and containers covered the rows of shelves, with an odd lamp or old appliance here and there. The top shelf held most of the boxes and that's where Chase began, pulling down one with a faded shipping label. He lifted the lid, but rather than documents the box held pictures in all shapes and sizes. A photo on the top caught his eye. He pulled it out and moved under the light to better see it.

It was a picture of him at a birthday party. He was maybe four or five. He wore a pointy birthday hat and sat in front of a cake almost as big as he was. A young boy about his age leaned toward the cake with him, his hair in curly dark waves. Could that be Robert?

He flipped the picture over. The names *Chase, Alexandra* and *Robert* were written in faded blue ink on the back. Frowning, he looked again at the old photograph. So if that was Robert, the chubby little girl beside him must be Alex. He shook his head and smiled.

He remembered the wall clock in the back. It had hung on the wall in the kitchen upstairs until recently. So, had his mother thrown him an actual birthday party and invited the Petersons? Mrs. Peterson was a blurry figure in the back, but he was pretty sure that was her and that was probably Aunt Rena with her. His mother wasn't in the picture, probably because she'd taken it, but she was there in the cake and decorations and smile on his young face.

"Twit," he said to his four-year-old self.

Look at those ears and that grin that spread from ear to ear. He looked…happy. This was probably the only birthday party he'd ever had and he hadn't remembered it.

He put the picture back into the box and closed it. There was no sense in meandering down memory lane. It was nice to know that happier times had once existed, but for how long? He'd been in school, in the first grade, when his mother had cut out on them. Those happy times were a blip on the radar. There one moment and then gone the next.

He should have appreciated them while he'd had them.

The next box looked more promising. He lifted the lid to reveal file folders with worn tabs displaying handwritten labels in varying inks and legibility. They marked everything from recipes to warranty paperwork. He flipped through the tabs, but they didn't seem to be in any order he could identify. Pursing his lips, he settled in to search the contents. With the number of other boxes on the shelves, this could take some time.

Some twenty minutes or more later, a door slammed upstairs. His father called out to him from above and Chase responded. The stairs creaked and a moment later his father stood facing him, his hands on his hips.

"Any luck?" he asked.

"Not yet, but maybe you can find it faster. I'm not sure how these are organized."

"Here, let me look. Most of these your mother started and then I tried to keep up with some of it. We can probably trash most of this."

He dug through one box and then moved on to another, while Chase also continued to search. "It was a license," Chase said. "And not from Mom, so maybe it would have been put somewhere else. Are some of these boxes from Kara's mom?"

"It's all mixed together. I remember seeing it…." He pulled the last box from the shelf. "Here we go. It's filed under *C* for *certificates*."

Chase shook his head. "But it's a license."

His father shrugged. "Same thing." He handed the document to Chase. "It's all yours. I have no need for it."

"Thanks, Dad." Chase stared at the aged paper. "You're not still married to her, are you?"

"I filed for divorce after she'd been gone a year. Did the same with your mother. I figured if they weren't back by then they weren't coming back."

He gripped Chase's shoulder. "I'm so very sorry, Chase. You know it was *me* she was leaving."

Chase shook his head. "I've been telling you that about Kara."

"Oh, that one. She was very high maintenance from the start. Her mother couldn't take it."

"Okay, Dad, whatever you say." Chase waved the marriage license. "This is going to help me gain guardianship of Ms. Kara Anders, and frankly, I'm looking forward to it."

"Well, good luck to you, son. You're going to need it."

ALEX HAD BARELY put the car in Park when Robert was unbuckled and out of the vehicle, shaking his head and muttering under his breath, moving with more speed than she'd seen in him since her arrival. She grabbed her purse and hurried after him.

"You are the *worst* driver," he said. "I'm driving myself tomorrow. There's no need for you to come along." He crossed the parking lot and headed for the double glass doors of the radiation unit marked with bold lettering.

Alex stared at the word *Radiation* as she pushed through after her brother. A shiver ran through her. Every patient who passed through these doors battled some form of cancer. How had her brother fallen into their numbers?

They immediately entered a waiting room with a windowed reception booth at the far wall, next to another door, beyond which was a visible hall and second waiting room. A sign with Patients Only Beyond This Point hung on the wall beside the door. Robert didn't slow, though. He moved on through the door, without looking back or saying anything to her.

A little out of breath, Alex glanced around the nearly empty room. A TV played quietly at one end, displaying the news with headlines scrolling across the bottom of the screen. A woman with a sparse sprinkling of gray in her hair sat in a seat midway along the closest wall, staring blankly at the screen.

Alex sat across from the woman and scanned the coffee table before her for something interesting, but the only thing that appealed was a *Forbes* magazine she'd read ages ago. She settled back in her seat empty-handed. But if the past sessions she'd brought him to were any indication, Robert wouldn't be too long.

"Was that your husband who went back just now?" the woman asked.

"Oh, no," Alex said, surprised the woman hadn't noticed her resemblance to Robert, but he'd been moving at a good pace. "That was my brother."

A sad smile curved the woman's lips and she nodded. "I'm so sorry." She gestured toward the door where Robert had disappeared. "I'm here waiting on my daughter. She's about halfway through her radiation treatments. Her burns have gotten pretty bad."

"Oh," Alex, said, uncertain how to speak to a mother whose child had cancer. What could one possibly say? "I'm so sorry, as well. How old is your daughter?"

"She just had her nineteenth birthday. She celebrated with a nice dose of Etoposide." The woman's voice cracked.

Empathy washed over Alex. How was it the woman wasn't always in tears? How did one bear such a burden?

"That's a type of chemo?" she asked. "I'm new to this and just arrived to help care for my brother. I'm still getting caught up on the reading, but I think he had that, too, along with a lot of other drugs I can't pronounce."

"Yes," the woman said, pulling herself together. "It sucks, doesn't it?"

"Yes."

It sucked and she'd just gotten started with it. What must it be like for all the other patients and caregivers? Heaviness pressed down on her. No wonder Robert was always in a bad mood. Who could stay cheery in the face of all of this?

"She's having this in conjunction with the chemo. We're counting down until she's finished with both. So far so good, but we still have a ways to go."

"Best of luck to you both," Alex said.

"You said your brother already had chemo, so they aren't treating him simultaneously?"

"No," Alex said. "He underwent a stem cell transplant, but it didn't work."

She gestured to her neck, since Robert's tumors were most evident in those lymph nodes. "The tumors came right back, so his transplant oncologist wants him to have another transplant, but using donor stem cells this time. The last time they used his own."

She inhaled, surprised at how her emotions rose speaking to this stranger about it. "The radiation is more to buy him some time until they find him a donor. We're hoping to find one in the family."

"Oh, my," the woman said, her expression grave. "That sounds dire."

"He's a fighter, though. I think he's too mean to let this thing beat him," Alex said, for lack of a better response.

The woman smiled. "I'll say a prayer for him, for you both."

"Thank you," Alex said as the heaviness threatened to crush her.

How bad was it that a mother whose nineteen-year-old child had cancer and was going through radiation and chemotherapy felt *their* situation was dire?

She closed her eyes. She couldn't think like that. Somehow, she had to keep her spirits up. God knew Robert wasn't the one to do that. If she let all this get to her, then the situation would be dire indeed.

"ROBERT PETERSON," a small woman in scrubs called from a side door of the waiting room at the North Fulton Blood and Marrow Transplant Group later that afternoon.

Robert stood and Alex rose with him. "I'm coming back with you."

"Do you have any respect for HIPAA regulations?"

She stopped short of the woman in scrubs, who eyed them curiously. "If you really don't want me to come with you," she said, "I won't, but one of us should take notes in case we need to follow up on anything and if I'm not there, that someone will have to be you."

Anger emanated from him as he frowned at the notebook and pen she held out to him. "Fine. Suit yourself."

Smiling tightly, she scooted along after him as he followed the woman down a hall then into a cramped office. The woman showed them to two seats set before a desk cluttered with files and medical journals.

"Dr. Braden will be with you shortly. He wants to give you an update and then we'll draw your blood work," she said before exiting.

The silence Alex was beginning to hate settled around them. The light fixture above the desk hummed. Alex racked her brain for something to say.

"Steven says hello," she said.

Robert glanced at her, but made no comment. Her frustration level rose. Why did he have to make this so difficult?

"He's sorry he can't get away right now."

"I don't want everyone coming here," Robert said angrily. "I get that everyone has lives and can't just drop whatever they're doing and travel to my bedside. It's bad enough *you're* here. Why would *he* need to be here, too?"

She blinked. "He doesn't need to be, I guess, unless he's a match and can be your donor, then I'm sure he'll work something out if that's the case. He was just thinking it would be nice for me if he came for a visit. I haven't seen him in a while."

"You two..." Robert shook his head. "What? Are you feeling outnumbered here? Need someone else on your team? Speaking of which, I saw Chase with you on the porch the other morning. Why was he at the house? I asked him not to come by. I guess I should have known he'd find an excuse to drop by to see you, though."

"He didn't even know I'd arrived yet. He was stopping by for you, and Chase is *not* on my team," she said. "That was actually the problem back then. That's why we broke up. That's why I also told him not to come by the house anymore."

"You're so unreasonable, Alex. When are you going to grow up? Forgive and forget. Dad did something stupid a million years ago and you let it tear this family apart."

Anger simmered through her. "Oh, *I* tore the family apart? The fact that *he* screwed the neighbor woman had nothing to do with that?"

The door opened and a man in a lab coat, presumably Dr. Braden, entered. He wore a side part in his overly thick hair, giving his head a lopsided look. He extended his hand to Robert. "Robert, how are you doing today?"

Robert shook the man's hand. "I'm doing okay. A little tired, like usual." He gestured to Alex. "This is my sister Alexandra."

Alex also shook the man's hand. "It's nice to meet you, Doctor."

"Likewise." The doctor settled into his chair behind the desk and faced them. "You're the sister from Baltimore who's come to help during the next transplant?"

"Yes," she said.

He pursed his lips and opened a manila folder, the contents of which he reviewed for a short while. She glanced at Robert, but he wouldn't look at her. *She* was unreasonable? How could he blame her for their family falling to pieces?

At last the doctor glanced up and removed his reading glasses. "Your father didn't come with you?"

"No," Robert said. "He's at his hardware store."

"We do disclosure statements with the typing, but I'm a little hesitant to discuss the results with you without him here," the doctor said.

Confused, Alex swung her gaze to Robert, then back to the doctor. "He sent me instead. Robert's the patient and he's okay with me being here. We'd like to hear the typing results."

"Do you have a number for your father? I think we should call him."

A feeling of unease crept over Alex as Robert frowned and pulled out his cell phone and made the call. "Dad?" he said. "Hey, we're with Dr. Braden and—"

The doctor gestured for Robert to pass him the phone.

"Hold on, Dad, he wants to talk to you." Robert handed the man his phone.

To Alex's surprise, Dr. Braden held up his finger to ask them to hold on and then he stepped from the room.

"I've got a bad feeling about this," Alex said.

Robert merely sat brooding beside her while the moments ticked by and the doctor's unintelligible mumbles sounded on the other side of the door. After a few interminable moments he stepped inside the room and handed Robert his phone, saying, "Thank you."

"Dr. Braden," Robert said as he leaned forward, "what was that about? If you don't have a match, why don't you just say so?"

The doctor settled again in his chair. "I needed clearance from your father to speak frankly about the results. We *have* gotten the results of all the typing and I'm sorry to say we don't have a suitable match from your family."

"None of my siblings match?" Robert asked.

"That's correct."

Robert shifted. "Out of four of them? Is that normal?"

"It happens, unfortunately."

"So, do we keep looking in the donor bank, or do we go with my dad? He's a fifty percent match, right? You said it's more complicated, but doable."

Dr. Braden cleared his throat. "We keep looking." He patted the folder. "Unfortunately, your father wasn't a match, either."

"Well, not a hundred percent match," Robert said, "but you said parents are always a fifty percent match and if we needed to go with that we would."

"That's true," the doctor said, "but in this case, your father *wasn't* a match. And that's why I needed to speak with him, but he's given me permission to disclose his results to you."

"Wait. What do you mean he wasn't a match? You mean not a fifty-percent match, not a match at all?" Alex asked.

"Correct."

"I don't understand." Robert shifted in his seat. "How is that possible?"

Dr. Braden again cleared his throat. "I'm not sure how to say this, but children get half their genes from each parent, so a *biological* parent will match four out of eight human leukocyte antigens. They'll be half matched. In this case there was a zero HLA match."

"What are you saying?" Robert asked.

Alex inhaled slowly. The moment took on a surreal feeling. "He's saying that Dad isn't your biological father. Isn't that right, Dr. Braden? That's what you're trying to tell us. That's why you had to talk to him first."

The man shook his head slowly. "We can rerun the typing to make sure there wasn't an error, but from what I see here and from the conversation with your father, I'm afraid that's correct."

Alex slumped in her chair. This couldn't be right. Robert stared at her in stunned silence. Why the hell had she insisted on coming with him today?

CHAPTER EIGHT

"CHASE, I'M FREAKING OUT here," Kara said, panic edging her voice.

"What's up, hon?" Chase straightened from his computer, where he'd been working on labels and catalog text for the new exhibition, and focused on the call.

"I'm not sure. Pansy and Carl are in some kind of trouble. I don't know what's going on. I think they were selling drugs or something. Shit. I can't believe this. I knew they weren't cool. There are cops and DFCS all over the place. This chick says I have to go with her."

"What? What chick? Let me talk to her."

"I hate this, Chase. They're going to put me in another foster home. This is crap. I was supposed to spend the night with you and they said I can't do that now."

"Let me talk to the woman, Kara," Chase said.

He pressed his lips together while Kara spoke briefly with someone on the other end.

"Hello? This is Rhonda Smith with the Division of Family and Children Services."

"Ms. Smith, this is Chase Carrolton. I'm Kara's stepbrother. Can you tell me what's happening there?"

"The DEA is taking her foster parents into custody, Mr. Carrolton. The officer in charge has requested emergency placement for the children, Kara included."

"What about me? Can't she be placed with me? I've already spoken to her caseworker and requested custody.

I'm her family. I'm waiting on the Relative Care Assessment to be completed. Can we expedite her placement with me?"

A short silence crackled across the line. "I can't make that decision, but I'll check with her caseworker to see where they are with the request."

Frustrated, he gripped the phone. "Thank you. What happens in the meantime?"

"She'll go to an emergency foster home until they can process your request, but that should be done relatively quickly."

"Thank you. Can I please talk to her?"

"Certainly."

Kara came back on the line. "Why won't they let me come stay with you?"

"I'm working on it, Kara. I made a request for custody and I think they can expedite it, especially under the circumstances."

"You did? Why didn't you tell me?"

"I didn't want to get your hopes up in case it didn't work out. I didn't know how long it would take. But Ms. Smith is going to check the status and get everything expedited."

"Will you call me and let me know what's happening?"

"Sure, hon, I'll call as soon as I know something. And you please keep me posted on where you are in the meanwhile and I'll try to get away to come see you later, okay?"

"Thanks, Chase. Hey, I love you."

His heart warmed. Maybe taking in his stepsister wouldn't be so bad. He could obtain some semblance of the home he longed for. "I love you, too, Kara. I'll talk to you soon."

RED FLASHED IN FRONT of Alex, drawing her thoughts from the ethers and bringing her attention back to the road in front of her. She slammed on her brakes, coming to an abrupt halt before the light, her arm flinging to the side instinctively, holding Robert back. Her heart thudded and she inhaled slowly.

"Sorry," she said.

"Christ, Alex, pay attention."

Pay attention? Since the dear doctor had dropped the little bomb that her brother wasn't her father's son, her mind was officially blown.

How was she supposed to focus on anything?

"I should have driven," Robert said. "I should never have let you come. You overreact to everything."

She gripped the wheel and shook her head. "This is insane. How can you sit there and *not* react? How can you be so calm? How is *any* of this happening?"

"Obviously, Dad isn't the only cheater in the family."

"Exactly. How is *that* possible?" The light changed and she accelerated through it. "What do we say to him? I'm… I can't wrap my brain around this. I can't imagine how this makes *you* feel."

A dry laugh worked its way from her brother's throat. "I've had a shit year. I guess this is just par for the course."

Empathy washed over her. How could she be concerned about herself when this meant that not only was Robert's parentage called into question, he was also out a donor for the transplant?

"Robert, I'm so sorry."

His eyebrows arched. "This doesn't just affect me, you know."

"Well, of course, it affects all of us. We'll have to tell everyone, or they won't understand why Dad isn't the donor. We'll talk to Dad first, for sure, but they're all going to flip out."

"Yes, but I was thinking this could affect *you,* as well. I mean, Mom cheated, right?"

"Obviously."

He leaned back and stared at her, his look smug. "But for how long?"

She glanced at him, then in the rearview mirror, before anchoring her gaze again to the road. She and Robert had the same blue eyes as their father, but then so did the rest of their siblings, and their mother was blue-eyed, as well, but the two of them alone shared the same dark wavy hair and fair skin tone missing from the rest of their family. People had always commented on how much they resembled each other.

"Oh, my God," she said, her heart pounding. "We have to talk to Dad."

"Do you think he knew?"

"I guess he wouldn't have gone through with the typing if he'd known, but surely he suspected," she said. "I mean, how does something like this…happen without anyone knowing?"

"There's only one way to find out. We'll ask him. He should be back from the hardware store by the time we get home."

Soon after, she turned onto their street and slowed. "I'm so not looking forward to this."

"I don't know," he said. "Maybe now you'll have to stop being mad at him, now that Mom's no longer the innocent wounded victim in this scenario. Maybe she got her just rewards."

A throbbing began in Alex's temples as they exited her car. People were just too complicated to comprehend. Her black-and-white assessment of the world had just gone gray.

"Chase, I think I have good news." Tony Abeline's voice crackled across the line. "I'm jumping on an elevator, so I'll make this quick. I have a contact at DFCS. Your stepsister was moved to an emergency foster home. These places are only meant to be temporary, so no permanent custody issues with them. DFCS has filed a motion for a hearing to transfer legal custody to you until she turns eighteen. They'll subpoena her parents, providing they can find them."

"Dad is easy to locate if they're counting him, but trust me, he doesn't want custody."

"All the better. Stay tuned for a hearing date. Meanwhile since she's in an emergency foster home, her caseworker is pushing for immediate placement with you. They just need satisfactory history, home and criminal background checks. Keep in mind, even if she gets placed with you right away, nothing is final until the hearing."

"So, when is the home assessment?"

"They should be calling you by the end of the day to schedule it. So, do what you have to do to get that place in tip-top shape and be ready."

"Should I call Kara and let her know, or is there a chance this still might not happen?" Chase asked.

"Man, it's never for sure. I've seen some crazy stuff when it comes to custody, but I'd say you can be optimistic. Relax and I'll get back to you if I hear anything else. Otherwise, you should hear from the caseworker yourself."

"Thanks, Tony. I really appreciate all your help."

"Well, I hope you're still feeling that way after you've had Kara with you awhile. Seventeen is a tough age, especially for a kid who's spent more time in foster care than not."

"It'll be all right," Chase said. "But maybe I'll wait until I hear something for sure before I call her."

"Probably not a bad idea. Elevator's here. Talk to you soon."

THUNDER RUMBLED in the distance as Alex trudged after Robert to their father's house. They followed the sound of a weather report broadcasting over the television to the back den. As they neared, Dad straightened from his easy chair and turned off the TV with the remote control.

"How did radiation go?" he asked, turning to them as they entered.

Robert waved his hand as he sat in the chair to his father's right. "Radiation was uneventful. I wish I could say the same about the appointment with Dr. Braden."

Dad inhaled slowly and shook his head. "I'm so sorry about that."

Alex exhaled. "You knew?"

His gaze met hers. "That I wasn't Robert's father? No, I didn't know that."

"But you knew about the affair—about *Mom's* affair." Alex's heart thudded dully.

This time he nodded. "Yes, I knew."

"Shit." Robert scrubbed his hands over his face. "Shit. So much for redoing the typing. There *was* no mistake. I'm screwed. I have no donor. The search of the national donor bank was a bust. This is just great."

"I'm so sorry, son."

"So am I, Dad, and I don't care what some blood test says. I'm still calling you Dad."

"God, I hope so." Their father straightened. "But what are you saying about the rest of the typing? None of them matched? I hoped we'd have a match from one of your sisters or Steven."

"He said it isn't uncommon to not find a match within a family." Robert spread his arms. "But we're not as much of a family as I'd thought. Are we?"

"Dr. Braden said they would keep looking. He said new donors sign on every day," Alex said.

"Yes, that's good," her father said. "We'll have a donor drive or something. We'll ask everyone we know to get typed. It can't hurt to ask them. Everybody wants to help somehow."

"Dad, I don't understand," Alex said. "That was way back at the beginning when you first got married. How is it you knew she was cheating on you and you stayed with her?"

He shrugged. "I loved her. And when she got pregnant I was so thrilled. Why would I leave her? She meant everything to me. She still does, but your mother is a hard-hearted woman. When *I* messed up, she couldn't forgive me."

Alex's throat tightened. "But *you* forgave *her*."

"I did," he said. "But so much time had passed. She wasn't happy with me. Till death do us part is a hell of a long time for some people. I guess your mother and I couldn't quite make it that long."

"She must have been losing her mind, even back then," Robert said.

Jacob narrowed his eyes. "You'll speak of your mother with a little more respect than that, young man."

"She cheated on you!" Robert said, his face flushed. "How could she do that? And she cheated first. And now I have no idea who the hell my real father is."

Alex stared at her father. "Do you know?"

He gazed back at her, his eyebrows arched. "Who Robert's biological father is?"

"Yes," Alex said, excitement coursing through her. "Maybe he can be Robert's donor."

"Hell, no," Robert said.

"Why not?" Alex said. "Dad, do you know?"

Her father shook his head, his gaze downcast. "No. She'd go out sometimes with that Rena Bartlett, you know, she was Grace Carrolton's sister. That's how we met them. The three of them were friends, but then when Grace left, your mother spent a good amount of time with Rena. They were always on the phone or doing something."

"Wait, so Mom used to hang out with Chase's aunt?" Alex asked.

"They were best friends," her father said.

"That's how Chase and I started being friends," Robert said. "I don't think his aunt had any kids, at least not when we knew her, but Mom and Chase's mother and his aunt would go out and leave us with whoever was home, either with Dad or Chase's father."

"I hadn't realized that." Alex frowned. Chase had been a part of their lives almost from the beginning. Did he know what their mothers and his aunt had been up to all those years ago?

"You think she met Robert's father while she was out with Chase's aunt?" Alex asked.

"Most likely, but Rena would have known everything that was going on. They were thick as thieves." Her father inhaled slowly. "I can't believe it. I just didn't want to think…"

"Dad," Alex began, but then she stopped. Did she really want to ask?

"Yes?"

She inhaled slowly, then blew out the breath before continuing. "How long did Mom's affair last?"

Her father frowned. "It went on for some time, I'm afraid, but to be honest I tried not to pay too much attention. I remember at some point I realized it was over and she was all mine again and then I just didn't think about it anymore. I tried to put it from my mind."

"I see," she said.

"Oh," he said, nodding, his eyes round, "I understand.

You're wondering because you and your brother favor each other."

"We do look more alike than anyone else," Robert said.

"I don't know, honey." Her father gestured toward the row of family photographs lined up along the mantel. "We had some dark-haired, fair-skinned relatives on my side, too. It's hard to say."

She nodded. What did it matter, anyway? Whether or not her father was her father, he'd still cheated on her mother. The fact that her mother had cheated on him all those years ago didn't make his actions any more forgivable. It only made Alex see her mother in a new light. She hadn't been the woman Alex had thought.

What good was marriage, if this was what came of it?

"It's okay." Robert rose and patted Dad's shoulder. "We can't change any of this, right? So, we'll just have to figure it out from here. But for now, I'm going to go kick back for a little while. I'm starting to feel a little puny."

"Robert, why don't I make you one of those smoothies you like?" Alex asked.

He turned to her, frowning. "I'm fine."

"You haven't eaten," she said. "I can make it the way you like with just a little bit of the kale, and I know to wash it, and any fruit, but nothing with seeds. They hurt your mouth."

She shrugged at the surprised look on his face. "Dad showed me how to do it last night when he made you one," she said. "Go ahead and lie down. I'll bring it to you."

Robert shrugged, still frowning. "Suit yourself."

As he headed out of the room, Alex turned to her father, refusing to let her brother's bad mood affect her. "Would you like a smoothie, too?"

Her father stood. "Actually, I think I'm going to have something a little stronger."

She followed him into the kitchen, where he pulled a bottle out of the cabinet over the sink. He poured the golden fluid into a shot glass and held it toward her. "Would you like one?"

"Tequila?" she asked as she took the glass.

He nodded and poured another one for himself. He raised the full shot glass to her. She clinked her glass to his.

"Cheers," he said and tossed back the shot.

She drank hers, swallowing quickly. The alcohol burned its way down her throat. Setting the glass on the table she asked, "What ever happened to Chase's aunt Rena?"

"I'm not sure. They moved years ago. I don't know, honey, I'm sorry. It was a long time ago. I wasn't really in the loop." A soft chuckle escaped him. "Not that I was in the loop while we were married."

"It doesn't matter. I was just wondering." She moved to the refrigerator. "Let me make Robert's smoothie."

Ten minutes later she knocked lightly on her brother's bedroom door. When he didn't answer, she quietly entered, his smoothie in hand. A strong wind gusted around the house and the rafters moaned overhead. The sound of the TV in the den drifted from below. Robert's soft breathing floated through the room. He lay on his side, curled into as small a ball as a five-foot-eleven-inch guy could fold into.

She hesitated for a moment, then placed the smoothie on his nightstand. The floorboard creaked as she turned to leave. Robert stirred, uncurling enough to peer at her.

"I'm sorry," she said. "I didn't mean to wake you." She pointed to his nightstand. "I brought your smoothie."

He offered no thanks, but merely grunted as he rolled to sitting.

"I added some peaches from the stash Chase brought."

Again, he made no comment in reply. She hesitated for a moment and then turned again to leave.

"Alex."

"Yes?" she asked, facing him again.

"Don't."

"Don't what?"

"You know."

She blinked. "What?"

"I don't want to know who my biological father is. I don't give a damn who he is. Whatever happened between him and Mom, it's done. For whatever reason, he was never a part of my life. I certainly don't want him to be a part of it now."

"Okay."

"Okay? I really mean it," he said with surprising force.

"Yes." With a shake of her head, she left, crossing the hall to her bedroom.

She sank to the bed. Though most everything else had changed, Megan had kept the same mint-green comforter and white eyelet pillows Alex had used in high school. Either that or Dad had pulled them out of storage for her. She preferred to think the former, otherwise she'd have to acknowledge that her father had been thoughtful and that didn't quite fit the image she held of him.

It was so odd to be back here again, to be back amid the family drama that had consumed her when she was last here. Why had she thought it would be any different this time around? No, this was infinitely worse. Robert had cancer, with little hope for a cure and, evidently, she had no idea who her mother really was.

And very possibly, her biological father was some guy her mother had cheated with.

Was anything what she'd thought it had been? All she

wanted was to get Robert better, so she could go home to Baltimore and start her life over again, away from all of this insanity.

Alex stroked the soft green fabric of the comforter. This, at least, had remained the same. She'd lost her virginity to Chase in this bed. A vision of him standing on the front porch that morning with the sun shining behind him flitted through her mind. She'd sent him away and that was a good thing.

She pulled his business card from her nightstand. Did he know how to reach his aunt, though? She could call and ask him for just this one favor, to put her in touch with the woman who'd known her mother so well, back in the early days of her parents' marriage, during the time when her mother would have been having the affair. All Alex needed was his aunt's phone number, maybe an address.

Before she could change her mind, she picked up her phone and unlocked it. She just wanted to talk to the woman. She needed to understand why her mother would do such a thing. And, whether Robert liked it or not, finding his biological father might be his best chance of finding a donor for the transplant.

Yes, Robert had made it clear he didn't want anything to do with the man. Chances were, she might not find him, and if she did, he might not be willing to be a donor. But she wouldn't be looking for the man just for Robert. Maybe she'd also be doing it for herself.

CHAPTER NINE

GRAVEL CRUNCHED UNDER Chase's tires as he maneuvered along the private road on his way to Paula Dixon's country estate. He'd only been here on two other occasions, first to view the original collection and then a year later to pay his respects after Albert Dixon's funeral.

Mrs. Dixon normally stayed at her Ansley Park home. Her story that she'd found the newest additions to the collection in a storage room at the country estate could very well be true. The place was large enough for a small mountain of crates to go missing. Albert had been so adamant about sharing his treasures with the world, though. It wouldn't have been like him to keep a special stash of treasures hidden for his own pleasure.

Ten minutes later, Paula herself answered the door. Normally her butler was always on hand. Had she given the man the day off?

"Well, good afternoon, Chase," she said. "I thought I was never going to get you out here."

"Mrs. Dixon." He took the fingertips of the gentle, ring-adorned hand she offered. "I'm sorry, my schedule has been impossible."

She gestured him in and then hooked her arm through his as they walked past the magnificent drawing room toward a back hallway. "You do so much, not just at the museum, but with still going to school to get your PhD. How is that coming along?"

"I'm close. I'm fortunate the university promoted me before I finished the program, but I'm almost there." He patted her hand. "And how are you doing these days? I see you're still very involved in all of the museum's fund-raising efforts."

"I do my best to keep busy. The gala should be spec-tacular." She sighed. "Things have never been the same for me since my Albert passed."

"I'm so sorry. I know you were together for a very long time. You must miss him."

They stopped before an all-white door in the all-white hall. "I do and when I found these artifacts I knew he would want me to use them to the best advantage. You know how he was. He's still taking care of me, even from the grave."

She opened the door. Sunlight streamed in through one long window at the back of the narrow room. Boxes, crates and sheet-draped objects filled the space. She moved to a large crate that sat on a pallet off to the left. The top had been removed and wrapped items sat nestled inside strawlike filler.

She pulled out one of the objects and, being careful to touch only the soft outer cloth and not the actual artifact, gently unwrapped it, to reveal a long wooden object with the body of an animal and head of a human. The body was long and slightly curved, likely carved from a tree branch in that shape.

"It's a neck rest." Chase pulled a pair of gloves from his pocket and put them on before holding out his hands for the object. "May I?"

"Of course." She handed him the neck rest. "And there are ritual headdresses and ceremonial masks, as well. Some of the pieces are quite interesting, though I admit I'm not familiar with what all of them are."

She unwrapped a number of the items for him to inspect.

"I'm sure I can help you to identify them all," he said as he examined them.

Chase's curiosity was piqued. The neck rest, as well as the ritual mask and bowl, were well preserved. If all of the items were in a similar state, they could, indeed, bring in a good price for the widow.

"I don't understand why these are just now coming to light, though," he said. "Albert wouldn't have kept a stash of artifacts for himself and if he did, why would they have been left in a crate all this time?"

Mrs. Dixon waved her hand in dismissal. "He had so much stuff at one point, I don't think he knew what all he had. These simply got lost in the shuffle."

Chase frowned. Albert would never have lost track of a find like this. It didn't make sense. "You have the provenance?"

Her gaze flitted away in a manner that had Chase's alarm bells ringing again. Her lips curved into a familiar sweet smile. "I'm sure it's around. I'll look through Albert's papers."

"Let me know when you find it. I'll be happy to help you find someone to do the appraisal, but you can't do anything with these, no matter how exquisite, if you don't have the ownership history."

"Of course," she said and laughed lightly. "It's not like I'd be involved with anything illegal. Of course I have the provenance."

She rewrapped the neck rest and tucked it back into the crate, then again looped her arm through his. "Now, Chase, I'm going to need all of these cataloged. You'll help me with that, won't you?"

He gritted his teeth. "I'll see what I can do to fit that in."

"And you did submit that exhibition proposal to Yale, didn't you?"

It was all he could do not to groan out loud. "Actually, I began the proposal this week."

"That's my boy," she said and patted his gloved hand. "And you will save me a dance at the gala?"

The gala. He groaned inwardly. He still had to find a date. He plastered on a smile and did his best to subdue the image of Alex that flashed through his mind. The woman had made it very clear she didn't want him around. "Of course, it'll be my pleasure."

EARLY THAT EVENING Chase swallowed and turned down the volume on his sound system. Coldplay should be a good choice. Straightening, he smoothed his hands over his slacks and button-down shirt. He inhaled slowly as he surveyed the area. He'd cleaned and scrubbed the way Tony had instructed, but had he missed something?

The doorbell rang and he jumped. His heart pounded as he hurried to the door. He'd been stunned when Kara's caseworker had called to say the home assessment was scheduled that afternoon. He'd left the museum early and rushed through getting his place in order.

A tall man in a gray suit stood on the front step, clipboard in hand. He extended his hand. "I'm Justin Harris with Children Services. Are you Mr. Chase Carrolton?"

"Yes," Chase said as he shook the man's hand. "Please come in."

The man nodded and gestured over his shoulder with his pen. "You have a loose board on your steps. One of the nail heads is protruding and needs to be resecured."

"Oh, of course. I'll take care of that right away."

Justin Harris nodded again and stepped across the

threshold. He turned to Chase. "I usually speak with the entire family first. Is your stepsister here?"

Chase glanced at his watch. "She should be here shortly. She's coming from work. I can call her, but I'm sure she's on her way."

"Do you mind if I just look around while we wait for her? I'll do the tour first."

"Help yourself."

Harris circled the living room, checking outlets, pulling furniture aside to check electrical cords and opening the coat closet. He stopped at the thermostat and adjusted the settings until the air conditioner kicked on. At several points he stopped to make notes on his clipboard. Each time, Chase pressed his lips together to keep from asking the man what he was writing.

After he finished with the living room, Harris moved to the kitchen. Chase folded his arms. Following the man would make him look anxious. He needed to play it cool. Besides he could see well enough from the entryway.

Water splashed from the faucet, and then the garbage disposal roared to life. Harris moved to the stove. The clicking of the gas burner starter sounded, stopped, then started again.

Chase straightened and called, "I don't use that front burner, or I light it from the back burner."

Harris made no reply, other than to bend his head again over the clipboard. *Shit*. Why hadn't he fixed that? The ringing of his cell phone had Chase jumping. He fumbled it out of his pocket as Harris moved down the hall. A moment later the toilet flushed.

It took him three tries to unlock his phone. "Hello?"

"Chase...it's Alex."

"Alex?" Surprise filled him. "Is Robert okay?"

"He's fine. Well, not really. I mean he's about the same

as when you last saw him, I guess, but I…I have something I need to ask you."

Harris reappeared from down the hall. He caught Chase's eye. Chase held up his index finger to show he'd be just a moment and the man stood in front of him holding his damn clipboard, frowning. Thankfully, at that moment Kara arrived, breathless, as though she'd run from the bus stop.

"Alex, I'm so sorry. Can I call you back? I'm in the middle of something."

"Can you meet me at Jocks and Jills in about an hour?"

He bit his lip. "I think so. I'm not sure how long this will take, but can we make it an hour and a half? I'll call you back if it looks like I'm going to be any later. Oh, and it isn't Jocks and Jills anymore. It's now Hudson Grille."

"Oh…okay, thanks, Chase. I'll see you then."

Chase ended the call, muted his phone and turned to Harris. "So, how else can I help you?"

"Can we sit down somewhere? I'd like to speak with you both together and then each of you separately. Also, do you have the three collateral contacts we spoke about? I'll want to contact them, as well."

"Of course," Chase said and directed the man to the living room. "Why don't you have a seat and I'll get that for you. Then we can have our talk."

THOUGH THE WOOD of the decor was darker now and the partially bricked walls covered with sports memorabilia had given way to a more upscale interior, a feeling of déjà vu came over Alex as she entered Hudson Grille a short while later. Why had she chosen this place? She and Chase had spent many a romantic evening here. But when he'd said he couldn't talk, she'd panicked. Their old hangout had been the first thing that had popped into her head. And it was probably better to ask him about his aunt in person.

Not that she had wanted to see him face-to-face again.

She glanced at the seating in the main dining area. The furniture was different, but the space still had booths lining the walls on either side, with tables and chairs grouped at the center. Her gaze fell on the back booth with its tan upholstery, and her cheeks warmed. She and Chase had experienced one too many intimate moments in that booth, though it had been covered in worn red fabric at that point.

Why hadn't she picked a dive diner with harsh lighting and truck drivers?

"Alex." Chase appeared at her elbow, out of breath.

She startled, heat filling her at his proximity. "Hi, I didn't see you. I thought you might be late."

"I literally ran here, well, when I wasn't driving, that is."

She smiled. "You didn't have to do that."

He shrugged. "My…thing took a little longer than I thought it would and you had me intrigued with your needing to ask me something. Besides, I was looking forward to seeing you again…and I think there's something I want to ask you, too."

Warmth and curiosity filled her. What did he want to ask her? She straightened, forcing her gaze from the strong line of his jaw, the breadth of his chest. She shouldn't be noticing these things. She was here only to get information about his aunt and for nothing more. She would not succumb again to Chase's charms.

No good would come of that.

"We should sit," she said. "I could use another drink."

"Another?" he asked as they moved past the seating hostess and into the bar.

"I had a shot of tequila with my dad earlier." She stopped at a square high-top table midway back. "Here, this one's good."

His gaze swung past the bar to the dining area. "Don't you want to sit in our old booth?"

"But we're legal now and can sit in the bar."

"If you're in the mood for a bar scene, we can always move next door to Pub 71."

"That place gets way too loud when the band gets going."

He leaned close to her ear, his hand warm on her arm. "So we'll have to sit close to hear each other."

Her skin warmed. Her heart thudded and she closed her eyes against the tempting vision of them snuggled close together in one of the pub's high-backed booths. "I like it here."

Shrugging, he pulled out her chair. "Works for me."

"Thanks." She breathed a sigh of relief and slipped into the tall seat, chiding herself not to be impressed with his good manners.

Instead of taking the chair across from her, he slid into the one to her right. "So, you and your dad did shots?"

She nodded.

"Together?"

"Yes, it was…an eventful day."

"What happened?"

She glanced around and to her relief a server approached their table. She ordered a Cosmo and Chase ordered cranberry juice. She smiled. "So, you're still drinking your juice? We're old enough to order the hard stuff for a change."

"No offense, but even the smell of alcohol bothers me. Brings up too many bad memories, I guess."

Empathy filled her. He had always seemed so okay

with the world, it was easy to forget how difficult his home life had actually been.

"So?" he asked when the server had gone. "Did something happen with Robert?"

She nodded. "You could say that. Honestly, I think I'd like to have that drink first. Tell me about your thing. What were you doing? And what did you want to ask me? You go first."

"Ah, well, first my thing. It was…trying. You remember my sister, Kara?"

"Yes, how is she? She must be all grown up by now."

"She's okay. She's seventeen and a little bit of a handful. A short while after you left my dad got busted on one DUI too many. She'd still been living with him since her mother split and no other relatives stepped forward for her.

"I had moved out and was fresh out of school and had just landed that security job at the museum. I was living in this dump with roommates I'd found online. I could barely support myself, let alone Kara. I tried to find someone, a relative, either of mine or hers, to help, but there just wasn't anyone."

"So, your father went to jail and she was left on her own? She was how old?"

"She was five. So young. DFCS took custody of her. She became a ward of the state and went into foster care. I hated it, but there really wasn't anything I could do about it at the time."

"I'm sorry to hear that, Chase. That must have been a difficult time." Before she realized she'd reached out, her hand was on his arm.

She quickly pulled it back and folded it into her lap. What she felt then was too close to guilt. She'd left and never looked back and he'd gone through so much on his own.

"It sucked. I wasn't in any position to take her on. The best I could do was to keep in close touch, maintain our relationship." He shrugged. "She's my family."

Family. Even though Alex had tried to keep a wide berth, her family still managed to wreak havoc on her life. What would it be like to have a loving and supportive family, like Chase had with Kara?

"So, she's still in foster care?" she asked.

"Technically, yes, for now, but it hasn't been going well. She has anger issues."

"Go figure. I can totally relate."

"Anyway, I've requested custody," he said.

"That's great, Chase."

"I had a home assessment just now. That was the thing."

"A home assessment, like DFCS comes out and inspects your place?" she asked.

"Yes, and asks all kinds of questions." He paused as their drinks arrived. After a long sip, he continued. "It was completely nerve-racking. The guy actually had a clipboard and was taking notes."

"Wow. I'm sure you did fine."

"I don't know." He shook his head. "I wish Kara didn't know about it, in case it doesn't work out. But there was all this drama with her foster parents getting arrested, which was great since the woman was a total bitch, but Kara went to an emergency foster home this week and it's been really stressful, though I think she actually likes it where she is now."

Alex took a long sip of her martini. "Is there a chance she can stay there if your request doesn't go through?"

"I don't think so," he said. "It was an emergency place-ment, so it's temporary by definition."

"When will you know about the custody?"

"I'm not sure. The caseworker grilled me after his clip-board tour. I was afraid to ask." He exhaled and then took another sip. "I think my traveling may be an issue. I hate it, too. I wish I could cut back on that. It's really getting old."

"I noticed on your business card you're a curator," she said. "Are you still at the university museum?"

"Yes, they were really great to give me the job, even though I was still working on my PhD."

Surprise filled her. "You're getting a PhD? In art his-tory, I presume?"

"I am. Surprised?"

A short chuckle escaped her. "I am. It doesn't quite go with the drifter you used to be."

"I still kind of drifted into it, though. You know, start-ing as a security guard there."

"That's great. It's a good jump from security."

"I got interested in art history while I was there. I took some classes, got a degree…and, as I said, am now work-ing on my PhD."

"That's…incredible. But you're not happy with it? At least with the traveling?"

"The work is okay, but being on the road sucks. Com-ing home to an empty house sucks."

"Well, maybe this custody thing will work out and you'll have Kara to come home to."

He nodded. "But then I wonder how that will be. We get along, but I've never had to be responsible for any-one but me."

"I don't know. I think I'd disagree with that. As I recall you were always pretty much taking care of your father."

"Yes, but this is different. I mean, he's always been a little screwed up. I've always done what I could to help him, and part of that was for my own good. I mean, if I didn't sober him up and make him go to work, we would have starved long ago. I had self-preservation as a motivator.

"When I went away to school I hated leaving Kara with him. He's great when he's sober, but he still struggles with that. I don't know if he's ever going to kick the drinking.

"But with Kara, it isn't her fault she ended up in foster care. She's been an innocent victim. She had crap parents. She's still young and impressionable. I feel like I could make a difference in her life. If this really happens I don't want to screw it up."

Alex resisted the urge to reach out to him again. "You'll do okay. You care about her and you have the best intentions. It's more of a break than a lot of kids get. I'm sure she appreciates all your efforts on her behalf, however they pan out."

"Thanks, I hope so." He nodded toward her empty glass. "You've had your drink, so now tell me. What's going on with you? Did you make amends with your dad?"

"Ah, I don't know, things are still pretty strained. I can't get past him cheating on Mom, but you could say I now have a new perspective on things."

"How so?"

"Well, I went with Robert to his appointment at the blood and marrow clinic today. We did get the results of the typing to see if any of us could be a donor for his stem cell transplant and it turns out that none of us is a match, which his doctor assured us isn't unusual, even in a family of our size, though in this case there was a good reason for it."

She shook her head and twirled the stem of her empty

glass. Chase signaled the waiter to bring another round and then she continued. "The tricky thing is that Dad was supposed to be the backup. Parents are always a half match and though they'd prefer a higher percentage match, they have a process with half matches that works." She met his gaze. "But Dad wasn't a match. At all, not fifty percent, not twenty-five, nothing. Zip. Nada."

"Did they make a mistake in the lab?" Chase asked as the waiter delivered the fresh drinks.

"We were kind of hoping that, but when Robert and I asked Dad about it, he admitted Mom had an affair very early in their marriage."

"Shit, so you're saying she had Robert by some other guy?"

"Apparently."

This time, his hand squeezed her arm and she resisted the urge to place her hand on top of his. "I can't believe it, Chase. Dad isn't Robert's biological father."

"Your mom cheated on him."

"And she had another man's child and Dad stayed with her." She lifted her glass. "Who does that?" She downed another long sip, the alcohol warming her. "Just when I think my family is one of the most dysfunctional ones out there I find out how screwed up it really is."

"Sweetheart, dysfunctional is the norm. You can't expect any family to be perfect, and for a long time, you guys came pretty damn close. You were the best family I ever had."

For some reason tears stung her eyes. She pushed the glass away. "It just sucks, and the search of the national donor bank came back negative. Now Robert is in this holding pattern on the transplant. Really what his doctor was saying today is that we just have to keep looking."

She pressed her lips together. "The transplant only

has a twenty-five percent chance of stopping the cancer
and they still say it's his best option. He's going to keep
having radiation to hold it at bay, but he's still wiped out
from the last transplant. I've never seen him so…fatigued.
I know Robert and I haven't been on the best of terms,
but I hate this for him."

"So, what did you want to ask me?"

The room blurred and she blinked. "Mom used to hang
out with your aunt Rena. I'm not sure I remember her,
but Robert does and Dad said they were best friends."

"They were. That's how Robert and I ended up being
friends. It started way back when my mother was still
around. She and Aunt Rena would go out with your mom
and they'd leave us together, usually with your dad." He
shook his head. "So, you wanted to ask me about my
aunt?"

"I'd like to talk to her. Dad said she'd know about that
time. That Mom and she shared everything and she'd
know all about the affair and the man my mother had
it with."

"You want to find your brother's biological father?"

She shook her head. "Robert is really against it, but
with none of us being matches and the national donor
bank coming up blank, this might be his best shot. But
Robert is adamant about not finding him. He doesn't want
anything to do with the man."

"But *you* want to find him?"

She inhaled slowly. "I do, for Robert, and I want to talk
to your aunt. I can't talk to Mom. She doesn't even know
who I am anymore. I just need to understand what happened. How it happened. I mean, did she love this guy?
Why would she do such a thing? I don't get it."

Chase stared at his glass for a long moment, his forehead creased. "I haven't been in touch with Aunt Rena since she left and that was years and years ago."

Disappointment filled her. "So, you don't know how to find her?"

"I have a cousin who may know. I can try to contact him and see if he has her address or phone number."

"Would you do that, Chase? It would mean a lot to me. I'll find a way to make it up to you."

"There is actually something you could help me with. Well, actually two things, but we'll get to the second one."

"Of course."

"It's Kara. Regardless of whether I get custody or not, she could really use a math tutor."

"Math?" She straightened. "I miss math. I'd love to help her."

He extended his hand. "Awesome, then we have a deal. You help Kara with math and I'll help you find my aunt."

She gripped his hand. "Yes, we have a deal."

They toasted and drank and then Alex cocked her head. "And what was the second thing?"

Chase shifted in his seat, looking decidedly uncomfortable. "You can, of course, say no, but first, it's for a good cause, raising funds for the university and museum, and second, I'd be forever in your debt if you'd do this for me."

"Now you have me really curious," she said. "What is it? A fund-raiser?"

"Yes, it's the Summer Soiree, I think they call it. It's a dress-up affair in a few weeks. I need a date. Would you please go with me?"

"A date?" Her heart thudded a little louder than she would have liked, but thankfully the bar music was loud enough to mask it. "You don't mean a *date* date?"

"No." He chuckled softly. "Just a date. I kind of need

someone to help me ward off this particularly aggressive docent we have."

"Oh, a female docent?"

"A wealthy female docent, at least she's been one of our biggest donors." He leaned forward. "So, should I text you the information?"

"I don't know, Chase. I'll have to check with my father to see if I can get away." She sighed. "But go ahead and send me the information and I'll see what I can do."

CHAPTER TEN

"THANKS FOR COMING to get me," Kara said, her smile wide. "I can't believe this is happening. I finally get to come live with you."

Chase shook his head as he merged onto I-85. Now that Kara had been placed with him, he was plagued with uncertainty. What if he wasn't cut out for this? He'd wanted to make his house more of a home, but was that really the best solution for his sister?

"I'm a little surprised myself," he said. "Even though it isn't official until the hearing, I didn't think it would happen so fast. And the home assessment had me worried. I didn't think that guy liked me at all. He had me freaked out with his clipboard and all his notes."

"What could they find to complain about with you? You're such a rule follower. Have you ever gotten so much as a speeding ticket? I'm glad Pansy turned out to be a drug dealer. I knew there was something wrong with her and Carl."

Chase silently shook his head. Thank God Kara didn't know about the indiscretions from his younger days. He couldn't let Kara turn out that way. At least, not any more so than she had already.

"We're going to have to set some ground rules," he said.

"Sure. I'll help out around the house. I'll cook and clean. You won't be sorry, Chase. I promise."

"Bring up your grades, so you can qualify for the Hope scholarship, and we'll call it even."

She blew out a breath. "I'll try, but trig is still not going well. I'm pretty sure I bombed that quiz. Why do I have to have all this math to graduate? When was the last time you used trig out in the real world?"

"I'm sorry we didn't get you in early to see your teacher. Do you want me to call her? Maybe you can retake it. It's not your fault this week was crazy. These were extenuating circumstances. Surely, they'll take that into consideration. Besides, I'll drop you early tomorrow."

"If I failed, which I'm pretty sure I did, and I'm still flunking that class, we can request recovery and they'll let me retake it."

"Great, we'll do that, then. I'll call your teacher first thing tomorrow. Oh, and I found you a tutor. Do you remember Alex Peterson? You were pretty young."

Kara rolled her eyes. "I remember you talking about her a million years ago."

He shrugged. "Maybe. But she's great and she's a math wiz and she's agreed to tutor you."

"Cool. But you should still contact my teacher. I think it's better to email her. I have a copy of the syllabus you can have. All her contact information is on it." She straightened in her seat. "I'm going to do better. I know this is a good thing, my coming to stay with you. I'm not going to blow it."

"I'll do everything I can to make it work, Kara." He exited the interstate and headed home.

ALEX GLANCED AT THE CHART on the refrigerator as she checked off the pills she'd placed in the medicine cup. It was a colorful assortment if nothing else: the anti pills, as she thought of them—an antibiotic, antifungal and antiviral. With Robert's weakened immune system his doctor wasn't taking any chances. Add to that his blood thinner doled out in fractions of a pill, depending on his lab work, and this was just the nightly dose. His morning medicine included these plus an assortment of supplements and vitamins, as well as a few others he still took to counter the lingering effects of the chemo.

He'd started on the blood thinner, she'd been told, when he'd suffered clotting from the original port they'd surgically implanted in his arm, because evidently chemo was too destructive on mere veins and needed to be administered via the device's artificial catheter. Prior to the first stem cell transplant he'd had a new port, a central line, inserted in his chest. To Robert's aggravation, her father had instructed Alex on how to care for the central line, how to check the cap and clamp on the tube exiting his chest, how to flush it if need be, but mostly how to check for infection around the site.

A tap at the back door sounded. Her pulse quickened. Chase was here already? She checked the clock over the stove. How had it gotten so late? She'd had trouble sleeping last night, wondering why she was even considering a date with him, even if it wasn't a *date* date.

After checking her reflection in the toaster she opened the door, smiling at Chase and suddenly feeling nostalgic. "It's a little like old times, you coming to the back door, but I don't remember you ever knocking."

He glanced past her. "Technically, it's a side door, and I've never been banned from coming by here before. Under the circumstances I thought knocking was a good compromise."

"Robert is upstairs. He spends a lot of time in his room these days. Come in." She stepped back and gestured him in.

A petite blonde followed him inside. "Hey."

"And look at you, Kara, the last time I saw you, you were this tiny thing," Alex said. "You probably don't remember me, do you?"

"Not really, but I remember Chase talking about you. You were the one that got away."

Heat filled Alex's cheeks.

Chase shifted beside her. "*Ran* away. She was the one who ran away."

Kara shrugged. "Same difference."

"Not…really," Chase said.

"Dad is still at the hardware store, but I have food ready, if either of you is hungry." She lifted her cup of pills. "I need to take Robert his medicine. I'll take him something to eat, but I don't think he'll want to come down. He hasn't been feeling up to much today."

"Why don't you let me take that up to him and you and Kara can get started on her homework?" Chase held out his hands for the pills and bowl of food.

"I'll let him know you're here, Chase, but let me take these. He's so touchy about these things and he's already said he doesn't want you helping him. We need to respect that. He's really not up to company. He's in a really bad mood."

"I'm not company." Chase spread his hands wide. "But I get it, and, of course, I want to respect his wishes."

She gestured to the wok on the stove. "I stir-fried a bunch of veggies and there's brown rice. I'm sorry, we don't have any meat, but you're welcome to help yourselves. I'll be right back."

"You up for stir-fry, Kara?" Chase asked.

"Sure."

When Alex moved toward the cabinet for dishes, Chase stopped her. "I remember my way around here. Go see your brother and please ask him if he's up to me saying hi."

Her heart sped at his close proximity and she quickly stepped away. With a nod, she headed for the stairs. Robert was sitting at his desk, his head propped up with his left hand, while he typed with his right hand. He didn't look up when she moved into the room. She set the pills and bowl on the desk beside him, and then refilled his water glass from the pitcher she'd left on his dresser earlier.

He continued to type, hunting and pecking at a slow, methodical pace, working on what appeared to be a blog of some sort. She hesitated for a moment, not sure if she should interrupt. His color wasn't good and he hadn't eaten much. He hadn't said anything, but he seemed to be having trouble keeping food down today. She'd called her dad and he wasn't sure what to make of that, since this hadn't been a side effect of the radiation. He had called Robert's oncology nurse and the woman had said to keep an eye on him.

Deciding to leave him to his task, Alex turned for the door.

"Who's here?" Robert asked, still without looking up. "Dad said he'd be at the hardware store late tonight. I heard voices."

"It's Chase and his sister, Kara. Do you remember her? She was maybe three or four the last time I saw her. She's all grown up, or close to it."

"Why are they here?"

"Kara isn't doing well in math. Chase brought her by for me to tutor her."

He made no comment, only continued his steady typing.

"Chase wants to respect your wishes," she said, "but he'd like to come say hello if you're up to it."

Sighing heavily, Robert at last stopped, cradling his head in both hands. "Tell him I appreciate his offer, but I feel like shit and I'd rather not be bothered right now."

"Maybe you should chill out for a while. You've been pushing yourself pretty hard. What are you working on?"

He glared at her, but answered, "It's just a thing."

"A blog?" she asked.

"Something like that. I have an online support group. We have a website."

"Oh," she said. "That's nice." She gestured toward the pills. "You should probably try to eat something before your nightly dosing. It's just stir-fry vegetables and rice. I'm sorry, I wasn't sure what else to fix. Tomorrow I'll look up some more of those recipes like the ones Dad downloaded."

He faced her, his eyebrows furrowed and eyes narrowed. "Quit coddling me. I don't need your help. I can pour my own water. I'm fine. I'll try to eat a little. I know better than to take those on an empty stomach."

Her throat tightened, but she straightened, swallowing back her hurt. He'd made it clear before that he didn't want her help and Becky had cautioned her not to do things for him. "Okay. I'm sorry. I will try not to coddle you."

He turned again to his monitor and made no further reply.

She hesitated another moment, hating to ask, but her father had mentioned they should monitor for fever. "Should we take your temperature? Do you feel like you have a fever?"

"No, I don't have a fever." Tension radiated in his tone. Scowling, he lifted the fork and peered into the bowl of stir-fry.

Listen to him. Just be there. Let him vent.

Shifting her weight, she said, "I'm sorry this all sucks for you."

"Yep, that it does."

She stood there a little longer, but he didn't elaborate. Either he didn't have anything to vent or he just didn't want to vent to her.

"If you're okay, then I'll head back down," she said. "You'll text me if you need anything, right?"

He nodded as he took a tentative bite.

THE XX PLAYED softly on Kara's phone as she bent her head over her math homework. Chase put the last dinner plate into the cabinet as Alex peered over Kara's work. He paused, letting his gaze rest on Alex while she was preoccupied.

The curve of her cheek still held him fascinated. How many times had he stroked his finger along that soft line? They'd had a good thing once, but then she'd been so unforgiving, cutting off her father and anyone who stood by him.

And when Chase had refused to take that hard stance with her, she'd left him, as well.

Chase had never supported her father's infidelity, but he hadn't been able to accept how easily Alex eliminated the man from her life. Yet, she was here now. Did that mean she was becoming more accepting in her thinking?

Alex leaned toward Kara. "Remember sine is odd and cosine is even."

Nodding, Kara rubbed her eraser across the page. Alex glanced at Chase. "She's getting it."

Kara smiled. "Only because you're sitting here with me while I do it and correcting me when I get it wrong."

"But you're still doing it. And you'll remember where you went wrong, right?"

Kara's shoulders shifted in a slight shrug. "I guess, but I'll probably be lost again tomorrow in class."

"Here," Alex said as she picked up Kara's phone. "Do you want me to put my number in here? Then if you have any questions you can call and I'll walk you through it."

"Sure," Kara said. "That would be cool."

"I can bring her by any evening, so you can work together." Chase settled into the seat across from Alex, enjoying the way the overhead light illuminated her cheekbones.

"That would be great," Kara said. "I'll make dinner for everyone the next time. That is, if you take me grocery shopping, Chase. Or I can make a list, if that's easier, and you can go without me."

"So, you're not driving yet, Kara?" Alex asked.

Kara shook her head. "What's the point when I don't have anything to drive?"

"It's good to learn," Alex said. "I'll bet Chase would let you drive his car."

Chase motioned toward Kara's paper. "That's a discussion for another day. Why don't we wrap this up? It's getting late and we both have an early start tomorrow."

Kara busied herself again over the page, scouring her eraser once more over her last entry. The muffled rumble of the garage door opening sounded from beyond the door leading to the garage.

"That would be my father," Alex said.

"How's everything going with you two?" Chase asked.

"We're okay."

Moments later, the door leading to the garage opened and Jacob entered. Chase rose to greet him, extending his hand. "Hello, Jacob."

"Chase," Jacob said as he shook Chase's hand. "I didn't think I'd see you back here."

"I brought my sister, Kara, by to work with Alex on her trig homework. Do you remember Kara?"

Jacob smiled. "I remember a little angel, but this is a lovely young woman. Look how grown up you are."

"Hi," Kara said as she glanced up from her homework. "Thanks for letting me come by. Alex has really been a big help. She explains it so I actually understand."

"She's always loved working with numbers," Jacob said. "She was balancing the store's checking account when she was ten, I think."

"How's your brother?" Jacob asked Alex.

She shook her head. "He's fatigued. I don't think he's been sleeping much. He's working on his computer, but he just looks wiped out. I tried to talk him into taking it easy, but he didn't seem much interested in that. He looked flushed and I wanted to take his temperature, but he insisted he was okay. He's not eating much."

"That's about normal, though his looking flushed has me a little concerned. I'll go check on him." Jacob nodded to Chase. "I'm glad you didn't let him scare you off. You and Kara are welcome here anytime."

"Thanks," Chase said. "I appreciate that."

After he left, Chase turned to Alex. For a brief moment her gaze met his and that old connection hummed between them. It was all he could do not to reach for her. "Thanks for helping Kara. And don't think I've forgotten my part of our deal."

Her eyebrows arched in question. "Have you found your aunt?"

"Sort of."

"You found a phone number?"

"Close," he said.

"An email address?"

He shook his head.

"Social media connection?"

"An address."

She cocked her head. "A street address?"

"That's right. Do you think you can get away this weekend?"

"*This* weekend? For how long? What about Kara?"

Kara waved her hand. "Go. I'm a big girl. I won't do anything crazy while he's gone."

Chase spread his arms. "Or she can come with us. What have you got to lose?"

"Where do we need to go? Can we do it in a day?"

"It's in northern Indiana. There isn't an easy way to get there. If we drive it's a day and a half each way. We'd probably want to plan to take the entire weekend."

"And all you have is an address? Can't we do a reverse lookup to get the number?"

"I tried that. Nothing. She must not have a landline," Chase said. "You can always write her a letter."

"That will take too long. What about flying?"

"I thought it made more sense to drive since we can be more flexible with our schedule then. She might not be home. We might need to hang out and wait."

"Or leave her a note and ask her to call."

"Okay," he said. "That'll work. We'll fly, though she's hours from an airport out in the middle of nowhere."

"So we'll rent a car when we get there."

Kara shook her head, but continued working without comment. Chase shrugged. "Whatever you want."

"I want just a day trip. It'll be hard enough for me to get away for that long," Alex said.

"So, it'll just be a day trip, then." Disappointment filled him. He'd hoped to have a little more time with her, even if they were only going together to find his aunt.

"Good." She nodded. "Let me check with my dad to

see if he can spare me. I'll have to figure out what to tell him and Robert." Her gaze swung to Kara.

"She knows about our deal," Chase said. "I hope that's okay."

"I guess. I just don't think they'll approve. Robert will think I'm looking for his father for his sake. He'll give me hell. I'll have to try to convince him otherwise."

"You think about it and let me know." Chase touched her arm. "We don't have to go if you're not comfortable with it."

"No, I want to go. Let me figure it out. I'll have an answer for you tomorrow after I talk to my father and make sure it works with his schedule."

"Cool," Chase said. "Did you ask him about the other, the night of the gala?"

Pink bloomed in Alex's cheeks. She nodded. "He said he'd make it work."

Chase smiled. If her reaction were any indication, she, too, felt the continued attraction between them.

"I'm done." Kara stood and shoved her notebook and textbook into her book bag. "Thanks again, Alex. I really couldn't have done it without you."

"No problem, Kara, I'm happy to help."

"I know how you can explain your going away for the trip," Kara said.

"How?" Chase and Alex asked in unison.

"Tell them the obvious. Tell them that you two are hooking up again."

CHAPTER ELEVEN

THE SCENT OF STRONG COFFEE enticed Alex down the stairs the following morning. She'd set her alarm to wake her early, before her father left for the hardware store. The sooner she could plan her trip with Chase, the sooner they'd know if they had a donor for Robert. And finding a donor would not only be a boon for her brother, but it would also put her that much closer to returning to Baltimore.

After lying awake deep into the night, she'd slept through her alarm. Thankfully, she'd still managed to catch her father. As she entered the brightly lit kitchen, he sat at the table, scrolling through his tablet. The morning news played quietly on the TV in the living room, visible from his chair.

He smiled up at her. "Good morning, Alexandra."

"Good morning," she said and headed straight for a mug and coffee.

"You look tired."

"I am. I didn't sleep well."

"Were you worrying about your brother, or what you're going to do about Chase?"

Tell them the obvious. Tell them you're hooking up again.

Kara's suggestion had been another of the disturbing thoughts interrupting her sleep last night. Why would the girl think that was obvious? Though Alex did need a reason to explain her trip to her father, she couldn't quite bring herself to tread that particular road.

Somewhere in the wee hours of the morning she'd determined that though she wasn't comfortable lying, she couldn't risk admitting the truth. Her father's loyalties lay with her brother. And Robert was too stubborn to ever support her plan.

"Why would I need to do anything about Chase?" she asked.

He glanced up from his tablet and sipped his own coffee before answering. "I think you two have unfinished business."

"What unfinished business?" She set her mug on the table and sank into the seat across from him. "We were finished way before I left for Baltimore. There's nothing more to do about Chase. He's only around because I'm helping Kara and he's concerned about Robert. I told you the gala thing is just to help him out. It isn't a *date* date."

Her father merely shrugged.

"I didn't sleep because I have a lot on my mind, what with all the insanity around here."

He reached across the table and patted her hand. "I'm sorry, honey, I know this hasn't been easy. Not only do you have to deal with your brother being sick and not having found a donor and your own plans being up in the air, but now you also have all these questions about Robert's father and whether he's *your* father. And you've got to deal with the fact that your mother wasn't as perfect as you thought she was. It's a lot to take in."

Whether it was the lack of sleep or something else, pain seared Alex's throat and tears gathered in her eyes. "I never thought she was perfect."

"She came close," he said, his voice rough. "I'm sure you find that a strange thing for me to say after all your mother and I have been through, but she was pretty much perfect as far as I was concerned."

"But you cheated on her." The tears spilled down her cheeks. "You can't love someone and do that."

"I don't expect you to understand. I couldn't explain it to you, anyway. I'm not sure I understand how I let that happen. It was a stupid thing for me to do and not a day goes by that I don't regret it. I'm sorry for what my actions did to my relationship with your mother and I'm sorry for what they did to my relationship with you and Steven. Things haven't been the same with Megan, either, though she's not been as vocal as you in her condemnation. Even though she's been the most adamant about reuniting this family, her disapproval has always been clear."

Alex closed her eyes. God, she was tired. Thinking about all this made her head hurt. "When I find someone, I hope it will be someone who will cherish me enough to not stray. I would never do that to someone I loved."

"I hope you find that," he said and leaned back in his chair. "I had hoped for the same thing at one point, but sometimes we have to settle for what we get. The heart can be a harsh master."

She shook her head, but made no response. What would it matter? If she remained single the rest of her life she'd be spared whatever further heartbreak a family of her own might bring her. She'd had enough of being dysfunctional with her birth family. Maybe it was best to spare a new generation more of the same. Why did people always hurt the ones they were supposed to love?

If that was what family was about, then count her out.

"I did need to ask you something," she said.

He folded his hands in front of him and gave her his full attention.

She dropped her gaze. "I've been thinking I'd like to

get away for a day to clear my head. Maybe head north into the mountains for some hiking."

Her father was silent a long moment. She held her breath. Did he suspect what she was planning? Finally, he nodded slowly. "I know it hasn't been easy around here, and we're just getting started. Your brother doesn't mean to be hard on you. This is just a very frustrating time for him. Of course, I understand your need to get away. You *should* have a break."

Relief coursed through her. Maybe slipping away wouldn't be as difficult as she'd anticipated. "I can't imagine what this must be like for Robert and he's already been through so much. I know I'm late to the game. I just… I want to be able to give this my all and I think I can do that better if I take a little time away. I hate that we still don't have a donor."

Her father nodded as he folded his hands around his coffee cup. "We're going to keep looking and even if we don't find a donor we're not out of options. Megan has been researching clinical trials for cancer treatments. We haven't begun to look at any of that. Then there are other alternative treatments we need to look into, as well."

"Of course we should explore all options, but with these clinical trials, aren't you talking about experimenting, Dad? Do we want that for Robert? Does *he* want that? Dr. Braden seems to believe the transplant is still the safest way to go."

"Ultimately, Robert is in the driver's seat on all of this. I'm supportive of whatever it is that he wants."

"What if the donor stem cell transplant *is* his best chance at kicking this thing, though?"

He held her gaze for a long moment before saying, "Then we have to trust in Dr. Braden that he'll keep looking until we find a donor, and in the meantime, it won't hurt for us to do all we can to recruit new donors."

Her breath caught. Was he telling her he would be supportive of her finding and recruiting Robert's biological father? "I'll see what I can do on that front, then. Surely I can find someone willing to donate, if not for Robert then for someone else."

"They can get typed specifically to see if they are a match to Robert and not have to sign up for the national bank. If we do all we can now, then hopefully we'll beat this thing, and if not…well, we won't have any regrets."

Surely, he meant what she thought. Without a doubt if she didn't find her brother's father and the worst happened, she'd regret it for the rest of her life. "So, if I were to take a day off…to clear my head…do you think you could spare me here?" she asked.

"It probably wouldn't hurt for you and your brother to have a break from each other."

She shrugged. "It's like a pressure cooker here. I hate not getting along with him. Maybe we're just too much alike to get along."

"You two are both stubborn, but you used to get along, back before…"

She shook her head. "I can't think about all that right now, or my head may explode."

Her father's shoulders rose as he drew in a long breath. "It's too bad you can't take Robert with you. A hike in the mountains might help his spirits. If he has the strength for it."

Her pulse thudded. She managed a small laugh. "That would kind of defeat the purpose, though."

"Of course." He eyed her again for a long moment. "Let me talk to Becky about the schedule at the store, but

I think we can work it out," he said. "Maybe for some-time this weekend."

"Thanks, Dad, I really appreciate it." She hesitated. "Maybe we shouldn't mention it to Robert. Things are tense enough between us, without him having to know I want a break already."

"Once we settle on a day, I'll plan something to keep him distracted. Maybe he won't notice you're missing."

"I'm not sure if that's good or bad," she said. "But I do think it's for the best."

TWILIGHT HAD FALLEN by the time Chase pulled into his driveway late on Tuesday. He was weary to the bone, but at least Kara was there to greet him. She'd been so appre-ciative since coming to live with him, she'd had dinner waiting every night when he got home.

What had she made for tonight?

His cell phone buzzed before he could exit his car. A glance at the display had him groaning as he accepted the call. "Mrs. Dixon."

"Hello, Chase, darling. I'm not interrupting anything, am I?"

"Well, I was just getting home—"

"Perfect, then, I won't keep you long. I was just think-ing about the lighting," she said.

"I'm sorry, what lighting?"

"Oh, you know, the lighting for the collection. We've had the same lights in there forever. We need to update them. I was thinking some LED lights with UV filters. And we'll want to spotlight some of the key pieces, too. I emailed you a list and how I think the lights should be mounted."

He squeezed his eyes shut. "How very thoughtful of you, Mrs. Dixon. I'm sure that's an excellent suggestion, but unfortunately, the museum's budget has been set and there isn't any room for additional lighting fixtures, especially when what we have is working perfectly well."

"But the new lighting would be the best thing for the collection, Chase. I'm sure something could be shifted in the budget. You'll do a little cost analysis and make the recommendation, won't you, dear? I wouldn't trust anyone else to do it."

After exhaling slowly, he said, "I'll see if I can carve out a little time in my schedule to look into it."

"Thank you, Chase. You are such a dear."

Impatience and self-loathing filling him, he ended the call as quickly as he could then finally exited his car. Why couldn't he just say no to the woman? He entered to find the house dark and quiet. He set down his briefcase and then wandered into the kitchen, but she wasn't there.

"Kara?" he called as he moved up the stairs.

He checked first her bedroom and then the rest of the house, but she was nowhere to be found. He called her cell phone, but she didn't answer. After leaving her a voice mail he headed back to the kitchen. Maybe if he got dinner started, she'd show up in time to help him. He cranked his music and opened the refrigerator.

As he marinated chicken and chopped vegetables to steam, he focused on not worrying about his stepsister. Kara had been on her best behavior so far. She'd studied with her teacher for her makeup test and had worked well with Alex, diligently finishing her homework every night.

She and Alex had seemed to hit it off. Warmth filled him as a vision of Alex's smiling face drifted through his mind. That smile had been such a big part of his earlier years, even before his relationship with her had taken a romantic turn. Alex had been an integral part of his life—of his family—for almost as long as he could remember.

Now that she was back, it was only natural that she'd be again a part of his life.

But in what capacity would that be? Alex had made it clear years ago that she was no longer interested in a romantic relationship with him. But was that what he wanted?

Tell them you're hooking up again.

Alex had made no comment in response to Kara's suggestion. What had gone through her head at that moment? And if she told her brother and father rekindling her relationship with Chase was the reason for their trip, would she only be using that as an excuse to cover her real plan to find Robert's biological father?

Or was there a chance for him and Alex to mend their relationship and start fresh?

He glanced at his watch. Maybe Alex knew where Kara was. Setting aside his knife, he picked up his phone and dialed her number. She picked up almost immediately.

"Hey," he said. "It's Chase."

"Hey, yes, I know. What's up?"

The sweet sound of her voice flowed over him. The woman didn't even have to try to sound sexy. She exuded a natural sensuality that had had him hanging on her every word in the past. Evidently, her effect on him hadn't waned over time. If anything, the mature tones of her voice added a smoky quality with even more allure. No doubt about it. The girl he'd known had become all woman.

He inhaled slowly. "I just got home and Kara isn't here. I was wondering if maybe you had heard from her. Do you know where she might be?"

"I'm sorry, Chase, I don't know. She texted me earlier to thank me again for helping her and to see if I could help her later in the week before her next test, but I was busy with Robert and I didn't respond until just a little while ago. She hasn't yet replied. Did you try calling her?"

A feeling of unease settled over him. "She didn't pick up."

"I can try to text her again."

"That would be great. I'll try that, too."

"I'm sure she's fine."

He blew out a breath. "I hope so. Is this how parents feel?"

"I guess so."

A dry laugh worked its way from his throat. "It sucks."

She chuckled softly and then she was quiet for a moment. "I talked to my father this morning."

"About the trip? What did you say to him?"

"I told him I needed a break, that I wanted a day to take a trip up into the mountains to clear my head. Maybe do some hiking. It was all I could think of. I hate lying to him, though."

"Did he buy that?"

"Yes. Things have been tense between Robert and me. It isn't a stretch. I really do need a break."

So, she'd decided against Kara's suggestion. It was probably a good thing she'd kept her real plans from her father, though. They really needed to find Robert's biological father and convince him to be a donor.

"And you don't think he suspected anything?" he asked.

"I'm not sure. There was one point where I almost thought he was trying to tell me he was supportive of doing whatever it takes to find a donor, but I really don't think so. I think it's better to ask forgiveness rather than permission on this one. He's going to talk to Becky about the schedule. He said that this weekend might work the best."

"Yes, I think I can get away at some point this weekend, though I should probably see what Kara has going on. I'll check out flights to get some idea, but we're taking Kara with us. After her no-show tonight, I don't think I can comfortably let her out of my sight again. Although…" He blew out a breath. "I do have to leave tomorrow on another trip for a traveling exhibition."

"For how long?"

"Just overnight, if all goes as planned. I'll be back Thursday."

His phone vibrated against his ear. He glanced at the display and relief filled him. "I've got Kara calling me now."

"Great. I'll let you go, then. We'll touch base later."

He clicked over to the incoming call. "Kara, where are you?"

"I'm at a friend's house."

"What friend's? You have to tell me these things. I've been worried."

"Chill, I'm fine. I didn't have to work and I'm allowed to have a life, aren't I?" she asked.

"What about homework?" he asked.

"I did it all already."

"Kara, don't be bullshitting me."

"Shit, Chase, get off my case," she said. "I'm not bullshitting."

"Okay, but I want you home by ten. It's a school night."

"Whatever. I know it's a school night."

"Don't whatever me, Kara," he said. "I thought we were both going to make an effort here."

"Fine. I'll be home by ten."

"Text me the address of where you're at."

"Seriously?" she asked.

"Yes, and your friend's name."

"I've never had to do this with any of my foster parents," she said, disbelief clear in her voice.

"Well, you're with someone now who gives a damn about where you are and what you're doing."

"Some of them cared about that. They just weren't jail wardens."

"Look, Kara, I don't like this any more than you do," he said. "But I also don't like not knowing where you are and if you're okay. I just need to not worry about you and I can only do that if you communicate with me."

"I'm fine. I've been fine. You don't need to worry about me. I can take care of myself."

"Fine, but text me where you're at and be home by ten. Please. Although, I can't believe I'm letting you run around Atlanta by yourself until ten o'clock at night."

"Okay. And I'm not by myself," she said and then disconnected.

He put down the phone and chopped at a carrot. So who was she with? And what were they doing? This being responsible for another human being was going to be the death of him.

CHAPTER TWELVE

"I'M GLAD YOU FEEL well enough to get out," Alex said as she walked beside Robert to Brookhaven Park near their neighborhood.

Robert's jaw tensed, but he made no response. He moved slowly. His doctor had added some heavy-hitting pain medication to his regimen to combat some of the discomfort from the radiation.

"It's a perfect day to get out," she said.

"It is, though I would have been okay on my own."

She smiled. She refused to let him get her down today. "I know you would have, but I wanted to get out, too, and why not venture out together? I haven't been to this park since forever. We used to come here all the time. Remember?"

He merely shook his head and continued his slow shuffle along the sidewalk.

"Should we schedule you a massage? It would make you feel better."

He shrugged. "You know, kissing my ass isn't going to make me any happier about you being here."

"Or how about some energy work?"

"That sounds like Megan's idea."

"It was," she admitted. "I can look online and find someone. I'd get referrals, of course. Do you think Dr. Braden knows any good energy workers he could recommend?"

A sarcastic chuckle escaped Robert. "I can't quite see that, but I'm open to it, if you want to find someone."

Satisfaction filled her. Maybe she *was* making progress with him. "Okay. I will then. I'll find you both a massage therapist and an energy worker. Maybe I can find one person to do both. It probably wouldn't hurt to get a nutritionist on board, either."

The wind blew softly around them. The late May breeze felt wonderful to Alex, maybe a little too warm even, but Robert pulled his old hoody closer around him. She hated that even on a good day, he seemed to suffer. No wonder he was so cranky.

"So what's going on with you and Chase these days?" he asked.

His question shouldn't have surprised her. Still, she tensed. Her breaking things off with his best friend had only been one more strike against her back in the days when everything fell apart. It had been a sore subject between them ever since.

"Nothing," she said. "I've told you. I'm just tutoring Kara."

"Have you asked him about his aunt Rena yet?"

"What do you mean by 'yet'?"

He shrugged. "If you haven't already you will at some point. I know you, Alex. Once you get an idea into your head it's only a matter of time. And the fact that I told you I don't want you to find my biological father wouldn't stop you if that's what *you* wanted."

The sweet scent of honeysuckle filled her nostrils as she inhaled slowly. The last thing she wanted was to fight with Robert. No good would come of that. Was she wrong to think she could just disappear for a day with Chase without her brother noticing?

She didn't want to lie to him. If she denied wanting to

find Chase's aunt he wouldn't believe her and he'd think she was up to something, but she couldn't very well admit to her plan to find his father and solicit the man's help for the son he'd never known.

"If I *did* ask about his aunt," she said at last, "I would do so only because I might want to talk to the woman. It would be nice to understand why Mom did what she did. Don't you want to know about that?"

"And you want to find my biological father." He stared straight ahead as he spoke.

"I would just want to talk to his aunt," she reiterated. "So she could tell me why Mom did what she did and how long the affair lasted."

He was silent a long moment and then he asked, "And?"

Her skin warmed. "And what?"

"And what did Chase say? Did he put you in touch with his aunt Rena?"

Maybe admitting she'd already talked to Chase would appease Robert for now. "She moved away some years ago and they lost touch."

"So, you're giving up on trying to find her?"

She bit her lip. Why couldn't he be reasonable and see that finding his biological father was a necessary evil? Was she the only one who saw the sense in it?

"I don't see what other choice I have," she said, hating being untruthful.

His eyebrows rose, but he only said, "So what about you possibly having the same father as me? What if this was a long affair lasting for years?"

At least he was focusing on that aspect of it. She shrugged. "Dad doesn't know how to find the man. Mom doesn't know who *we* are most of the time, let alone who a man she hasn't seen in decades is. How would you propose I go about looking for him?"

"You could ask Dad to take a paternity test. He'd do it for you. He isn't the evil person you make him out to be." He kicked a branch in his path. "Maybe he *is* your real father. Maybe that's why you weren't a match."

That did stop her short. She hadn't thought of a paternity test. "I don't think I could ask him to do that."

Robert scowled. "What? So, *now* you're afraid of hurting his feelings? After all these years of cutting him out of your life, you step back in only because circumstances are dire around here and suddenly, you can't ask him to take a simple test to determine if he's actually genetically linked to you."

He laughed softly. "That's rich, Alex. You're all heart. I'd think you'd jump at the chance to prove you aren't related to him. Ah, but then of course, if the test proves he isn't your father, you'd share the blood of the dick who slept with Mom while she was married to Dad and then impregnated her, but never claimed his offspring."

Her face warmed and tears pricked her eyes. Why did he have to be so hateful to her? It wasn't as if he'd made any effort to repair things between them over the years. He'd been happy to wash his hands of her.

And she was here now, trying as hard as she could to help him, while all the while *he* was a dick to her. Did she really deserve this?

"I think you and I could use a break from each other." She tried to keep her voice steady. "I asked Dad if he'd be okay with me taking some time to clear my head. He's checking with Becky to see if he can find a day when she can be at the store or has someone else to cover for them, so he can be home for you."

"I don't need a babysitter."

"We know that," she said and then inhaled a calming breath. "It makes us feel better to have one of us around, though. Besides, you'll need to get used to it. Once you start the transplant you're stuck with at least one of us hovering around 24/7."

"Yeah, I know the drill. And that's *if* we start the transplant," he said, his gaze sweeping hers before shifting away. "If we don't find a donor soon, I may want to schedule my surgery to remove the central line."

"No, why would you do that?" Alex asked. "You need that for the transplant."

"I hate having this hunk of metal in my chest when we don't know if I'll even need it." He laughed a derisive laugh. "It's a real babe magnet, you know? It's bad enough I have this thing." He lifted his left arm, with the scar just above the inside of his left elbow, indicating the portacath. "I'll have this taken out, too. It's done nothing but give me trouble."

"It got you through your initial chemo and from what Dad says, they've used it plenty since then, as well."

"And a lot of good all of it has done me." He gestured with his arms wide.

Her heart squeezed. He may be a dick, but he was going through the worst of times. Maybe she needed to cut him some slack. "We'll find a donor, Robert."

"I hope you're right," he said as he trudged along the path. "Because if we don't find one soon, I'm ready to call it quits on all this bullshit and live whatever time I have left with what little remaining dignity I have."

Her throat tightened. "Then we'll find a donor, Robert. We just have to."

STEAM CURLED UP from the pot on the back of the stove. Alex stirred the quinoa, checking to see if the small grains had cooked. "This looks ready."

Becky shifted beside her as she removed one medium-size baked potato from the microwave. She stabbed the potato with a fork. "Potato is done. That's organic quinoa, right?"

Alex pulled the box from the recycling and showed it to her sister. "It's what you brought in with you in that big bag you shouldn't have been lugging around."

"Honey, come sit and prop up your feet." Becky's husband, Michael, patted the empty chair beside him.

He sat at the table, slicing a tomato for the platter of toppings Alex's father was preparing at the adjacent counter. Robert, who'd been feeling a little better after their walk, sat across from Becky's husband, husking ears of corn.

"Yes, Becky, please sit. I've got this," Alex said.

They had way too many people in this kitchen. When her father had called to tell her Becky and Michael were coming to dinner, apprehension had knotted her stomach. Could this have anything to do with her talk with her father that morning? Her sister hadn't been by since Alex's arrival. What else could have prompted her sudden craving for southwest quinoa veggie burgers at their father's house?

"Well, someone needs to toast the buns," Becky said.

Alex turned from the stove. "I'll take care of it once I get the patties made and in the oven. Just relax. It's going to be another half an hour before everything is ready. Do you want to go stretch out on the sofa while you wait?"

"No," Becky said. "I like being here with everyone. Isn't it nice to have us all together? Alex, I'm so happy to see you here. I didn't think it would ever happen. Now, if only we could get Steven and Megan to come down, as well. We could have a family reunion."

"Steven can't get away and Megan won't come for just a weekend. It's too far and she won't pull Carly out of preschool for a longer visit," Alex said as she put all the ingredients for the burgers into the food processor, consulting the recipe on her father's tablet as she went.

"We don't need everyone to come right now, Becky," Robert said. He might be feeling better, but his sour mood had remained.

"Well, surely they'll come after Baxter is born. They'll want to meet their new nephew. That or they'll come to celebrate your victory over this awful cancer." Becky finally eased herself into the chair, swinging her feet up into her husband's lap and leaning back with her hands folded over her rounded belly.

Alex glanced at Robert. His frown had deepened. He shook his head as he stripped another ear of corn. He said, "The transplant is a big fat maybe at this point and if I do get it it'll be a long process. And even then, you'd be better to shoot for a baptism or some other celebration for your son. I don't see any other opportunities for celebrations on the horizon."

"But they're doing another donor search, right?" Becky asked.

"Yes," Dad said as he turned from slicing an onion. "And I've put the word out that we're looking for a donor. Megan has, too. I know of three people already who have contacted the donor bank for typing."

Alex touched Robert's shoulder. She wasn't usually as optimistic as her sisters, but she had to keep hopeful in this case. "We're going to find a donor."

Robert didn't respond and a short silence fell over them, filled first by the whirring of the food processor and then by the soft tones of Dave Matthews playing on the satellite radio in the living room.

"So, Alex, what's up with you and Chase Carrolton?"

Becky asked after a long moment. "I hear he's been coming by."

Alex inhaled slowly. "He's been bringing his sister, Kara, by and I've been tutoring her. She's having a tough time with math. Trigonometry isn't easy for everyone."

"And I hear you and Chase are going to a big-time ball together. Are you two rekindling the old flame?" Becky asked.

A short laugh escaped Alex. She shook her head as she formed the patties and dropped them onto a baking sheet. "No, not at all. It's a fund-raiser for the museum where he works and it isn't a real date. I'm going as a favor to him to help fend off unwanted attention from at least one of the museum's benefactors. We're just going as friends."

"That may be true for you," Robert said. "But what about Chase?"

"What do you mean? I told you. Chase and I are ancient history. He's taking me only for appearance's sake. That's all it's about."

"Okay, if you say so," Robert said.

"You two were so good together, though. I miss having Chase around. I haven't seen him in forever," Becky said. "What happened with the two of you?" she asked Robert. "How come you stopped hanging out with him?"

Robert shrugged. "We kept in touch for a long time. It was tough when I was out in Seattle and he's had his father to deal with all this time and I guess Kara has always been a little bit of a handful, as well, even though she hasn't been living with him. Chase has always been a part of her life."

"And his job keeps him pretty busy. He travels a lot and he's getting his PhD in art history," Alex added.

"Wow, he sounds so accomplished," Becky said. "How can you not be interested, Alex?"

"I'm plenty busy with Robert, and Chase has Kara to occupy his free time these days. She's already giving him gray hair."

"Maybe she acts out because of the foster care," Becky said. "I'm sure she's had some good families, but I always thought that was so sad. Chase has custody now, though, right?"

"For almost a week now," Alex said. "Though they still have to go through a hearing to make it final."

"That's so great of him. He's such a good guy, Alex. So, really, what's the problem?" Becky asked. "Has he gotten fat and bald? Has he completely let himself go?"

Warmth that had nothing to do with the fact she was sliding the southwestern veggie burgers into the preheated oven crept into Alex's cheeks. "No, he hasn't let himself go."

Becky grinned. "He's looking good still, though? Chase was always so hot." She patted Michael's shoulder. "Not as hot as you, babe, but Alex always found him irresistible."

"He is *not* irresistible," Alex said as the warmth in her cheeks intensified. She could and she would resist Chase's appeal. "I'm heading back to Baltimore as soon as Robert is in the clear. There's no way I'm starting up again with Chase Carrolton."

"That's a shame," her father said. "I like the boy."

Becky laughed. "He's, what, thirty-two now? He's no boy. He's got to be *all* man. We should invite him and Kara to dinner. I'd love to see him again."

Alex shook her head and opened the bag of buns. She saw no sense in continuing this conversation. "Who wants their bun toasted?"

BY MIDNIGHT, Chase's worry had escalated into a near panic. He glanced again at his cell phone display, but he found no response from Kara to his numerous follow-up texts and calls. He paced onto the front porch, breathing in the cooler air to help calm his nerves.

How did parents handle this? When he had his own kids, which, hopefully, wouldn't be too far in the future, he was going to teach them from the start to communicate with him. They'd have cell phones as soon as they could talk and learn to operate them and not lose them.

Had Kara done this to all of her foster parents? No wonder life in foster care had been a struggle.

The low rumble of an engine sounded up the street as a car approached, its headlights illuminating the quiet neighborhood. Chase tensed as the vehicle stopped in front of the house. He had to hold himself back from storming to the curb and yanking open the door to see if Kara was inside.

Instead, he forced himself to relax as the passenger door opened. Rap music boomed at a barely tolerable decibel and laughter drifted over the night air. At last Kara emerged from the vehicle. Chase remained on the porch as she sauntered up the front walkway to the stairs.

When she hit the porch, he unfolded his arms. "Kara, where have you been?"

She startled and pressed her hand to her chest. "Shit, Chase, you scared the bezeesus out of me."

"Good, that makes us even. We agreed you'd be back by ten. That was over two hours ago. Do you have any idea how worried I've been? Anything could have happened to you. If I'd thought it would do any good, I would have called the police."

"Jesus, you're overreacting. I'm sorry, my friend offered to give me a ride, and I figured that was safer than taking MARTA and then the bus. But he had to run an errand first and then it got later than I realized."

"So, you could have called. I would have come and gotten you."

She jiggled her purse. "My phone died."

"And your friend didn't have a phone you could borrow?" he asked, folding his arms across his chest.

"What good would his phone do me, when your number was in my phone and it was dead?"

He took a step closer to her and was hit by the distinct scent of alcohol. Disappointment filled him. "Shit, Kara, I can't believe you've been drinking."

With a shake of her head, she turned from him and headed for the door. "It's not like it's a big deal. You can't tell me you didn't do it at my age."

He snorted in disgust. "Do you actually think that after all the crap I've been through with my father and his drinking that I'd have any taste for alcohol?"

Her hand stilled on the doorknob. "Never? Not even a sip?"

"Why would I?" He leaned closer to her. "It's a stupid thing to do."

She shrugged and pushed open the door. "That's actually kind of sad. You need to learn how to have fun."

Anger simmered through him. How could she be this callous? His father's drinking had ruined her life every bit as much as it had ruined Chase's. Why would she drink?

Ignoring her comment, he followed her inside. "I'm sorry, Kara, but you're grounded."

She paused on her way up the stairs, but didn't turn to him. "Fine."

He stood at the foot of the stairs long after her bedroom door slammed closed from above. She was a seventeen-year-old girl who'd been having her run of Atlanta doing as she pleased with no one but him to call her on it.

Guilt worried its way up his spine. Why hadn't he been

more diligent in looking out for her in the past? How had a night like this become acceptable to her? He'd assumed it was safe to leave her discipline and oversight in the hands of her foster parents, but if tonight were any indication, Kara had been running on her own for years.

For her own safety, Chase would have to find a way to rein her in.

CHAPTER THIRTEEN

"SOME OLD HIPPY Caught Another Hippy Tripping On Acid." Kara grinned. "I can remember that. Cool."

Alex smiled, pleased by Kara's delight. The girl was really starting to grasp the lessons. "It's the way I learned the formulas."

"I think that's going to help me on this next test. I've had the hardest time with keeping sine, cosine and tangent straight. This is totally cool," Kara said, turning to face Alex. "Thanks for coming by. I know you only came because Chase asked you to, so you could make sure I was here and behaving while he's out of town, but I still appreciate it."

"I *wanted* to come by. This is my big night out away from my father's house—my break from my family."

"I'm sorry about everything that's going on with your brother. That must really suck. I mean, the whole cancer thing is awful enough, but then you finding out about your dad not being his dad and maybe not being your dad has got to totally blow."

"It does. And did you know to top it all off I was just laid off from my job?"

"No way."

"Yes," Alex said. "That's how I was able to pick up and come here at the drop of a hat."

"That's wild. They must have been really strapped to lay *you* off. You're probably better off without them, though. Maybe the universe was trying to tell you something."

"And what was it trying to tell me?"

"I don't know, that you're supposed to come back here and fix everything, maybe."

Alex shook her head. "I don't know if any of it is fixable. And I doubt I'm the one meant to do the fixing. I can't believe we haven't found a match for Robert. I guess it's understandable under the circumstances that none of us in the family was a match, but you'd think I might have been. Everyone has always thought we were so alike, at least from a physical aspect. If any of us was going to match him, I thought it would be me."

"Maybe it's because he *is* only your half brother. Maybe you weren't a match because you don't have the same father that he does."

"Maybe, but still, his doctor says it's not unusual for even full siblings not to match. You'd think having the same mother would make it more likely we'd match than someone out of a random bunch of strangers, but they find totally unrelated donors from the national donor bank all the time." She sighed. "It just sucks that he doesn't have a donor yet. He needs this transplant."

"I think it's really cool, what you're doing with Chase—finding your brother's real dad."

Alex tapped her fingers against the table in frustration. "I wish *Robert* thought it was really cool. I haven't figured out how I'll handle it if we find the guy and he doesn't agree to be a donor. Actually, I'm not sure what to do if he *does* agree. I just know I have to find him."

"I don't really know your brother that well, but I know if it were Chase who had cancer and I had to find his donor, I wouldn't stop until I found him or her. And when I found that donor, if the person didn't want to donate his bone marrow or whatever it is, then I'd find a way to convince him. Then if Chase didn't, for whatever stupid reason, want to use the dude's stuff, then I'd find a way to convince him. I wouldn't stop until *my* brother had gotten what he needed and I knew he was going to be all right."

Warmth filled Alex. "You really care about Chase, don't you?"

"Hell, yeah, I love him. He's all I have. I've never been able to count on anyone in my entire life but Chase. He is the one and only person who has ever really totally been there for me. I know I can count on him, no matter what."

"You put him through the wringer last night, Kara."

Kara drummed her pencil against the tabletop. "I know. But I don't get why he was so freaked out. I've been running on my own for years. I know how to get around and no one messes with me. I give attitude when I'm on the street. People don't want anything to do with me that way."

"But, Kara, Chase isn't used to that—to your being out at all hours and not checking in. It would freak *me* out if you were staying with me and you were late like that and I couldn't reach you. My mind tends to veer toward the worst-case scenario. And Chase takes being responsible for you very seriously."

"He should just chill."

"Maybe, but maybe you could cut him a little slack. Meet him halfway. He's never done this before. Is it a bad thing that he cares about you?"

"No," Kara said, her voice low. "I really want this to work. I do have a life, though."

"That's true of most teenagers." She cocked her head. "Does that mean there's a special guy keeping you out late?"

A slow smile curved Kara's lips. "Maybe."

Alex leaned toward her. "So tell me about him, so I can live vicariously through you. My love life is sadly lacking."

"He's just a friend, but I really like him and I think he likes me. His name is Bruce and he's blond-haired and brown-eyed. We match, you know? But he's really cool. He works at the ice cream shop with me and he rides a Harley, so he's environmentally conscious."

"I have a feeling Chase wouldn't quite see it that way."

Kara straightened and her gaze held Alex's. "Maybe if Chase had a life, too, he'd ease up a little on me."

Alex shook her head. "Don't look at me."

"Why not?"

"Besides the fact that Chase is not the guy for me, I'm only here for a couple of months or so. Once we get Robert through this stem cell transplant I'm going back to my old life."

Kara's expression darkened. "That sucks. But what's so wrong with my brother? He's got a good heart. He really cares about people. And he's great eye candy. Girls are always hitting on him and he hardly notices half the time."

"So why isn't he dating anyone…or is he?" Alex's heart thudded. Why should she care if Chase had a girlfriend?

"Don't get me wrong. He's had his share of women, but most of them don't stick around. They can't handle his old man. He takes up any time Chase has left over after working and checking up on me and studying." Kara hung her head. "I don't get why he still tries to help his dad. The dude is a mess. He's pretty much ruined everybody's life he's ever come in contact with."

Alex inhaled slowly. She had no idea why Chase hadn't washed his hands of his father. She'd have done so long ago, but admitting that to Kara didn't seem prudent. "Your brother doesn't believe in giving up on people."

"I don't know why. His mother gave up on him, just like mine gave up on me."

"Maybe that's why." Alex frowned. "He knows how it feels to be given up on and he doesn't wish it on anyone else. Not even his father."

Her cell phone vibrated in her pocket. Her dad was with Robert, but she'd asked him to call if he needed her to come home for any reason. She pulled out her phone and grinned. "Speak of the devil. It's Chase." With a shake of her head she accepted his call. "Your ears must be burning."

"Were you talking about me?" he asked, the rumble of his voice rolling over her, familiar, yet intriguing with its deeper, more mature tones.

"Kara and I were just talking about your inability to give up on people."

"Ah, well, I hope you see that as a good quality," he said.

"I think the jury is still out on that."

He was quiet a moment, likely thinking she'd given up on him way back when. Had he expected her to stay when he had failed to emotionally support her? And if he could be supportive still of her father after he'd cheated on her mother, could Alex have trusted Chase to remain true to her?

"How's she doing?" Chase asked, drawing Alex back to the present.

"I don't see what all the trouble was. She's been picking it up without any problem."

"That's because you know how to explain it to me so I can understand," Kara said.

"Thanks for working with her, Alex."

"No problem," Alex said, glancing at his stepsister.

"Kara is a great kid, even if she likes to roam the streets of Atlanta like a vagabond."

Kara rolled her eyes and muttered, "I told you, no one messes with me."

"She's going to be the death of me," Chase said.

"I'm trying to convince her to take it easy on you."

"If you can do that I'll really owe you."

"So, you'll be back tomorrow?" Alex asked, not wanting to explore her reasons for asking.

"My flight gets in around seven. Do you miss me?"

Her cheeks warmed and she laughed a short little laugh that made her feel way too vulnerable. "I talked to my father about this weekend's schedule."

"You did? What did he say?"

"He talked to Becky and she has the store covered on Sunday, so he can stay with Robert as needed and I'm free to go. Did you look at flights?"

"We have several options. I was thinking we should take an early flight, though, so we can spend as much time there as possible," he said.

"Okay, that sounds good. I'm okay with whatever you feel would work. Just let me know what you book and I'll book the same."

"I'll look at it tonight and let you know. Could you please put Kara on?"

"Sure." She held the phone out to Kara. "He wants to talk to you."

"Thanks," Kara said. She pressed the phone to her ear. "Hey, Chase, what's up?"

Alex checked over Kara's work, pleased with the limited errors, while Kara chatted with Chase. After a few minutes, Kara handed the phone back to her, saying, "He wants to talk to you again."

Thanking Kara, she pressed the phone to her ear. "Hi."

"Hi. I just wanted to hear your voice again. You sound really sexy on the phone."

Her face again warmed. She turned from Kara, in case the girl noticed the pink that was surely blossoming in her cheeks. It had been way too long since a man had spoken to her in this way.

"Chase…"

"You didn't answer my question."

She bit her lip. "What question?"

"You know what question. Do you miss me?"

"I'm not answering that."

"Why not, Alex? It's been fifteen years. Can't we let bygones be bygones?"

"We made a truce," she said, stepping into the next room as she glanced to make sure Kara was busy again with her homework.

"And that was a great start, but it isn't enough," he said. "Tell me it isn't just me that remembers how great we were."

You two were so good together, though.

She closed her eyes. She would not, could not, open herself up to being crushed again by him, regardless of his appeal. "I remember how you let me down."

Silence hummed across the line. She shifted her weight and glanced again at Kara. If she didn't need Chase to find his aunt, she might have walked away at this point, but she did need him. She had no choice but to bide her time and continue to resist any attempts he made to resurrect a romantic connection with her.

"We'll have a long time to talk about it this weekend," he said at long last. "And for the record…I miss you."

I-85 TRAFFIC CRAWLED at an agonizing pace as Chase headed home from the airport the following evening. Aggravated, he gripped his steering wheel and cranked up his air conditioner a notch. The temperatures had jumped over the past week, reaching record highs for May in Atlanta. With this heat he wasn't looking forward to June.

At least Kara would be finished with school soon and could take a little break from the books. Maybe he should plan a beach trip or something fun for them to do over her summer break. She'd enjoy that and he'd enjoy it, too, especially if he could convince Alex to come along.

He frowned. Of course, her availability depended on what was happening with Robert. And things were not looking too promising on that front. Chase peered at the long line of cars behind and in front of him.

Why was there still so much traffic this late? An accident must be slowing down all the rubberneckers. He inhaled slowly as he inched along.

When he came to a full stop he glanced at his cell phone. He'd called Alex last night to give her the flight information, but she hadn't picked up or returned his call.

Well, she could act as if she hadn't missed him all she wanted. He'd felt that certain something between them and he'd bet his bottom dollar she'd felt it, too. They still had that connection. He was tired of letting work and his father dictate his life. It was time to make some changes and if Chase had any say in the matter, having Alex in his life again was going to be a part of those changes.

Red and blue lights flashed ahead to his right. At last, he'd reached the accident. He exhaled as he rolled slowly past a huge pickup truck and a crumpled sedan flanked by emergency vehicles. Finally, the bottleneck opened.

Within twenty minutes he turned the corner to his street. As he drew closer to his house a low rhythmic booming vibrated through him. Cars lined the road on both sides. The booming grew louder, joined by the strains of a squealing guitar. Laughter drifted on the air, along with the murmur of a crowd.

"Oh, no, no, no," Chase said as he drew near his house.

Light shone through every window. The front door stood wide-open as a swarm of kids moved between the house and the porch, and throughout the yard. No wonder Kara hadn't responded when he'd texted her that he'd landed.

Since the driveway was filled with cars, he drove up the street another block before finding a spot alongside the curb. With a shake of his head he exited his car and then strode up the street, anger simmering through him. What was Kara thinking to have a party like this?

A boy around Kara's age stumbled toward him. He stopped in front of Chase, holding his stomach. *Shit.* From the look and smell of it the kid was roaring drunk. Chase grabbed the kid's arm and asked, "Where are you going, buddy?"

The kid shook his head, cupped his hand to his mouth, then turned and threw up in the gutter. Another boy ran over to them. "I've got him, mister. He's okay."

"He's not okay," Chase said. "He's drunk…or something."

"It's the punch." The kid gestured toward Chase's house, grinning. "It's killer."

"God, I hope not literally." He glanced over his shoulder, expecting to see DFCS agents descending on the place, intent on swooping Kara away.

"But I'm cool." The kid dangled a set of car keys. "I'm the designated driver."

"You look twelve. Is that supposed to make me feel any better?"

The kid frowned at him as he looped his arm around

his friend. "I'm a senior and I've been driving for two years. I'll get him home."

"Great," Chase said as the youths moved up the street and he reached his driveway.

He pushed his way into the first cluster of high schoolers in the yard. "This party's over, but no one is driving until I've cleared them to do so."

"Fine," a dark-eyed girl with blue streaks in her hair said. "But you'll have to talk to that blonde girl. She took everyone's keys."

A small amount of relief flowed through him. "Super. Where is this blonde girl?"

A guy in sunglasses, wearing sagging pants and a hoody, gestured toward the house. "She was in the kitchen when the keg came."

"Awesome," Chase said. "A keg, of course."

He maneuvered through the crowd, squeezed around a big guy in the doorway and then shouldered his way into the living room. He turned off the television, which was hooked to his surround-sound speakers. The music stopped and kids turned to him, questioning looks on their faces. Murmurs of protest broke out.

"The party is over," Chase said. "Everyone needs to leave, but no one is driving until I have cleared them."

A small commotion erupted near the kitchen. Kara pushed through a knot of people and headed toward him, clutching a plastic pitcher under her arm. "Chase," she said. "Thank God you're here."

"What is going on, Kara? I can't believe you did this. And on a school night."

"I am *so* sorry, but I did *not* do this. I swear. I had one friend over and then I don't know where all these people came from. I tried to get them to leave, but they started drinking and it just got crazy."

He nodded toward the pitcher. "You did good by taking their keys."

"I had to get tough with them."

"If you were so tough you would have gotten them to go in the first place," Chase said.

"Hey, can I have my keys? This party blows." A freckled kid held his hand out to Kara.

"Hold up," Chase said. "I want to see you walk a straight line."

The kid walked a straight line forward and then backward without looking. He smirked at Kara and held out his hand. Chase nodded to Kara and she pulled off the lid to the pitcher. The boy fished out his keys from the pile inside, waving them in triumph as more kids crowded around Kara.

"Line up," Chase said. "One at a time. And you." He grabbed the first kid. "Pick a buddy in need to drive home."

The kid rolled his eyes, but gestured toward a glazed-eyed boy sitting on the stairs. "Come on, man, let's roll."

"Thanks, Chase," Kara said.

"No problem, but don't think you're getting off easy. I'll deal with you once we get this place cleared out."

She nodded, her gaze lowered.

Chase steeled himself against softening toward her. If ever there was a case for tough love, this was it.

He turned to the row of kids. "Next."

CHAPTER FOURTEEN

ALEX PEERED THROUGH the entryway of the brightly lit common room, but her mother was nowhere to be seen. Frowning, she moved toward the wide French doors leading onto the patio near the enclosed garden. Had her mother ventured out into the heat?

She found her sitting on a shaded bench, a surprising breeze ruffling her hair, her eyes closed and her face turned up and smiling. Alex slowed her approach, unsure if she should interrupt her mother's blissful moment. As if sensing her, her mother opened her eyes and spread her arms wide.

"Alex," she said. "It's so good to see you. Come give me a hug."

Tears stung Alex's eyes as she slipped onto the bench and her mother enfolded her in her embrace. "Mom, I'm so happy to see you."

Her mother held her close and rubbed her back. "I can't believe how you've grown, honey."

She pulled back and tucked Alex's hair behind her ears. "I like the shorter length, though what does Chase have to say about it?"

"Chase? He really hasn't said anything."

"He *is* taking you to prom, right?" Light danced in her mom's blue eyes. "We'll have to find you a dress and I'm sure we can find a way to put your hair up that will look nice."

Prom? Disappointment flickered through Alex, but she shook it off. At least she wasn't some stranger today. She dredged up a smile. "I'm sure we can figure something out."

"He's such a nice boy. I'm so glad he finally came to his senses and noticed what was right there under his nose all these years." She laughed lightly. "Of course you were too young for him to date most of that time, but anyone with eyes knew it was inevitable."

Alex gripped her mother's hands. Should she ask her about the affair? Should she ruin what might be the last semi lucid visit they shared? "Mom, do you remember Chase's aunt Rena?"

She again laughed. "I think I remember my best friend."

"I know you two spend a lot of time together." She cocked her head. "Where's your favorite place to go with her? Who do you hang out with, besides Rena?"

"Did you know we went to school together? Rena and I go way back." She shook her head and her smile faded. "We like to go dancing. Your father doesn't care to dance, but I decided that wouldn't stop me from kicking up my heels."

Shifting on the bench, she faced Alex more fully. "Listen, honey, I want to talk to you about Chase."

"Mom, Chase and I…"

"Relationships are hard and they require a lot of work. I know you're frustrated with his go-with-the-flow attitude, but I do think Chase will make something of himself one of these days. True, he lacks direction, but he's come such a long way. He's doing great considering all the drama he has at home." She patted Alex's hand. "Cut him some slack, okay? I think he'll surprise you. When you find someone who cares about you the way Chase does you should hold on tight to that."

"I'm not sure if I can do that, though. It's not that easy."

Her mother folded her hands into her lap. "I just want you to be happy, Alex."

"Are *you* happy, Mom?"

Sadness flickered through her mother's eyes, but then she smiled. "I have my beautiful children, a faithful husband who adores me. Everyone's healthy and happy. What more could I hope for?"

Alex's throat tightened. Tears pricked her eyes and she pressed her lips together, lest the terrible truth spill from her.

"I really like Chase," her mother said. "He's more like his aunt than his mother. And he's good for Robert. He keeps him from being too serious all the time. Promise me," she said.

"Promise you what?"

Her eyebrows furrowed. "Promise me you'll give Chase a chance, a real chance."

Alex nodded. "Okay, Mom."

"WHERE ARE YOU going?" Kara asked as Chase headed for the door.

He paused with his hand on the doorknob. He was leaving for his trip with Alex on Sunday and thanks to traveling for work and Kara's shenanigans, he hadn't been by to see his father in over a week.

"I'm going to see my dad," he said.

"Can I come?" She grabbed her book bag and hurried toward him.

"Are you sure you want to?"

She stopped, staring at him with her eyes narrowed. "He was kind of my dad, too, at one time."

"But that was ages ago. You were a little kid. Do you

remember him at all, except for the yelling and scream-
ing and cursing and breaking of things?"

"I do, actually. He read to me," she said.

"He read to you?" Chase shook his head. "When did
that happen? I thought you two didn't get along."

"Okay, maybe it was just the one time, but he did read
to me. He read me *The Cat in the Hat*."

"Are you sure this is a memory? You didn't dream it?
I honestly can't imagine him doing that. The man never
once read to *me*."

"I'm sorry, Chase. I guess I'm special." She gestured
toward the door. "So, let's go. I want to see him."

"But why? He's not even nice to you. Not that he's
overly nice to anyone else."

Her gaze dropped. "Well, maybe I want to change
that," she said quietly. "It's not like I have a real family.
At least not one I know of. You and your dad are the closest thing I have. I want to try again with him."

"Kara, we *are* family, but I don't think it's a good idea.
He still blames you for your mom running off. I know
it's wrong and he's an idiot and I've told him it was his
drinking that sent her and everyone else he's ever cared
about packing, but you know he's never going to be able
to admit it was his fault. He's not well. As your guardian
I'm not sure I even want you around him. He's unpredict-
able when he drinks and, yes, he's been back at it again."

"Except for you," she said. "He's sent everyone packing except for you."

Frustration had him shaking his head. "I get that you
want to try to fix him. So did I, for years. I tried to help
him by making sure he kept a job and paid his bills. But
I was spending all my time making sure he was okay and
he wasn't and all I was actually doing was enabling him.

I even dragged him to counseling and AA meetings, but he's got to want to change. We can't make him."

"So we'll both be there for him when he hits rock bottom and makes that choice to change."

"Do you know how many times I've thought he hit rock bottom?" he asked. "Honestly, I don't know how much longer I can take him. Sometimes I feel like I'm beating my head against a wall."

"So it will be easier if I help you with him." She gestured with her hands. "You've given me so much, Chase. Not just taking me in this time, which is damn awesome, but in how you've always been there for me, no matter how bad it got. I would have been on the streets years ago if not for you. Please, let me go with you. Let me help you with your dad. Let me do something in return for all you've done and continue to do for me, even though sometimes I inadvertently get into trouble."

He touched her cheek. "You're still grounded, you know. Indefinitely."

"Yes, I know, though I can't believe you're punishing me for something I had no control over."

He held her gaze. "You have total control over who you choose for your friends, Kara. You need to look at all those times you've gotten into trouble and ask yourself if it was because of the company you were keeping."

She rolled her eyes. "Fine. I'll keep better company. Can we go?"

He opened the door and stepped onto the porch. "Don't get your hopes up. This could be unpleasant if he's been drinking."

"Or he might be sober and I'll be able to win him over," she said as she followed him out the door.

His spirits lightened at the thought of his father having to deal with the girl's optimism. Fifteen minutes later they walked through his father's open garage door and pushed through his kitchen door, which was unlocked, as usual. The smell of decaying food emanated from a pile of dirty dishes in the sink.

"Gag me," Kara said as she dropped her book bag in one of the kitchen chairs. She headed straight for the sink, obviously determined to make short work of the dishes.

"Don't you want to say hello first?" Chase asked.

"I can't be in this house with this smell. It probably reeks all the way upstairs. How does he live like this?"

Chase chuckled softly. "Years of conditioning."

Her eyes rounded as she scraped the contents of a plate into the trash. "Well, we're just going to have to recondition the man."

She shooed him on with a flick of her wrist. "Go on and say hello. I'll come find you guys when I'm finished here."

Grinning, Chase went in search of his old man. He made his rounds of the entire house to no avail. As he stood in the back bedroom, a banging sounded from the shed in the backyard.

Curious, he made his way through the tall grass and weeds to the structure. His father had built it from a kit when Chase had been about ten. He'd helped and his mother had brought them iced tea and cookies on a break. It was one of his fondest memories from back in the days before everything had fallen apart.

The paint was peeling and the boards showed the weathering of all those years, but the building appeared sound. He peered through the open door. His father stood with his back to him, squatting over an inverted lawn mower.

"Does that thing actually work?" Chase asked. At least his dad was being productive. That was a good sign.

His father turned, his eyebrows arched. "It did, until I hit that rock." He flipped the mower upright. "I just put a new blade on. It should be okay. Of course, it needs a tune-up, but I think I can get it going another time or two."

"Do you need help?" Chase asked. "I can sweep through and look for more rocks."

"That would be good." His father stepped into the tall grass with him. "There are probably some big limbs, as well, from those storms." He gestured along one side. "I'll take this area, if you want to take over there."

"Sure." Chase grabbed a rake to search through the grass. "It's been a while, hasn't it?"

His father scanned the area in front of him. "Since I last cleaned up the yard? Obviously. Since I last saw you? Not too bad this go-round. Since I last attended a meeting?" He paused as he stooped to pick up a large limb, the bark crumbling from the surface. "I've been every day for the past nine days, ever since I last saw you."

"That's great, Dad. I'm glad to hear it."

"I know I've said this a million times and you don't believe it anymore, but I'm going to stick with it this time."

Chase didn't respond. How many times had they had this conversation? He found it harder and harder to maintain any optimism on that front. Maybe it was a good thing Kara had tagged along.

"I brought you a present," he said, glancing at his father.

"You didn't have to do that."

"Actually, I did. She didn't give me much of a choice."

His father frowned. "She?"

Setting aside the rake, Chase motioned for his father to follow him. "It's Kara. She insisted on coming. Why don't you come say hello?"

His father shook his head, frowning. "She's a trouble-maker. Why did you bring her?"

"I won't deny she tends to stir up trouble, though she doesn't do it on purpose. She wanted to come with me. She wants to see you."

"Why?"

"You can ask her. She's cleaning up your kitchen." Chase turned and headed toward the house.

"Shit. I don't like this," his father said, but he followed.

The scent of bleach drifted on the air as they entered the kitchen. Kara turned to them, drying her hands on a dish towel. She smiled. "I was just coming to find you."

"I saved you the trouble," Chase said. "He couldn't wait to see you."

His father scowled at him, then addressed Kara. "What are you doing, miss?"

"Getting rid of the stink around here, but you don't have to thank me, Roy. This is what family does for each other." Her eyes shone and an angelic smile curved her lips. "How are you doing? It's been a long time."

"Family." His father stood stiffly in front of the girl. "You were…" He held his hand to indicate her height the last time he'd seen her. "You were a little thing."

"I was." She glanced at Chase. "Hey, Roy, didn't you read to me once? Chase doesn't believe me, but I remember it."

His forehead furrowed. "I'm not sure. My memory isn't so good." He brightened. "Wait, was it one of those rhyming books?"

"Yes! It was *The Cat in the Hat*." She grinned at Chase. "See? I told you."

"Thanks, Dad. You never read to *me*."

His father pointed at Kara. "You never hounded me

like that one. Even as a little person she was always insisting on having her way."

"Things haven't changed in that department," Chase said and winked at Kara.

"Well, they've changed in other ways. Look at you, miss. You're all grown up." His father's voice grew rough. He straightened. "I can clean my own kitchen."

"Of course you can, but I wanted to pitch in. Besides, it reeked. And I'm not finished. I was going to mop the floor." She opened the refrigerator and frowned. "We need to grocery shop. I can make dinner."

"You don't need to," his father said as he closed the refrigerator. "I'm capable of taking care of myself."

"Of course you are," she said. "But we're family. And family helps each other."

He turned to Chase. "Why does she keep saying that?" He faced her again. "We have no blood between us."

"Family isn't always blood." She walked to Chase and hooked her arm through his. "This man is my family. He is all I have." She stood before Chase's father. "And you're *his* family, so you're my family by default."

"That's nuts," he said. "I'm going to mow the lawn."

Kara frowned as he left. Chase squeezed her shoulder. "Don't let him get to you. He's been cranky most of his life. He'll come around."

"Yes." She smiled. "I'm not giving up until he does."

The lawn mower roared to life in the yard. "He got it going," Chase said. "I should go help him."

"I'll finish cleaning in here. The entire house needs a good scouring, actually. I won't be able to finish it all today." She cocked her head. "Is my airline ticket refundable?"

"It is, but we caught a good deal. Why?"

"How about if I come over here on Sunday and stay while you and Alex go find your aunt?"

He nodded slowly. "Maybe, but what if he falls off the wagon again?"

She turned him toward the door. "Then I'll deal with it. If I have trouble I'll call you. Besides, you can't think about that. It's counterproductive."

"We could get the number of his AA sponsor, in case you needed someone immediately."

"Perfect," she said.

"But Dad might not want you to come over."

"Well, then I'll just have to make myself indispensable."

With a shake of his head, he headed after his father. If Kara was truly determined to make herself indispensable, it might actually be a good thing for all of them. The sun warmed him as he turned his face up to its rays. For the first time in a long time he had hope they might salvage something out of this family.

CHAPTER FIFTEEN

ADRENALINE PUMPED THROUGH Chase as he climbed the steps to the Petersons' side door early Sunday morning. He was going to spend the day with Alex and hopefully they'd find Robert's father. He raised his hand to knock.

How many times had he walked through that door without knocking, feeling completely welcome? This place had been a second home to him. If he were truthful with himself, he had to admit it was actually the only real home he'd ever had.

But that was before.

He rapped lightly on the door. A few moments later the door opened and Robert narrowed his eyes on him. The circles under his eyes looked darker. "You're here for Alex."

"Yes," Chase said. "We're spending the day together."

"I see." Robert stood aside for him to enter, saying, "Good morning."

"Good morning," Chase said as he stepped inside. He shook Robert's hand. "What's up?"

"Just having breakfast. Want some?" He gestured toward the stove and then coughed into the crook of his arm. "We've got scrambled tofu this morning. There's plenty to go around."

"No, I'm good, thanks."

"I hear Kara is giving you a run for your money. Any second thoughts on taking her in?" Robert asked.

"No, though I can't leave her alone. She almost brought the house down the last time I did that."

"She had a little party while you were out of town?"

"*Little* doesn't begin to describe it."

Robert chuckled softly. "I thought you might be biting off more than you could chew with that one."

Chase shook his head. "She didn't mean for it to happen. Things got out of control. You remember how it is. High school."

"Honestly," Robert said, "I think it's a good thing you're doing with your sister. I wish you luck."

"Thanks," Chase said. "Where's Alex? Is she ready?"

Robert's eyebrows arched. He coughed again, before he could answer. "She heard your car and ran upstairs. Said to tell you she'd be down in a little bit. I'm sure she's primping for you."

"Really?" Chase smiled. "That's nice to know."

"I knew you were still into her."

Chase shrugged. "I wasn't the one who left."

Robert gripped his shoulder. "I don't know what to tell you. She holds on to stuff."

"But she's here. You and your dad needed her and she came."

"That doesn't mean she's forgiven and forgotten. Even in light of the blood typing results, she's still here more because of a sense of obligation than anything else." He gestured wide with his hands. "She's taking this day with you, so she can clear her head. That's code for get away from the rest of us. There's still a bit of friction around here."

"I don't think that's entirely true that she's only here because she feels obligated, Robert," Chase said. "She cares about you."

He shrugged. "Maybe, but we're not best buds or anything. She's still sore at Dad and sore at me for stand-ing by him." He gestured to Chase. "And you're in that same boat."

"I was always neutral."

"Evidently that wasn't good enough for my sister, though. Just be careful. Don't go falling for her again. You're likely to get your heart busted just like before."

"I'm playing it by ear. We'll see how it goes."

"Playing what by ear?" Alex asked as she entered from the hallway. She wore faded jeans and a T-shirt and she looked soft and inviting in an almost irresistibly vulner-able way.

Chase straightened. "Oh, today, this…outing," he said. "We can play it by ear, unless you have a better plan."

She pursed her lips and her gaze swung from Chase to Robert and then back. "Sure. We can play it by ear."

"Excellent. Are you ready?" Chase asked.

"Where's Kara? I thought she was coming with us," Alex said.

"Actually, she's at my father's house."

"I thought your dad was anti-Kara," Robert said.

Chase shrugged. "She's working on him. Personally, I don't think he stands a chance."

"And you're sure it's okay for her to be there…with him?" Alex asked.

"I walked her in and he was sober and tolerating hav-ing her there. She's cleaning his house. He should be thrilled to have her. She has the number for his sponsor if anything gets out of control. She's okay." He chuckled. "It's him I'm worried about. She'll have him scrubbing floors by the time we get back."

"If you're sure, let's go, then," Alex said. "Traffic looks clear, but you just never know."

Chase offered his hand to Robert. "Thanks for letting me steal her away. You have a good one."

"No problem," Robert said as he gripped Chase's hand. "And good luck with everything you've got going on."

"There's a mango and grape tomato salad and some hummus in the fridge," Alex said to Robert. "We won't be too late, but no one needs to wait up for me."

Robert coughed as he nodded. "I hope it all works out and you get your head nice and clear. And do me a favor."

"You don't look so good. Are you okay?" Alex asked, frowning.

Robert waved the question aside. He nodded toward Chase. "Take it easy on this guy. He's more fragile than he appears."

Alex's gaze swept over Chase and she frowned. "We're just hanging out."

Chase glared at Robert as he took Alex's arm. "Come on, let's go."

AN OVERHEAD SPEAKER in Atlanta's Hartsfield Airport announced final boarding for a flight to Phoenix as Alex settled beside Chase to wait for their flight to be called. A young girl took a seat opposite them, her thumbs flying over her phone keypad, her earphones in, her head bobbing to a beat discernible even across the aisle.

"That can't be good for her ears," Alex said, nodding toward the girl. "Do you think Kara is really okay?"

"She's fine. She was determined to spend the day with Dad. She's set on winning him over and making him family again," Chase said. "And after this week I didn't have the energy to try to talk her out of it."

"So, what was the verdict after her little soiree?"

"She's grounded at least until the end of the month. She can go to school and work, but then she's to come straight

home. No friends visiting. That's what started this whole mess. Apparently she invited one of her friends over and had unfortunately mentioned that I'd be out of town. That friend invited another and that one another and it snowballed. I feel a little bad that she invited the first friend because she didn't want to be alone and then her friends actually took advantage of her because I was out of town. But she was grounded. She shouldn't have had anyone over. I hate that I have to travel so much."

"It's high school. This kind of thing happens all the time. You're lucky none of your neighbors called the cops, though."

"We talked about that. At least she was upset about the whole thing. DFCS wouldn't have looked too kindly on it." He shook his head. "She's giving me gray hair."

She patted his arm. "She's worth it, though."

He nodded and pressed his hand over hers, his gaze locking with hers. "So, admit it. You missed me just a little while I was gone, didn't you?"

Her heart thudded. "I'm not admitting anything, Chase."

"But you're not denying it."

Frustration swelled through her. "As soon as Robert is in the clear I'm heading back to my life in Baltimore."

"What life do you have there? You're starting fresh with your job search." He shrugged. "You could easily do that here. I'll bet Atlanta has tons of openings for number gurus. You might miss your sister, but you have more family here. And you're not seeing anyone there, right?"

She tried to tug her hand away, but he held her fast. "Why are you doing this?"

"Because I want you in my life."

She looked out the window where a plane taxied away

from the gate. "I'm in your life as much as I can be, Chase."

He tugged her around until she faced him and then he locked his gaze with hers. "I don't want us to just be friends, Alex. I want to share my life with you. The way we did before. Don't you remember how it was? You were my best friend. We told each other everything. I know you and you know me in a way no one else does. Tell me you don't miss that and I'll leave you alone."

She closed her eyes. Why did he have to do this now, when she was feeling more vulnerable than ever? Robert had hidden it well this morning, even with his coughing, which concerned her even more so because he'd been up in the wee hours. He'd had a worse night than she had and she'd not slept a wink fretting about Chase doing exactly what he was presently doing.

"Can we please just focus on finding your aunt for now?" she asked.

He lifted his hand, freeing her. "Sure, sweetheart, whatever you say." He glanced away and then back again. "I want to find Robert's real dad as much as you do, you know."

Her throat tightened. "Robert doesn't like to show it, but he isn't doing well. He talked about having his central line and portacath removed if he doesn't have a donor soon. He said he's tired of the bullshit and is close to walking away from all of it. He needs that donor."

"He's not going to do anything with his central line. He'll be ready when they *do* find a donor, which they will, and hopefully we'll find his biological father and the man will be willing."

"Oh, God, I hope so," she said.

On the plane, she traded seats with Chase and sat beside an older woman, who had traveled the world three times over. They passed the time chatting, and for a while, Alex didn't think about Robert, her father or Chase.

Shortly after they landed she rushed to a red SUV on the rental-car lot. "This one."

Chase smiled. "Really? You like this? Isn't it a little showy for you?"

"Maybe you don't know me as well as you think you do," she said.

"We'll just have to remedy that." He paused as he opened the door for her. "Do you think Kara is okay?"

"You can call her."

"Should I? Maybe I should trust that they're getting along and he's staying sober."

"Call her so you won't worry, but I don't want you to drive while you talk to her. I hate when people do that. It isn't safe and you need to set a good example for her. She *will* eventually want to drive, you know."

"Right." He nodded. "So, we'll hang out here for a minute?"

"Works for me," she said. "We have all day, right? And we don't even know if your aunt will be there when we get to her place."

Funny how now that they were this close she didn't feel any urgency in moving forward with their search. Were they doing the right thing? Doubt and uncertainty had her biting her lip. What if they couldn't find Chase's aunt? What if they did, but she didn't know how to reach Robert's father? What would happen to Robert if they didn't find a donor for the transplant? Would he really stop all the treatment?

Chase leaned against the car, his cell phone to his ear. "Hey, Kara, what's up? How's the old man?"

While he talked, Alex settled into the passenger seat, leaning her head back and closing her eyes. Fatigue pulled at her. She'd have to get Chase to stop for coffee once they got going.

"I'm glad it's going well," Chase said. "Oh, no, I don't care if you turn him into the next saint. You're still grounded. Don't even go there with me. You have to face your consequences. What if DFCS had caught wind of your little get-together?"

A smile worked across Alex's lips. Chase was sounding so...fatherly. It was a new side to him. Why did she have to find it so appealing?

"So you'll be eighteen. And then what?" Chase asked as he moved around to the driver's seat. "It's a tough world out there. Are you really in such a hurry to get out in it?"

He frowned and glanced at Alex as he listened to whatever his sister was saying. "Why would you think you have to leave when you turn eighteen? I mean, I know you want to go to Georgia State and that's cool if you want to live in the dorm, but there's no deadline on how long you can live with me. You can drive to school or take MARTA, since you're so fond of it. Shit, Kara, you just got there. Why are you in a hurry to leave? My home is your home, indefinitely."

In spite of his frustrations with his sister, Chase seemed very resistant to her moving out. Had he been lonely before Kara had moved in? Alex could relate to that. Lately she'd been so engrossed in work she'd drifted away from most of her friends. She'd have to make it a point to reconnect once she returned to Baltimore.

Sunlight streamed through the windshield, highlighting the curve of his cheek and his clean-shaven chin. Alex's heart quickened as her gaze fell to his lips. Was his kiss still as exciting as it had been all those years ago? He glanced again in her direction. She looked away and her cheeks heated.

"Well, it's something to think about," Chase said. "Yes, thanks. I'll tell her. See you tonight....No, we'll definitely be back. If my aunt isn't there, we'll leave a note. Hopefully, she'll be there, or we'll hear from her before we have to head back for our return flight....Okay, you, too. Talk to you later."

He hung up and then entered Rena's address into the GPS. "She said to tell you good luck and she hopes we find my aunt and Robert's father."

"That's nice," she said, still not looking at him for fear her cheeks were pink.

It wasn't right that the man could get her worked up without trying. What was wrong with her? And that he seemed intent on winning her over again only made her response worse. Resisting Chase would be so much easier if she didn't find him so attractive. She inhaled slowly and reminded herself of all his faults.

He hadn't stood by her and her mother when her father's infidelity had come to light.

He was a drifter, never planning or setting goals.

The fact that he was doing well in his work was only accidental.

The man did not understand boundaries.

"You up for coffee?" he asked.

Shit. He had a knack for anticipating her needs.

He had always been that way. Giving in, she turned to him and a small smile curved her lips. "Absolutely. That would actually be really awesome."

"You've got it," he said as they exited the airport. "See, I know what you need. Caffeine fix for my girl."

"*Your* girl?"

"That's right. You might as well get used to it. I think Kara's rubbing off on me. I'm a determined man."

Alex opened her mouth, but no response flowed readily

to her lips, so she closed her mouth and settled in for the ride as Chase clicked on the radio and the strains of Snow Patrol filled the air. This was going to be one long day.

CHAPTER SIXTEEN

As THE RENTAL CAR bumped along the never-ending dirt road, Chase stole a glance at Alex. She was slumped in the seat, fast asleep, her head bobbing with the movement of the SUV. Her dark lashes lay curled against her freckled cheeks. Her hair streamed over her shoulders in disarray. Soft snoring escaped through her partially open mouth, but somehow she maintained her appeal.

And the woman was maddeningly appealing, even though her attitude toward family and "till death do us part" was more than lacking. Why was she so bent on fleeing back to Baltimore at the first opportunity? Wasn't she here working things out with her family?

Somehow, he'd have to convince her to stay.

"Destination on the right." The computerized voice of the GPS announced their arrival at the address his cousin had given him.

By the looks of it, the house had stood on this hill for decades, though it must have been magnificent in its heyday. An abundance of French doors and wide porches wrapping around the ground level and balconies surrounding the upper floor spoke of summer evenings welcoming guests who spilled out onto the outdoor spaces.

As the SUV rolled to a stop, Alex stirred in the seat beside him. She yawned and stretched, arching her spine and covering her mouth with the back of her hand. He resisted the urge to undo her seat belt and slip his hand into the space at the small of her back, to pull her over to him.

"We're here," he said, letting his gaze sweep her face still flushed with sleep.

As she fumbled with her seat belt, he exited the car and moved to the passenger side. He opened her door and, before she could protest, pulled her out and into his arms.

Her eyes widened as he held her close, enjoying the soft warmth of her pressed against him. When her gaze dipped to his mouth, he moaned softly and it was all he could do not to press his lips to hers. She tipped her face up to him, the movement triggering an automatic response in him. He came so very close to kissing her, but he found restraint in the fact they were here on a matter that might very well save her brother's life.

"I'm giving you full warning," he said, still holding her close. "When we're finished here, I plan to take complete advantage of that promise in your eyes."

Her lips parted and she inhaled a sharp breath. He loosened his hold, but she neither stepped away nor disputed his claim. Smart woman. She'd been caught and the color rising in her cheeks proved she knew it. Satisfaction filled him.

He had proof positive she was still attracted to him. Now that he knew her weakness he planned to fully exploit it when the timing was right. He'd do whatever it took to keep her in Atlanta, where she belonged with her family *and* with him.

At long last he stepped back, taking her hand. "Are you ready?"

She closed her eyes for a brief moment and then nodded. "As ready as I'll ever be."

He squeezed her hand as they walked up the gravel

driveway. Wildflowers bloomed along an embankment to one side. The sun pressed down on them, weighing the air as the buzz of insects filled the early afternoon.

"It doesn't look like anyone is home," Alex said as they ascended the stairs to the wide front porch.

Keeping his fingers curled around hers, Chase pressed the doorbell with his free hand. The sound reverberated through the house. They stood expectantly, waiting. Chase cocked his head, straining to make out a sound beyond the chirping of birds and buzzing of insects.

After a few seemingly endless moments, Alex leaned forward and banged the heavy brass knocker. Long moments stretched by as they again waited. A butterfly drifted by in an aimless pattern of flight.

Chase smiled, his worry over finding Robert's father easing. "This place is like a land without time."

"Maybe we should write the note." Disappointment weighed her words.

The worry in her eyes was enough to make him want to wrap his arms around her and kiss her to distraction. He gestured toward a white wicker sitting area to the right, with a table suitable for afternoon tea, and four wide-armed chairs. A swing hung beyond it, in the corner where the porch began its long wrap around the house's perimeter.

"We could sit here and write it," he said. "And then maybe she'll come while we're still here."

"Okay, but I'm not sitting in that swing with you, Chase," she said.

Chuckling, he tugged her again into his arms. At least she was worrying about *him* and not her brother at the moment. It was a little too much to resist.

"I don't need a swing to kiss you," he said.

With that he claimed her mouth. Her lips were as soft as he remembered, but she had a hunger he hadn't experienced with her before. She opened to him, welcoming his tongue with the steady stroke of her own. He pulled her close, loving the feel of her soft length, running his hands down her back, but stopping short of her luscious ass. He needed to keep this clean, so he didn't scare her away.

He drank his fill, not wanting the kiss to end, but they did have the letter to write and now that he knew he could still stir up Alex's passionate side, he'd be sure to set aside more time for that going forward.

With regret, he broke the kiss and pressed his forehead to hers. "I'm sorry, I couldn't resist."

She closed her eyes and inhaled slowly before pushing back from him and reaching for her backpack. "I…I brought some stationery."

Nodding, he followed her to the wicker chairs, feasting his eyes on the gentle sway of her backside. He'd been way too long without a woman, but being with Alex again was like coming home. This time, they'd find a way to make it work.

He took the seat beside her as she pulled out her stationery and a pen. She glanced at him. "Do you want to write it, or do you want me to?"

He sobered as he focused on the task at hand. "I don't mind doing it, if you think it will be better coming from me."

"Maybe that would be best, since she knows you. I doubt she'd remember me." She handed him the pen.

"I don't know, you're pretty unforgettable," he said. "And you were one really cute kid."

Pink tinged her cheeks. "Chase, can we please forget about that kiss?"

He arched his eyebrows in question. "Sweetheart, I don't know about you, but I plan to savor the memory of that kiss, and—" he leaned in closer to her "—I plan to kiss you like that again the first chance we get."

She shook her head. "I can't think about that now. Let's write the letter."

He placed his hand over hers. "Fine, but admit that we've got something here, that we can make another go of this."

"Chase, please…"

He held her gaze. "You know, in Al-Anon they say *I'm* the one who's supposed to have the problem with taking everything too seriously and not wanting to commit."

"I didn't know you'd been attending those meetings. Have they helped?"

"Yes, I think so. They at least remind me other people have to deal with the same shit and that I'm really not nuts. I hope I've learned how to be supportive without enabling his drinking. I should probably try to get Kara to go with me some, too, especially if she wants Dad to be part of her life." He shrugged. "It might make a difference to him if he knew she were going, though she may be going a little overboard on the whole 'we're in this all together' thing. I don't think my dad is ready yet for all her family bonding."

"I think that's really sweet," she said. "I love how you are with Kara. I'm not sure I get how she can be so supportive of your father after all he's done. I think it would be really hard for her not to blame him for her having been thrown into foster care, but I guess it shows a lot about her character."

"Or how much she wants to erase where she's come from, being passed from family to family. The girl wants roots." He nudged her with his elbow. "Unlike some people I know."

Her gaze fell to the tabletop. "When those roots have been torn from the ground, it's really hard to trust in them again."

Frustrated, he took a piece of stationery. Why couldn't she trust? If *he* could trust in a relationship, how hard could it be?

"Family is family," he said, because wasn't that really all that mattered in the end?

Dear Aunt Rena,
This is your nephew, Chase Carrolton.

He stopped. "Don't you want a family of your own one day?"

The crease between her eyebrows deepened. "So I can carry on another generation of dysfunction? Why would I want to do that?"

"Your family is not that bad. Besides, what family isn't dysfunctional? We figure out how to deal with all the bullshit, because we love each other."

"Then why do we hurt each other?" She looked away, over the hill blooming with wildflowers. "Maybe it's so hard because I once thought I *did* have it all, the perfect family, the best boyfriend, and it all evaporated in the blink of an eye. Maybe I'm just not as tough as you are. I don't think I can take that kind of grief again."

Once more, he placed his hand over hers. "But you'd like to have that again, the part before all the drama? You'd like to be in a loving relationship, to have your family healed and together again?"

Moisture gathered in her eyes. "Yes," she said, her voice rough. "I'd like to have that again."

Satisfaction filled him. "Good, I can work with that. Now let's find Robert's father."

I know it's been a long time, but I need to see you.

He glanced at Alex before continuing.

You remember the Peterson family. You were once best friends with Ruth Peterson. Her daughter Alexandra and I have traveled here specifically to ask you something important about her mother.

We are only here for the day, but you can reach either one of us on our cell phones at any time. Our flight doesn't depart until around nine tonight. We plan to remain in the area, in case we hear from you and you're willing and available to see us, in which case we'll return to your house or meet you anywhere that might be more convenient.

He signed his name and listed both of their cell phones at the bottom, then handed the letter to Alex. She read through it and nodded as she folded it and then slipped it into an envelope.

"Thanks for doing this for me, Chase," she said. "This is such a huge favor. You actually flew out here with me and drove all that way. Whether we ever hear from your aunt or not, or whether she can help us find Robert's biological father or not, I owe you big-time. I'm not sure how I'll ever repay you."

His heart warmed for this woman. She wasn't perfect by any means, but neither was he, and her intentions in trying to find a donor for her brother were sound, whether Robert agreed with them or not. And didn't that really mean her family mattered to her?

He took both of her hands in his. "I wanted to do this for Robert every bit as much as you did. You don't owe me anything. I just hope that what we're doing here today will make a difference."

He took the letter and rose. "Let's tuck this in the door so she's sure to see it as soon as she arrives."

Alex followed him to the door. The birds continued their song and a soft breeze swept along the porch. He wedged the letter in the crack above the doorknob, and then turned to Alex as large drops of rain spattered the roof and ground around the porch. In moments, the sky opened, pouring down rain in sheets. Then, as quickly as it had started, the rain stopped.

"If this doesn't work, we'll find another way to help Robert," he said.

She nodded, though worry still creased her brow. If only he could soothe away her concern, then hold her close so nothing else could ever upset her again. He hugged her once more, because it at least made him feel better.

The floorboards of the porch creaked, startling them both. Footsteps sounded along the far side of the wrap-around porch. A woman's voice called out, "Hello?"

They parted, turning as his aunt Rena rounded the corner, a basket of wildflowers hung on her arm, rainwater running from her hair. There was no mistaking her, though her hair held streaks of gray she hadn't had the last time he'd seen her, she was a little thicker in the middle and creases formed at the corners of her eyes when she spied them and smiled. Those were the same fun-loving eyes his aunt had always had.

He opened his arms as she did the same. "Hello, Aunt Rena."

"Chase, my boy," she said as she wrapped her arms around him. "I'd recognize you anywhere. What a surprise!"

THE BRASSY NOTES of a saxophone floated softly through the air as Alex tried to relax beside Chase on the red leather sofa that somehow managed to appear tasteful in his aunt's huge drawing room. Maybe it was the sunshine streaming through the windows and the spaciousness of the house that lent acceptance to all things bright and big. Huge paintings of wildflowers in bold colors graced the walls, and the furniture competed equally for attention with its reds and purples and greens in bright hues that made the eyes widen, but in a pleasant kind of way.

Aunt Rena herself was surely the inspiration for the decor; whether she had selected it or paid someone to decorate for her, it had been money well spent. Any visitor, be they weary or weighed with worry as Alex found herself that afternoon, when faced with the brilliance of Aunt Rena's drawing room, could only feel the need to celebrate life in all its glory. Alex felt a hint of this sitting on that red leather sofa, even though her nap in the car had been full of nightmares and had left her more tired than ever.

Aunt Rena smiled as she finished reading the letter and glanced up at them. "Alexandra Peterson, what a beauty you turned out to be. I'd recognize you anywhere, as well. You are so much like your mother." She turned to Chase. "And you, Chase, I see my sister, Ruby, in you clear as day."

"You look great, Aunt Rena," Chase said. "The years have been kind to you."

His aunt patted her hair. "I do what I have to do to take care of myself. I want to keep husband number four." She waved with her hand. "The first three were just a warm-up. This one is a keeper."

"Is he here?" Chase asked. "We'd love to meet him."

"Oh, so sorry, sweetie, he's on the road. He drives a big rig and won't be back until late tomorrow. I hate that he missed you."

She gestured to the tray of sweet cakes and tea sitting on the big oak coffee table. "Help yourselves. I love having company. This place is too big for me to be bumping around in all by myself, now that all the kids are gone. You two have to promise you'll stay the rest of the day until you have to leave for the airport. You can rest in your own room and I'll make us a nice meal. I can't send you on your way without feeding you properly."

Chase scooped Alex's hand into his, and warmth again filled her as the memory of that kiss washed over her. He smiled at her and said, "That sounds wonderful. We don't have any other plans."

"Excellent," she said and then turned to Alex. "So tell me, Alex, what is it you wanted to ask me about your mother?" She frowned. "Wait, but first, how *is* your mother? I hate that we lost touch."

Alex glanced at Chase before answering. He kept his fingers entwined with hers. His hand holding hers was such an old familiar feeling and it calmed her. "She was diagnosed with early-onset Alzheimer's about a year and a half ago. She was having trouble taking care of herself and she wasn't eating. My sister Becky found her in her kitchen bleeding. She'd sliced her hand badly. We had to put her in a home."

"Oh, my God, poor Ruth. Sweetie, I'm so sorry."

"It's…been difficult, but she seems happy there. At least she's safe."

"She is such a beautiful soul, your mother. Lord, she

liked to dance the night away. We used to have a blast when we went out. I hate to hear she isn't doing better." Aunt Rena sighed. "I should have kept in touch, not that it would have helped her any." She gestured with her hands. "We're a little out of touch here. I love being out in the middle of nowhere, absolutely. It's a life like no other, but we don't have an internet connection or much cell phone coverage."

"I wanted to ask about my mother," Alex said and glanced at Chase. "I'm sorry. I don't know how to put this without just saying it."

Chase's aunt nodded. "No worries, I think I know what you want to ask me. It's the only thing I can think of that would have you trekking all the way out here. I'm guessing she may have mentioned him in her state. My mother was that way sometimes with the dementia, living in her past. You want to know about Charles."

Alex's pulse quickened. "Who is Charles?"

"I'm not sure how to explain the man. I'm not sure your mother ever understood him or his effect on her." She shook her head. "No disrespect to your father. Jacob was a wonderful man and Ruth adored him, make no mistake about it, but Charles McMann was a force to be dealt with. I don't think your mother ever stood a chance when it came to that man."

Distressed, Alex leaned against Chase and he swept his arm around her. "I hadn't realized until just now that a part of me had hoped it wasn't true," she said. "I thought maybe it was a mistake with the blood sample, maybe it was contaminated or switched or something."

"Blood sample?" Aunt Rena asked. "I don't understand. Was that something to do with your mother?"

"Alex's brother Robert has cancer," Chase said. "He needs a stem cell transplant."

"Oh, my, Robert? He was such a fine boy. I'm so sorry to hear that. You poor thing." Aunt Rena pressed her hand to her chest. "Your family has seen such tragedy."

Alex nodded. "The transplant is sort of like a bone marrow transplant. We all had our blood typed, with the exception of my mother. She's not an option in her condition. It was surprising that none of us siblings were a match to Robert, though, so we were counting on my father."

"You were hoping your father would be the donor."

"Yes, but *he* wasn't a match, either. Parents are supposed to be half matches, but Dad wasn't."

"Because he isn't your brother's father." Aunt Rena blew out a heavy sigh. "Oh, what a mess."

Chase squeezed her hand. "He'd known about the affair, but hadn't known for sure about Robert."

"What a mess," Aunt Rena repeated. "And here you are trying to clean it all up. Honestly, I don't believe your mother ever knew for sure, either. What a horrible way for you all to find out such a terrible truth. I tried to talk sense into your mother. To be honest that was part of the reason we lost touch. I never quite saw eye to eye with her on that, though I completely understand why she couldn't stay away from that man. He was downright mesmerizing. Oh, and he truly loved her. When a man wants you the way that man wanted Ruth, well, it's a powerful aphrodisiac."

Her eyes widened. "Oh, my, I'm guessing you came here to find Charles, then."

Alex drew a deep breath. "Yes, I know it sounds crazy, but the national donor bank hasn't been able to find a match. My brother's oncologist says the stem cell transplant is his best bet at beating this cancer. I was hoping you would know where to find my mother's… Where to find Charles. Maybe he'd be willing to be the donor. He *is* Robert's father, after all."

"Was," Aunt Rena said, a pained expression on her face. "I'm so sorry, sweetie, but he passed away last year. I didn't keep in touch, but I happened to see his obituary in the newspaper."

"Oh, my God," Alex said, finding it hard to breathe. The room blurred. She turned to Chase. "I hadn't thought of that. What will we do?"

He rubbed her back and held her close. "It will be all right. His oncologist will keep looking. We'll do like your father said and have a donor drive. I don't think that's typical, but we'll do whatever it takes. I'll get typed. Who knows, if a stranger in a donor bank can be a match, maybe I can, too."

"You look exhausted and I've given you some bad news. I'm so very sorry." Aunt Rena rose. "Let me show you to your room. Sweetie, you should lie down for a spell. A nap will do you wonders."

Chase stood and pulled Alex up with him. "She's probably right, sweetheart."

Alex nodded. Exhaustion threatened to overwhelm her. How could they have come all this way just to reach a dead end?

Chase's aunt showed them the way up a wide staircase with a landing large enough for a nook with more chairs and a bookcase. "This way," she said as they headed down an equally wide hall. Finally, she escorted them into a large bedroom with splashes of bright yellows and oranges. "You should be comfortable here. There's a washroom through that door. Please make yourselves at home and let me know if I can get you anything. You just come down whenever you're feeling rested and I'll have something yummy ready for you before you head out again."

"Thank you," Alex said, too discouraged to worry about the appropriateness of Chase's aunt putting them in a room together.

"I can't leave you without hugs," his aunt said, opening her arms first to Alex and then to Chase before she quietly left them.

The bed was too inviting to resist. Alex sank to the mattress, weary to the bone. Tears trickled down her face as she hugged a pillow. "I'm just tired. That's why I'm upset. I haven't been sleeping, because Robert hasn't been sleeping and I hear him up at all hours. I hate that he's sick, Chase. I hate that my mom is someone completely different than the woman who raised me. In so many ways she's different. She had an affair. She cheated with Charles and now he's gone and he can't help my brother. And my mom can't even comprehend that any of this is even going on."

Chase sat beside her, stroking her back. "Just rest. Sleep and you'll feel better. I'll stay with you until you're asleep if you'd like."

Her heart warmed. He was truly a good man. Was he right? Was it possible that they could work things out this time? She patted the bed beside her. "Stay. Hold me, Chase."

He stretched out beside her, wrapping his arm around her and pulling her close. "It's going to all work out in the end. I'm so sorry about Charles." He exhaled. "At least we won't have to try to talk Robert into accepting him as a donor."

"I'm worried about him," Alex said. "He's sick from the chemo and the radiation. And the cancer. It's horrible. And he's depressed. I try to get him to talk to me, but he doesn't seem to want to. Things are still kind of strained between us and I hate that, but I'm not sure how to change it."

He wiped his thumb across her cheek. "When you cry like this, it makes me want to take on the world for you."

"I wish you could do something to fix this, to fix Robert, to fix my broken family."

His gaze held hers. "I'll do everything in my power to make this better for you, Alex."

Her tears fell in earnest then, because she could feel that he meant it and it had been so long since anyone had cared like that for her. She cupped his face. "I missed you."

He shut his eyes briefly and he pressed his lips together. When he looked again into her eyes, his were misted and his voice was rough as he said, "I missed you, too."

His lips closed over hers with a gentleness and a passion that took her breath away. She turned to get closer, to get as close to him as possible, all the while delving into the depths of his kiss. His body, lean and hard, pressed her into the bed as he settled over her.

She wrapped her arms around him and tugged him closer when he started to pull away. He gave in easily, kissing her again with renewed vigor. She lost herself in the sheer pleasure of being with him.

At last he broke the kiss and pulled back to look at her. "Sweetheart, you need to sleep."

She shook her head. "I need you." She ran her hand down his chest, to the bottom of his T-shirt, then up under, over his bare skin.

He sucked in his breath. "God, I love it when you touch me."

"Then let me touch you," she said and tugged his shirt off over his head.

This time he rolled to his back and carried her with him so she was spread on top of him. She kissed him long and deep, his mouth warm and soft, his tongue sending pleasure rippling through her. Why had she resisted this?

She drew back, straddling him, rising up far enough to pull off her own T-shirt. His eyes widened in appreciation as he ran his hand along her abdomen. "Sweetheart," he said, "you are so beautiful."

He rose to meet her, locking his arms around her and kissing her again, the heat of his bare torso pressing against hers. His hands skimmed her ribs, then over the lace of her bra, but he made no move to take it off her.

Heat spread through her and she rocked against him, gasping as she seated herself more securely over the hard ridge in his jeans. He groaned into her mouth and grabbed her hips, first urging her to grind against him and then suddenly stopping.

"Yes," she said against his mouth as she shifted to undo her jeans. "These have got to go."

"Wait." A pained expression marked his face. "We can't."

She pulled back to better see him. "What?"

"I want you so much, Alex, but I wasn't expecting this."

"Neither was I," she said as she slipped off her jeans. "But it's a pleasant surprise." She slid her fingers into his waistband to unbutton his jeans. "For both of us."

A groan worked its way from his throat. "Woman, I don't have a condom."

"Oh." She rolled off him. How had she not thought of that? She bit her lip and calculated the days in her head. Would it be worth the risk? "Shit. You're probably right."

His eyes rounded and he swung his legs over the side

of the bed as he opened the nightstand drawer. "Wait, maybe Aunt Rena keeps a stash."

"For guests?"

"Bingo." Smiling, he held up a small packet.

"Yes." Relief flooded her. She needed this distraction, but mostly, she just needed Chase.

Within moments they had stripped off their remaining clothes. He kissed her again and this time there was nothing between them to keep them from being as close as she craved. She sighed and lost herself in the wonder that was Chase.

CHAPTER SEVENTEEN

THE SUN SLANTED lower in the sky as Chase dressed. They had both spent themselves and then fallen asleep together. Alex shifted in the bed and for the second time that day he indulged in watching her sleep.

They'd had many stolen times together when they were younger, but they'd had only a few nights where they'd slept until morning in the same bed. More often than not, Chase would slip out of her bedroom window before anyone else in the house woke up. What would it be like to sleep with her every night and wake with her in his bed?

Her eyes opened and a slow smile curved her lips. He leaned down and kissed her. She wrapped her arms around his neck and attempted to pull him back into the bed with her.

"I wish we could," he said, "but we have to get moving."

A shadow flickered in her eyes and she nodded. "Maybe Robert will get some good news from his oncologist."

He handed her her clothes and she dressed quietly. His aunt's news was apparently still sinking in, but at least Alex looked more rested. And he couldn't deny the small amount of satisfaction he felt knowing that his plan to woo her during their day together had been a success.

They followed the sounds of clanking pots and the scent of roasting herbs to the kitchen, where Aunt Rena was obviously in her element. Aunt Rena had her salt-and-pepper hair pulled up in a ponytail and she wore a "Kiss the Cook" apron. She wiped her hands on a dish towel as they entered.

"There you are and looking so much more rested." She hugged Alex. "Look at the bloom in your cheeks, sweetie. Much better."

The pink in Alex's cheeks deepened. She glanced at Chase. "Yes, I feel much better, thanks."

"Is anyone hungry? I don't feel like I've done my job as hostess if I haven't properly fed my guests," his aunt said.

"We definitely want to be good guests," Chase said. He glanced at Alex and winked. "And I, for one, have worked up quite an appetite."

His aunt gestured to the breakfast bar, where she'd set out an assortment of dishes: a spinach salad, roasted chicken, rice pilaf, a vegetable medley and a basket of rolls. "Here, sweeties, grab a plate and help yourselves. We can eat in here or out on the porch."

"Oh, the porch, please," Alex said. "It's so beautiful out there."

A smile shone in Aunt Rena's eyes. "It's what sold me on this place. Believe it or not, I used to be a city girl, but when my Buck brought me out here and told me he'd built this house with the hopes of filling it with a family, well, I don't know if I fell more in love with this home or with the man."

They filled their plates and she led them out onto a different area of the wraparound porch, one that overlooked the hillside of wildflowers. "There's a nice breeze here, but I can turn on the ceiling fan, if you'd like."

"This is great." Chase pulled out a chair for first his aunt and then for Alex.

"You know, sweetie, I was thinking." His aunt touched

Alex's hand. "I'm guessing you've had your earful already today and I don't want to stir up anything that might cause you more distress, but our time together is so limited and you must have more questions about Charles."

Alex's fork stilled. Chase reached for her hand. She laced her fingers with his and held tight as she said, "I do, actually, Aunt Rena. I'm not completely sure I want to ask, but exactly how long did the affair last?"

"I've been thinking about that and I'm sorry to say I can't narrow it down to precise dates, but you should know it was a long-lasting affair. It started shortly after your parents married and continued for a number of years. Your mama was fairly discreet about it and I suspect she saw Charles more often than even I realized and perhaps for longer than I knew.

"As I said, it was a touchy subject between us. I loved your mother, but I hated watching her take such a risk with what she had with your father, and he was so good to her. I hated how he turned his head and looked the other way. Sometimes I just wanted to shake the man and make him put his foot down."

"So…" Alex's shoulders heaved. "You're saying, given the timing and my unique resemblance to Robert, that this Charles McMann could also be my father?"

"I'm afraid so, sweetie, but the only way to know for sure would be for Jacob to take a paternity test."

Alex nodded slowly. "I don't really see the point of that. Charles is dead and I'm not sure how I'd feel about him if he weren't. I hadn't really thought about him in those terms. My interest in him was purely to see if he could be a donor for the transplant."

"Of course. I just know if I were you that would be a question rattling around in my head."

"It has been," Alex said.

"Would you like to see a picture of him?"

Alex straightened and looked at Chase. "I don't know."

Chase nodded, his heart heavy. Alex had gone through so much lately. He hated that she had to deal with all of this on top of it. "I think you should. You might regret it if you don't and maybe once you see him, you can lay this whole mess to rest."

She inhaled slowly, and then nodded. "Okay."

Aunt Rena excused herself to get the picture. While she was gone, Chase scooped his arm around Alex and pulled her close. "I know you aren't getting answers you want to hear today, but none of this changes who you are, or who your brother and father are."

"It changes who my mother was and, in all fairness, it does change who I thought my father was." She shook her head. "I don't understand the kind of love my parents had that they could do that to each other."

"Love is so complicated," Aunt Rena said as she returned with an old photo album. "Who among us can ever truly explain the ins and outs of our relationships to each other, let alone to anyone outside that relationship? We can all look in and judge, but I can tell you without a shadow of a doubt that your parents loved each other with a passion few of us are lucky enough to ever know. That they both eventually hurt each other is only something they can understand. We're all only human."

She retook her seat and opened the album, turning the pages with a nostalgic smile. "My, we were young. Here we go," she said and handed the album to Alex, indicating a particular picture. "This one. I thought I remembered this one shot of him. Ruth wouldn't ever allow me to take pictures of them together, but I managed to sneak this one. I didn't show it to her until years later and then she burst into tears when she saw it. I never knew if they were tears of longing or regret. Maybe it was a little of both."

Chase kept his arm around Alex as she ran her hand over the photograph. It depicted a much younger version of her mother sitting on a sofa in what appeared to be a nightclub. She held a half-full martini glass, and a dark-haired man sat beside her, his hand on her knee. While he smiled at the camera, her focus was entirely on him, and the look in her eyes was one of adoration.

Alex shook her head as she passed the album back across the table. "I hardly recognize her, in those clothes, in that setting…with that man. I have no idea who that woman is and it makes me so sad to see how she appears completely devoted to him."

"That feeling went both ways." Aunt Rena closed the album and set it in the chair beside her. "He lived for those stolen moments with your mother. He was a beautiful, single, stable man. He could have found someone available and started a family of his own. But he remained true to your mother. It's tragic, really."

"Did he know about Robert?" Alex asked.

Aunt Rena shook her head. "Oh, no, Ruth was adamant about him not knowing. I'm sure he suspected, but she told him your brother wasn't his child. He was heartbroken about it." She again shook her head. "Who knows how he rationalized it?"

"Thank you, Rena, for sharing all this with me," Alex said.

Chase again nodded. "You've been so hospitable with us dropping by without any notice."

"And we haven't had a chance to catch up," his aunt said to him. She frowned. "I hope that father of yours has sobered up and gotten his act together."

"He's still working on it."

"You deserved better and you definitely deserved better than that no-good sister of mine, cutting out on you—on all of us—the way she did. Have you heard from her?" A hopeful look shone in her eyes.

He shook his head, numb to even disappointment at this point. He'd written his mother off so long ago the memory of her was as if it were from a previous life. "Not a word."

"Ever?"

"No, and I'm fine with that."

This time it was Alex who slipped her hand in his. He was happy to have the connection with her, though she should know his mother's abandonment didn't keep him up at night. "I really am perfectly okay with that. We've done just as well on our own."

"I get the occasional postcard," his aunt said, "and I mean once-in-a-decade occasional, but as far as I can tell she still hasn't settled anywhere permanently. And for you, as I recall, your real home was always with Alex's family anyway."

"It was and I'm working on making it that way again." He checked his watch. "This has been really wonderful, but we need to get on the road again."

Alex rose with him. "I'm ready."

THE ROAR OF THE CAR'S ENGINE and Chase's calm presence soothed Alex as they headed back toward civilization. She fiddled with the radio, but nothing came in clearly. A comfortable silence fell over them and Chase reached over to take her hand.

"I'm glad we came, even if we didn't find Robert a donor," he said.

"Me, too. It was very nice seeing your aunt. She's a special lady."

"Kara will want to come see her. She's stockpiling family members every chance she gets. The fact that there is no blood between her and them doesn't faze her. Maybe the silver lining is making that connection again."

"Definitely." She patted his hand, her heart filling at the thought of what life for him as a child had been. "I'm sorry about your mom. I don't know if I ever told you that."

"Honestly, sweetheart, that's history." He chuckled. "My dad, now, *that's* another story. I'm definitely scarred for life there."

"Then I'm sorry about your dad," she said.

He glanced at her, then back at the road. The muscle in his jaw twitched. "Makes us stronger, right?"

"Right, and obviously you're superstrong. Is that why I'm such a wuss? Not enough trauma in my early childhood?"

"First of all, you're not a wuss, and second of all, I hate to break it to you, but your family is full of trauma and drama and whatever else you want to throw in. You just weren't aware of it in early childhood, but you, my love, are part of the norm. Dysfunctional, like all the rest of us."

"Thanks," she said, smiling. "I'm glad we came, too."

"Hey," he said and he paused until she looked at him. "This *is* a new beginning for us. I'm not letting you go again. Let's get that straight right now. You get that things might not have all been your dad's fault back then and that I never chose sides, because I was neutral, because I didn't want to see the only real family I'd ever known fall to pieces and not because I sided with Robert or your dad, or wasn't supportive of you."

A sliver of unease rippled through her. "My dad was still wrong, though, Chase. Just because my mother was also wrong by cheating on him years ago, that doesn't really negate his actions."

"But he turned the other cheek for her. You said that made you see him in a different light."

"It does, but it isn't a 'get out of jail free' card."

The chirping of her cell phone announced the arrival of several texts and missed calls. Chase's phone also started pinging. She pulled out her phone and checked the display. "We must have hit cell range."

"At least text range," Chase said as he checked his phone. "I have a missed call from your dad, but I'm trying to call him back and it isn't going through."

"Oh, dear, he called you, too? I have missed calls from him and my sister Becky, and they both texted me. This can't be good."

Dr. Braden called with bad scan results. Cancer has spread. Robert is upset.

"That one is from my dad. I can't believe the cancer spread. For Dr. Braden to have called on a Saturday must mean it's spread to the next level," Alex said. "Shit. Here's Becky's text."

At Dad's w Robert nd Dad. Roberts freakn out. He's trashing his room. Could use a hand.

She tried to call her father, but the connection failed. "Damn it. Let me see if I can get voice mail."

But that didn't work either. Frustration and guilt welled up in her. She'd been busy making love with Chase and her brother's life had come apart. Another ding sounded on her phone.

"It's another text from Becky," she said.

He's running fever and can't swallow. Maybe pneumonia.
We r taking him to hospital. Where r u??

"Oh, my God, I can't believe this is happening." She
pressed Reply and then started to text. "What do I say?
We're not even near the airport. They think we're hiking
in north Georgia."

"Maybe we can get an earlier flight," Chase said as he
swiped his screen.

"I'll look," she said. "You focus on the road. We're
hours away. We probably couldn't make an earlier flight
even if there was one." She inhaled a deep breath and
then entered her reply.

On r way. Have been out of range. B there asap. Will call
when we r closer.

She closed her eyes and leaned her head back against
the headrest. Robert's biological father was dead, no other
donor was in sight, her brother was headed to the hospital and she was MIA.

"He's going to be all right, isn't he?" she asked, still
with her eyes closed.

Chase squeezed her hand. "I don't know. All we can
do is be there for him."

"Which we're not." She nearly laughed at the irony of
it. They'd come on this trip to help Robert and now they
were letting him down. They were letting her whole family down. "I hate this."

"Me, too."

Several times during the long drive, Alex tried unsuc-
cessfully to call her father. She finally got through when
they were about half an hour from the airport.

"It's going into voice mail," she said. "Hi, Dad, I'm so

sorry we aren't there. We've been out of cell phone range all day and didn't get your messages until we were heading back. We're on our way and will be there as soon as we can possibly get there. I'll call when we get closer."

She turned to Chase. "It's still conceivable we've been hiking all this time, right? I mean, there's no reason to upset Robert by letting him know that we went looking for his biological father when he expressly asked us not to."

"It's reasonable," Chase said. "There's no need for him to know, especially since it turned out to be a bust. He's got enough on his mind."

"What will they do now that the cancer has spread? How are they going to stop it without the transplant?"

"Sweetheart, I'm sure his oncologist has a plan. He probably deals with these situations all the time. We'll find out more when we get there."

"I can't believe they had to take him to the hospital. He's so stubborn. I knew he was running a fever the other night. If he'd just let me take his temperature then we might have nipped this in the bud. He's so frustrating."

Twenty minutes later they dropped off the SUV and rushed into the airport. They'd just made it to their gate when Alex's cell phone rang. She pulled it from her bag. "It's Becky."

Pressing her finger to one ear to try to shut out some of the airport noise, she answered. "Becky, we're still a ways out, but we'll be there as soon as we can. How's Robert?"

"He's not good. The cancer has spread. He's got pneumonia and his mood sucks. How do you think he is? I've never seen him this down. Alex, where are you? What's all that noise?"

Shit. "We had a stop along the way, but we'll be there as soon as we can."

"Did I just hear them call for boarding? Are you in an airport?"

Alex glanced at Chase, who was closely following their conversation. She had to come clean with her sister. "Yes, we're in an airport, but please don't say anything to anyone. I'll explain when we get there."

"Alex, I'm in Robert's hospital room with him and Dad. Megan is on her way. Steven still can't make it, but he's been at least checking in. I can't believe you're in an airport. Where the hell are you?"

"We just...took a day trip." She closed her eyes. Robert would no doubt figure out exactly where they'd gone. "Listen, Becky, I've got to go. I'll call you when we land."

She hung up and sighed. "Oh, man, we are so busted."

Chase nodded and pulled her close. "It'll be all right."

CHAPTER EIGHTEEN

"WHY WERE YOU..." Robert stopped and coughed hard enough to bring him up off the bed.

Alex bit her lip, her stomach tightening. They'd barely made it to the hospital and the inquisition was in full bloom. She had to keep Robert calm. Maybe if she explained he'd understand.

An oxygen tube fed Robert air through his nose, a blood pressure cuff hummed on his arm and he was plugged up to several IVs via his central line and portacath. "...at the airport? What airport? Where did you go, Alex?"

He kept his voice low, but there was an underlying tone of anger to his words. Becky patted his shoulder. "Maybe we should just leave it at it was a romantic getaway with Chase. Look at them. They're totally back together again, can't you tell?"

Chase placed his hands on Alex's shoulders. "Robert, we—"

"Chase, let me explain," Alex interrupted him.

"Yes, please explain to me, so I can underst—" Another coughing fit took hold of Robert.

His father gripped his shoulder. "Calm down, son. Let your sister talk."

"You went looking for him, didn't you? After I specifically asked you not to." Anger resonated in Robert's words. "Why would you do that?"

Dad's gaze caught hers. "He's had a really bad day."

"I don't blame him for being pissed off," Becky said, her hand resting on her rounded belly. "I don't blame him for not wanting some no-good cheat's stem cells."

Alex braced herself. "Chase helped me to find his aunt Rena. She lives out in the middle of nowhere Indiana. That's where we went. We just talked to her. I needed to understand—"

"You had no right to go there and dig up the past," Robert said.

Becky chimed in with, "I thought you were just supposed to go hiking for a few hours. I can't believe you just left like that. We've had our hands full all day. I can't believe how selfish you are, Alex. And why would you go when you knew Robert didn't want you to?"

"Honey, I know you meant well, but you should have left well enough alone." Her father stood beside Robert's bed and shook his head.

"She needed to understand how your mother did what she did." Chase kept his arm firmly around Alex's shoulders.

Alex shook her head. Since it was all out about their trip, she might as well tell them everything. "His name was Charles, your biological father."

Robert cursed and looked away. Becky's mouth gaped. Her father stared at a spot on the floor.

"And he died last year." To her frustration, her voice cracked and tears gathered in her eyes. "So you don't have to worry about whether or not he could have been your donor. Now we'll never know."

Silence fell over the room. Alex breathed slowly as tears rolled down her cheeks. Why were they getting all bent out of shape? She'd been trying to help.

At long last, Robert turned to her. "I think you've done enough here."

She stared at him in disbelief. "What do you mean?"

Her father raised his hand in pleading. "He's had a rough time of it. This isn't easy for anyone."

Becky cocked her head. "Maybe you should give him some space, Alex. We need him to calm down. The coughing is wearing him out and he needs to rest."

"Give him some space? Shit. Really? I try to help and you all lambaste me for it? Fine. I'm out of here." She gave them all one last glance, but none of them would look at her. She jerked out of Chase's hold and headed out the door.

The hum of the blood pressure cuff contracting on Robert's arm and the beeping of the monitor standing to the side of the bed filled the room as Chase stood facing Alex's family after she'd gone. His heart ached for all of them, especially for Robert, who looked ashen as he struggled with another coughing fit.

"We meant well," Chase said.

Robert settled again on his pillow, exhausted. "I knew letting you come around again would mean trouble."

Anger shot through Chase, but he held his tongue. Robert wasn't his old self. He was hurting and striking out at everyone around him. Chase had experienced that in spades with his father. He'd grown practically immune to it.

He nodded. "I'm sorry to have done anything to upset anyone in this family. You all mean a lot to me. If there's anything you need from me ever, please don't hesitate to let me know."

Without waiting for a response he left to search for Alex. He found her in a nook off the main waiting area.

She sat huddled into herself, with her arms wrapped around her middle, and she was crying. His heart broke into a million pieces seeing her so distraught.

He knelt beside her and brushed her hair from her face. "Sweetheart, it will be okay. Everyone's emotions are running on high right now. They're just upset in general. Anything above and beyond that is too much for them. We've all had a lot to digest today. Just give them time. They'll calm down."

She raised her gaze to his, her eyes swollen and red. "But it *isn't* okay and it will never be okay. It's always like this with us. I can't keep doing this with them, Chase. I don't have the heart for it. I don't understand how they can be like that. They're stubborn and closed-minded and unforgiving."

"Wait, are you hearing what you're saying? Do you think maybe they aren't the only ones being unforgiving?"

"Really?" Her eyes rounded. "*I'm* being unforgiving? I came back here. I moved into my father's house. I have been caring for my brother. How much more forgiveness do they need?"

"Everyone just needs to calm down. It's late. We've all had an extraordinarily trying day. We'll go home and get a good night's sleep. It will all seem better tomorrow. You'll see. It will be all right."

She straightened. "Please stop saying that. It isn't going to be all right. Ever. I give up."

A sense of impending doom descended over him. "What do you mean?"

"I mean, I quit. I give up on family, on the idea of family and on this particular family. They don't want me here. You heard them all."

"They're upset, sweetheart. They didn't mean any of

that. Just like you're upset. I know you don't mean this. No one gives up on family."

"Well, you're wrong. I do. I just did."

He stood, his distress mounting. "I don't believe that. I don't accept it. You can't mean that, Alex. They're your *family.* You can't turn your back on the people who love you and at a time when they need you most."

"If that's what family is about—sneaking around in nightclubs with other men, instead of being home with your husband, or sleeping with the divorcée next door, or hating on the person who's trying to help you, well, then, I don't want anything to do with family."

"I would do anything for your family if I was truly a part of it. I'd do anything for them and I'm *not* a part of it. At one time I really felt like I was. I felt more loved and more accepted in your home growing up than I ever felt anywhere else, even in my own house." He took her by the shoulders and turned her toward him, his throat tight with emotion. "I would do *anything* anyone in your family needed of me. You're so fortunate to be a part of them."

Tears streamed unchecked down her cheeks. "Is that the only reason you wanted to be with me, Chase? Were you so in love with my family that you would stoop to dating your best friend's sister, just to make sure you had a good in with them? I think you want all of them more than you want me."

The knot in Chase's stomach intensified. His own eyes filled and her beautiful face blurred, distorted by the tears he refused to let fall. "If that's really what you think, then there's no future for us. I'm sorry, Alex. I can't take your side in this and we all know if I'm not with you, I'm against you.

"I hate that I was wrong to think we could have a new beginning, but I can't be with someone who doesn't value her family. If you're truly incapable of making amends with the people who love you, then I won't be a part of your further destroying your relationship with them."

Without another word, he turned and walked away.

ALEX AWOKE THE NEXT MORNING to the sound of cicadas buzzing. After Chase had gone, she'd called a taxi to bring her back to her father's house. She cocked her head, listening, but no sound of life, other than the insects outside, greeted her ears. Her father had obviously stayed at the hospital with Robert. She was alone in this empty shell of a house. She'd thought it had been home at one time, but it was as though her entire childhood had been an illusion.

Home. She missed home—*her* home—where everything was in order and no one was ever there to get upset with her. So maybe it was lonely there sometimes, but it was so very peaceful. And once she returned to Baltimore she'd reconnect with all of her friends she'd lost touch with along the way.

She rolled to her back and stared at the ceiling. She had hardly slept, mostly cried through the night. How had she let Chase mean so much to her again in such a short time? She couldn't get the image of him turning his back on her and walking away out of her head.

I won't be a part of your further destroying your relationship with them.

What did that even mean? What further destroying could there be? They'd effectively kicked her out last night. Booted her from her brother's hospital bedside. She'd uprooted herself and returned to a place she'd avoided for the past fifteen years, just to try to help her brother. And it had seemed she'd been on her way to repairing all the old relationships with her family. *They'd* kicked her out. Her washing her hands of them was just to make her feel better.

But then Chase.

The pain seared through her, burning her throat and curling her into a ball on her side. Why did his betrayal hurt worse than the rest? She hadn't thought she'd had any more tears to cry, but they came in heaving spasms.

Her phone vibrated on the nightstand, but she ignored it. She was having an emotional wringing-out and whoever it was was either calling to tell her off some more or needed something from her. She couldn't handle either right now.

She cried until she lay limp and exhausted from the outburst. Her throat hurt. Her stomach ached and her eyes felt raw. She pulled the covers over her head in an effort to sleep her way through her misery, but her phone again vibrated, knocking a note with Aunt Rena's address on it from the nightstand.

She rolled over and stared at the paper. It had been a horrible mistake to take that trip with Chase. She should have never gone. If only she could take it all back, erase the knowledge of her mother's affair and her adoration of the man she cheated with, go back to being ignorant about the fact that the man was dead and completely useless to her brother, and obliterate her afternoon of lovemaking with Chase.

How had she let it happen?

Once more the vibrating of her phone shook the nightstand. Heaving out a breath, she grabbed the phone and checked the display before answering, a small sliver of relief filling her when she recognized the caller.

"Steven."

"You sound like shit."

She almost laughed, but she'd exhausted every muscle in her body with her last crying spasm. "I feel like shit."

And then she started to cry again.

"Christ, Alex, I've been trying to finish this project so I can take off, but they just loaded another one on me. What the hell is going on down there? Becky called and gave me a tongue-lashing and I have no idea what's happening."

"They're all pissed at me and you must be guilty by association."

"Hell, what did you do?" he asked.

"I tried to freaking help."

"I knew when you told me about the typing results you were going to get into trouble. I heard that you went on a hunt for Robert's real father."

"And please tell me why exactly that was such a horrific thing to do? He would have been a match. He could have been Robert's donor." She shook her head as fresh tears rolled down her cheeks. "Robert is running out of time, Steven."

"Yeah, I know, Becky says he's advanced to stage four now. They found more tumors in the last scan. They're getting close to infiltrating his lungs. Sounds like he'll have to up the radiation to stave it off until he finds a donor."

"Shit." Her shoulders shook with the next wave of tears. She inhaled another deep breath to try to compose herself. "I hadn't heard all the details. We got to the hospital and they went on the attack."

"He didn't want you to find the man. You should have just respected his wishes."

"God, Steven, please don't you turn on me, too."

"I'm not turning on you, but what good did it do for you to go looking for the guy? I take it you didn't find him?"

"He died last year, but Mom was evidently crazy about him." She wiped her nose with her sleeve. "I should have never gone. I should have never asked Chase to help me. The entire thing is a huge disaster."

"Megan texted me," Steven said. "She says you're unnecessarily upsetting Robert and he needs to cut out all stress. She's pissed, too."

"Of course she is."

"I can't get down there. Are you going to be okay?"

"No."

"You'll be fine. I'll try to soothe their ruffled feathers, but for Christ's sake, Alex, the man is ill and you disrespected him. Don't do that again. They're killing me over this."

She stared at the phone, unable to think of a reply. She'd disrespected Robert by trying to find him what should have been a sure shot at a donor, after the national donor bank had come up with nothing?

"What are you going to do?" he asked.

"Hell if I know. I don't even know if they want me here anymore. I guess I'll start looking for a job back home."

"It all sucks. All right, I've got to go. You'll keep me posted?"

"It doesn't sound like you need me to, since you're getting the scoop from Becky and Megan, but I'll let you know when I figure out where I'm going from here."

She hung up and headed for the shower. She felt horribly…tarnished. If only she could wash all this away and come out clean again. She needed to think and come up with a plan.

And there was only one place where she could do that. But first, she'd clean the house. Nothing cleared her mind better than a good scrub-down.

CHAPTER NINETEEN

CHASE SQUEEZED his eyes shut, trying to focus on the concept proposal for the new exhibit he'd so vividly imagined last week. Timing was everything and if he didn't get the approval to move forward with this he'd lose the dates he wanted to use for the collection. He opened his eyes and stared at the screen, rereading what he'd written so far.

His phone rang and the display showed an unknown number. Frowning, he accepted the call. "Hello?"

"Is this Chase Carrolton?" a clipped male voice asked.

"Yes, this is he."

"Mr. Carrolton, this is Officer Downs with the Fulton County Police."

He shook his head in disappointment. What had his father gotten into this time? "Is he okay? He didn't hurt anyone, did he?"

"I'm sorry, I'm not sure who you're asking about."

"Aren't you calling about my father?" he asked.

"No, I'm not calling about your father, Mr. Carrolton. You're the legal guardian of Kara Anders, correct?"

"Kara? Yes, she's my sister, my stepsister, actually. We haven't had the final hearing yet on the guardianship, but she is staying with me and I'm responsible for her. What's this about? Is *she* okay?"

"I'm not aware of Miss Anders's state of being at this time, but we would like to talk to her. We want to question her in connection with some recent robberies and vandalism in the area."

"Whoa, Kara wouldn't do anything like that. She has a bit of a wild streak, but she'd never be involved in that kind of thing."

"She isn't a suspect, Mr. Carrolton. We'd just like you to bring her in for questioning."

"Bring her in?"

"Yes, sir, will that be a problem?"

"No," Chase said as he glanced at the clock. "She won't be out of school for another hour, though. I should be able to bring her after that."

"That would be good."

"Can you tell me anything more about this? Why Kara? You think she knows whoever committed these crimes?"

"We have a known suspect we've put out an APB on, but we have reason to believe your stepsister knows this individual and was with him around the time of the latest incident. Mr. Carrolton, this is gang-related violence. These were armed robberies. If I were you, I'd keep a tighter watch over whom she's fraternizing with. This character is a bad element."

"Shit. Excuse me, I'm sorry. Yes, of course I'll bring her by. I'm sure she'll be completely cooperative." Chase jotted down the officer's name, where the precinct was located and the case number before ending the call.

Cursing under his breath, he texted Kara. She was probably still in class and unable to receive phone calls, but hopefully she'd get back to him at her next break.

THE DIGITAL DISPLAY on the stove clicked over to six twenty-five as Chase paced the kitchen and tried to call Kara one more time. His concern growing, he left her another voice mail.

"Kara, you have *got* to call me. I called the ice cream shop, but they said you weren't working tonight. I'm heading to the school to look for you. I doubt you're there this late, but I'm not sure where else to look. I'm really concerned and need to talk to you."

With a shake of his head, he grabbed his keys and headed out the door. Atlanta traffic was still heavy as he navigated I-75 onto the connector. Seeing an opening, he swung into a clear lane and managed to make it to Kara's high school within twenty minutes. He rolled through the parking lot, not sure where to start, so he parked in a section that still had cars. As he approached the building strains of music floated in the air. He pushed through the glass side door and followed the sound down a hall to an auditorium.

He peeked his head inside. Numerous kids dotted the tiered seats, while an orchestra rehearsed onstage. He scanned both the seats and the stage, but Kara was nowhere to be found. A tall dark-skinned boy passed Chase on his way out of the auditorium.

Chase exited and hurried after the boy. "Excuse me."

The boy turned and gave him a questioning look.

"Do you happen to know Kara Anders?"

"Kara?" The boy's eyebrows knitted. "I don't think so. Sorry."

"It's cool, thanks. Are there kids anywhere else here?"

The boy's expression brightened. "I think there's track practice out in the high field."

He directed Chase to where the practice was, and then wished him luck. Chase thanked him, but his stomach had a bad feeling as he surveyed the field. Kara wouldn't have had any interest in any of these events.

Where could she be? He checked his phone display again, but no new message alerts had appeared in the past five minutes since he'd last checked it. Inhaling a deep breath he called his father. Could she have gone back there for more cleaning and Roy time, as she liked to call it?

He counted four rings and then it rolled into his father's voice mail. "Hey, Dad, I'm…looking for Kara. She's late getting home and hasn't checked in. I'm a little worried about her, so if by some chance she happens to show up there, could you please have her call me? It's very important. Thanks and hope you're doing okay."

He hung up and frowned. If he didn't hear back from his father soon, maybe he should stop by there. He tried to ignore the little voice in his head that reminded him his father never answered the phone when he was drinking. At least the man was staying out of trouble with the law these days. And hopefully, he was sober and attending his meetings.

The mall. He blew out a breath and headed to his car. Kara was a teenage girl and teenage girls liked to hang out at the mall. That she was grounded and not supposed to be hanging out at the mall sent a dose of doubt coursing through him, but he continued there anyway.

Half an hour later he strode into the food court, scanning the tables and food kiosks as he moved through the area. By the time he'd circled halfway through the top floor, passing not only teens in packs, teens in couples and teens in small clusters, but also families with small children, and older couples who spread out along the walkway, moving at a slow shuffle, panic had set in. How would he ever find her?

Gritting his teeth, he headed again for his car. He had as much of a chance of finding her here as he had of finding a needle in a haystack. The quiet of the parking garage was a welcome relief after the chaos of the mall. He drew a calming breath. Where next?

This wasn't the first time Kara had gone missing, but the sick feeling in his gut told him something wasn't right with the girl this time. He swung by his father's house on his way home.

The house was quiet when he pulled into the driveway. The door was open, as usual. The scent of pine filled the air. Was that from Kara's cleaning yesterday or had she returned after school?

"Dad?"

A chair scraped the floor in the kitchen. "In here."

"Hey," Chase said. "Did you get my voice mail? I'm looking for Kara."

"No, I'm sorry, I haven't seen her today." His father sat at the kitchen table, a pen and pad of paper before him.

"I'm really worried about her. Did she say anything yesterday about plans she might have today?"

His father frowned and shook his head. "Not that I remember. She likes to talk, though."

"What did she talk about? Did she mention anyone?" Chase grabbed the back of a chair. "I should know who she's hanging out with."

"It isn't easy being responsible for someone, is it? And that one has a wild streak, always did, even when she was a wee bit of nothing."

"I don't know if *wild* is the right word. She's more of a free spirit, and I need to find her." He gestured to the spiral notebook where his father had written almost a complete page. "What are you writing?"

"Oh." His father closed the notebook and tucked his pen in the spiral binding. "It's homework…twelve step stuff."

"That's great, Dad. I'm glad to see you're sticking to it." Guilt from doubting his father earlier when the police had called filled him. "You can do it."

A small smile curved his father's lips. "Thank you, son. I appreciate that." His eyebrows arched. "You should call Alexandra. Kara talked about her nonstop. She really likes her. Maybe she knows where she is."

The knot in Chase's stomach tightened. He closed his eyes briefly. "I'm not so sure Alex wants to hear from me right now."

"Uh-oh, did you two have a fight? I thought you were getting along. From what Kara said Alex is still sweet on you. I'm sorry I was asleep when you came for Kara last night. How did the trip go?"

Chase hesitated. "It was…complicated. We found Aunt Rena and she was great, but we didn't find a donor. Alex was pretty upset and then we had to hurry back, because Robert was in the hospital. He's got pneumonia and to top everything off the tumors have spread."

"That's a tough break."

"I really need to find Kara. The police want to question her in relation to some gang-related crimes."

"My God, I knew that girl was trouble and she comes here sweet-talking me and trying to get in good with me. What is up with her?" His father's eyes went wide behind his glasses.

"Now, let's not judge until we know what's going on," Chase said.

"You need to find that girl. I'd call Alex if I were you."

Slowly, Chase nodded. He hated to admit it, but he did need Alex. "You're right," he said as he pulled out his phone. "I'll call her."

IT WAS EARLY EVENING before Alex left the house. She'd spent the day cleaning and left knowing that whenever her father arrived home he'd at least have a clean home to return to. She parked in the far parking lot at the Chattahoochee River National Recreation Area.

A dragonfly hovered for a few seconds in front of her before zipping away. She stepped onto the gravel path at the end of the parking lot, beginning the familiar journey she'd taken so many times, usually on her own, but also often with Chase. Robert had first brought her here ages ago, back in their early years, when bicycles had been their main form of transportation. But then she'd continued to come, and Robert had moved on to other pursuits.

For Alex, the long hike through the woods was a calming experience. She inhaled deeply. With luck, the fresh air would wipe away the pounding in her head. She continued on the gravel path for another fifteen minutes before coming to the old footpath. The woods had grown all around it and the path itself hadn't been as well maintained as the rest of the trails. She nearly missed it, passing it by and then circling back only when the graveled trail had taken an unfamiliar turn.

Sweeping aside a spiderweb, she moved forward on the pine-straw-covered path. The last time she'd been here had been when she'd learned about her parents' divorce. She shook her head. The events of those times took on new meaning now.

How had her mother been so angry with her father when she'd done the same thing to him? Alex spent the rest of her journey to the river lost in thought, imagining her mother in the alternate life she'd lived without her family. Why would her father allow it? A part of her was absolutely angry over her mother's actions. She felt betrayed, as if her happy family life had been a lie.

In spite of the shaded path, sweat dripped down her nose by the time she reached the river. Without hesitation, she pulled off her shoes and stepped into the water and her feet went numb with cold on entry. The river swirled around her shins.

She stepped along the rocks, carefully placing each foot, one in front of the other, feeling her way along the uneven river bottom, the soft moss squishing between her toes. She tied her sneakers together and draped them around her neck before making her way to where the water broke over an outcropping of rocks in the middle of the river. Geese drifted by near the far shore, passed by an occasional duck. A light breeze ruffled her hair as she slipped up onto the rocks, dangling her feet in the river. The water that had been painfully cold now felt amazingly refreshing. She inhaled deeply and let the peace and tranquility flow over her.

She'd come here so many times in the past, just for the sheer enjoyment of it. She and Chase had spent many summer days drifting in inner tubes, swimming and swinging from the rope swing tied to a branch overhanging the far shore.

She searched the bank, but found no sign of not only the rope swing, but the branch that had supported it. Melancholy filled her. Her days of fun and laughter had ended fifteen years ago when her family had fallen to pieces. Then this place had become a refuge for her, as it was now.

She stared into the water swirling around her ankles. Too bad she couldn't stay here forever. Unfortunately, she had to decide what to do with herself. Should she pack up and head back to Baltimore?

Sighing, she swung her feet in circles, stirring ripples in the water. A crow cawed overhead as a bee buzzed by. She couldn't leave. As much as she hated to admit it, Chase had been right. Yesterday had been full of turbulence. With all her family was going through with her brother they were living in a pressure cooker of emotions. She needed to cut everyone a little slack and then maybe they'd do the same for her.

She didn't want to leave. And though she might be tempted to walk away from her family at this point, would she be able to live with herself if she did? What if things got even worse for Robert? What if he lost this battle? Then how would she feel?

Her phone vibrated in her pocket. She checked the display and her pulse quickened. It was Chase.

She stared at her phone a long moment, before pressing Accept right before his call rolled to voice mail. "Hey."

"Hey," he said, his tone hesitant.

She closed her eyes. Why was he calling? Hadn't he said it all last night?

"Have you had any more news on Robert?"

"I haven't talked to anyone since I left the hospital," she said. "But Steven called me this morning. Becky told him Robert is now a stage four and that the tumors may be encroaching on his lungs. I think they're increasing the radiation until they find a donor."

"I scheduled an appointment to have the typing done."

She nodded, but made no reply. Her throat burned and the tears again threatened. "Thanks. You could probably call my dad directly to get an update."

"Okay, I can do that. Actually, that wasn't the only reason I called." He paused. "Kara didn't come home after school today and I'm worried about her."

"I'm sure she's fine, Chase. She's a big girl, she's street-smart and she's been out on her own for a long time. She's just not used to having to check in all the time. You need to give her more time to adjust."

"The police want her for questioning."

"Oh, my God, what do they want to question her about? Is she in some kind of trouble?"

"I don't know. That's why I'm worried. They want to question her about some break-ins and robberies. They say it's gang related."

"I'm so sorry. I'm out on the river. I don't know where she is."

He paused another moment and she thought she almost heard him smile. "Are you by the rope swing?"

"There is no more rope swing."

"Oh," he said and then cleared his throat. "Well, did she say anything to you, about where she likes to go, what she likes to do? I've called her work, looked at the school and the mall, and even checked at my dad's. He's actually the one who suggested I call you. He said all she did when she was at his place was talk about you. He thought maybe she might have said something to you that might help us find her."

Alex frowned. What kind of trouble had the girl gotten involved with? "I don't know. There's a boy she likes. She said his name was…Bruce, I think that was it, and he's blond, like her. She said they matched. I don't know his last name, but he works at the ice cream parlor. Does that help?"

"I'm not sure, but maybe the police will know who he is and how to find him."

"Chase…" She bit her lip. She wanted to be with him, to comfort him and help him find Kara, but did he want her there? And, besides, what more could she do, other than to just be a calm presence for him? She almost laughed. After the past twenty-four hours, if she were the calm one, then he was really in trouble.

"Alex, I know this is a lot to ask, especially after all that's happened between us, but would you mind stopping by? I just think if she shows up, it'll be easier for her if you're here."

Alex's throat burned. He wanted her there, but for Kara, not for himself. She nodded a few times, before she could manage to speak without her voice betraying her emotions.

"Sure," she said. "I'll be right there."

CHAPTER TWENTY

DUSK HAD FALLEN as Chase paced along the length of his porch. He'd called the police and admitted to them that Kara was missing and he hadn't heard from her. He hated to do so, but given the circumstances and the knot in his gut that hadn't let up since he'd first gotten the call from the police, he'd felt it was the only thing he could do. He'd given the officer who answered the phone the information on the mystery blond-headed boy that Alex had told him about.

He shook his head. He'd thought he'd known Kara, understood her in a way no one else had, but here was Alex, sweeping in after a fifteen-year absence, winning over the girl and getting her to confide her secret crush. Chase hadn't even known Kara had a crush.

For the hundredth time, he checked his phone display. Still no message from Kara. And where was Alex? Under the circumstances, he probably shouldn't have asked her to come over, but the police thought they knew who the boy was, a suspected gangbanger, and they were checking out all the places he frequented. All Chase could think of was the police descending on wherever the kid was and finding Kara there with him. She'd be completely freaked out and would likely feel betrayed that Chase had sent the police after them.

If that were the case, she was going to be a handful when she arrived home, and Chase felt better about having Alex with him as a show of solidarity. Headlights shone across the yard as a car pulled into his driveway. He squinted into the darkening night and surprise filled him. It was his father.

He exited the vehicle, seeming more nimble than he'd been previously, his usual shuffle replaced with a determined gait. As he neared, he waved to Chase, asking, "Any news?"

Chase gestured for him to join him inside. "I called Alex, like you suggested. Kara wasn't with her and she hadn't seen her, but Kara had told her about a boy she likes. I gave his description to the police and they think they know who he is."

His father frowned. "He's in a gang?"

"If he's who they think he is." He offered his father a seat in his living room and took a seat at a right angle to him. "They were heading out to look for him the last I heard. I don't know what would be worse, if they find Kara with him or they don't."

"There isn't a chance she went back to her old foster home? Maybe she left something there?"

Chase shook his head. "The place is deserted, as far as I know, but I suppose it's possible. She should be answering her phone, though."

"Unless it died on her again."

"True."

"Well, I couldn't sit by myself and wait to hear from you, so I thought I'd come hold vigil." His gaze met Chase's. "I know I'm a proven failure when it comes to being there for you, but I want you to know how much I appreciate how you've always been there for me, even when you shouldn't have been."

Gratitude clogged Chase's throat. What was wrong with him that he kept getting emotional over everything?

But that his father was there in a show of support for not only Chase, but for Kara, as well, was nearly overwhelming.

"Thanks, Dad," he said. "I really appreciate that." And then to lighten things up, he added, "I knew Kara would get to you. She's a pain in the ass, but she's a loveable pain in the ass." He frowned. "I just want her to be okay."

"I know you're worried about her, son. I've said a prayer for her."

Chase stared at his father in surprise. Those were words he'd never heard come out of the man's mouth. "Did I just hear you say *prayer?*"

A small smile played across his father's lips. "Make fun all you want, but I'm truly embracing the twelve steps, and this time I'm taking the whole higher-power part seriously." He ducked his head. "I was really just going through the motions before, but now…I don't know, but something about that girl got to me. Why she would care enough about an old goat like me to come spend a day mucking out my pigsty and drawing me out of my stupor is beyond understanding, especially when I pretty much abandoned her as much as her own mother did."

Pride filled Chase. "She's kind of hard to resist that way."

A rap on his storm door sounded. The porch light shone on Alex as she stood on the other side, carryout bags in hand. He opened the door and the enticing aroma of sesame chicken filled the air.

She stepped inside and nodded to his father. "Mr. Carrolton, it's so nice to see you."

His father rose to greet her. "Alexandra Peterson, look how you've grown up. You look wonderful, darlin'."

Pink tinged Alex's cheeks as she moved to the coffee table to deposit the bags. "I didn't know you'd be here, but

I got plenty, since I couldn't decide and I was hungry and I've fallen off the vegan diet. I wanted meat and I needed a selection." She announced the various containers as she pulled them from the bags. "Sesame chicken, *moo goo gai pan,* Mongolian beef, shrimp with snow peas, egg drop and wonton soups and two orders of spring rolls."

Chase stared at all the containers. "You thought the two of us would eat all of this?"

"No, silly, but Chinese makes for great leftovers."

"I'll eat my fill and take a doggy bag, if that'll help," his father said, rubbing his hands together.

With a sigh, Chase rose to get them plates and silverware from the kitchen. He hadn't thought he was hungry, but the aromas emanating from the open containers made his mouth water. He dished out a healthy serving for himself from each of the entrees.

"I shouldn't be surprised," he said to Alex. "As I recall, you always used to order like this, wherever we ate."

She shrugged as she squeezed duck sauce over a spring roll. "You could never decide between menu items, so we always ordered a little of everything. We never let it go to waste. I remember you always inhaling it all."

He nodded. He hadn't remembered that, but she was probably right. Had he been so unable to commit to anything that he couldn't choose a single entrée on a menu? Yet, hadn't he been committed to her at one time?

His father turned to Alex. "I'm so sorry to hear about your brother. Chase has been keeping me abreast of the situation. I hear he's in the hospital and not doing well."

Sadness passed across her features. "That's right. I called my sister on my way over here and his condition hasn't changed. Everyone is in town, with the exception of my brother Steven. He's a project manager for a marketing company and they keep piling projects on him, so he isn't able to get away."

"I'm surprised Robert is allowing everyone to come. He seems a little touchy about that kind of thing," Chase said, trying not to take it personally that Robert hadn't been too thrilled to see him last night.

"He isn't happy about it," Alex said. "But besides me, it's just my sister Megan who came down and she came without her daughter, so she's only here for a couple of days. Becky lives here and she's been around, so she doesn't really count." She glanced at Chase. "Megan tore me a new one over us going to see your aunt."

Chase frowned. "I'm sorry we made everyone upset about that. They should see that we were well-intentioned and meant Robert no disrespect."

"They're having a tough go of it. Whenever a family member gets cancer it becomes stressful for all involved," his father said. "Give them some time."

"Well, one night wasn't enough. I should have waited to call," Alex said. "But I wanted to see if there had been any change in Robert's condition. Next time I'll just call the hospital and get his status. I'm giving the rest of them a wide berth."

Frustration had Chase stabbing his food. Why did this have to be so difficult? He wanted Alex to take a stand *with* her family, not against them, and steering clear of them just didn't seem right. Yet, who was he to judge her? At least the woman always knew what she wanted.

His phone buzzed and he nearly jumped. He fumbled to unlock it. The display showed another unfamiliar number.

"Chase Carrolton."

"Mr. Carrolton, this is Officer Downs. We found your

stepsister. She was with the individual you called us about. She came with us willingly for questioning."

He glanced at Alex and his father. "And she's all right? She's with you at the precinct?"

"Yes, sir, she's here. She's been very cooperative and she's free to go. You are welcome to come and pick her up, unless you prefer for a squad car to drop her at home."

Chase could only imagine how stressful Kara's night had already been. "Thank you, Officer Downs, but I'll come get her. Please let her know I'm on the way."

ALEX HURRIED AFTER CHASE as he climbed the front steps to the police station two at a time. She'd been relieved to hear Kara was all right, but concern filled her when she thought about the boy Kara had been with. Chase had said the police believed he was affiliated with a gang. Had Kara known?

They stopped at a windowed counter where Chase was directed down a hall into an open office area with rows of desks and ample activity, even for the late hour. They found Kara at one of the desks, her bright blond ponytail incongruous to the sullen expression on her face.

She stood and shouldered her book bag as they approached, said goodbye to the female officer at the desk and headed toward the door, passing by them without a word. Chase looked from her to the female officer, who rose and gestured him forward as he approached.

"I'll go after her," Alex said and Chase nodded.

She looked in the hall and the waiting area near the entrance without finding the girl. Finally, she pushed open the main exterior door. Kara leaned against the front wall, her arms folded. She didn't acknowledge Alex as she stopped in front of her.

Alex searched for words. "I know you must be upset, Kara."

The girl glared at her, but remained silent.

"I suppose if I liked a boy and I told someone I trusted about that and then they told someone and it got him in trouble I might be upset, but the thing is that none of us got Bruce in trouble. Whatever Bruce did got Bruce in trouble and I, for one, don't think you should be hanging around a guy who's involved with a gang."

"I didn't think he was. He has friends who are, but he said he stayed out of that stuff."

Alex nodded. "And I guess you believed him."

Kara shrugged.

"I don't know what's happening with this guy you like, but I do know that you went missing again today and that really worried everyone."

A short laugh burst from her. "Everyone?"

"Yes, Chase, his father and me."

Kara's gaze swung to hers. "Roy was worried about me?"

"He was just with us over at Chase's, waiting until we had word of you." She shrugged. "You should try to see this from our point of view. We didn't know where you were or if you were okay. And the police had called and said they wanted to talk to you in connection with some gang-related violence. How would you have felt?"

Kara exhaled loudly. "I suppose I'd be concerned."

"Well, we were. We all really care about you, Kara. Chase was frantic to find you. He asked me if there was anything I could tell him to help locate you, so I told him about Bruce, because I was worried about you. I'm really sorry if you told me about him in confidence, but we don't know this guy. We have no idea what he's capable of. Young girls go missing every day. You may be street tough, but you're still a target, every time you're out wandering around by yourself. A simple call or text to let one of us know you were okay would have been much appreciated," Alex said.

Chase stepped outside and glanced around for them. Kara ducked her head as he approached. He stood with his hands on his hips, his feet spread wide.

"I'm glad you're okay," he said.

She nodded slowly. "I'm always okay. You have to learn not to worry about me."

"Well, as long as you pick assholes for friends, that isn't going to happen. I thought we had a deal and you weren't going to go MIA on me again. Today was a pretty shitty day to do that, Kara. What were you doing with that guy anyway? You're still grounded, not that that seems to mean anything to you."

"I missed the bus and he offered to give me a ride. But he didn't bring me home."

"And you didn't call because?" Chase asked.

"My phone died again. I was going to ask to borrow his, but he was freaking glued to the thing. He kept saying 'in a minute' and then another call or text came in that he had to freaking take."

She crossed her arms. "Okay, you're right, whether he's in a gang or not, he's an asshole. I'm sorry I made you worry. I swear I didn't mean for any of this to happen."

"Did they show you the video?" he asked Kara.

She nodded slowly, her gaze downcast.

Chase said to Alex, "They have him on video robbing a convenience store at gunpoint." He turned to Alex. "He's wearing a mask, but he takes it off when he leaves and the outside camera gets him."

"Do you know how angry it makes me that you were hanging around with this guy?" he asked Kara.

"I didn't know he was doing that shit. I'm not going to hang around him anymore."

"You're damn right. He's not going to *be* around anymore. He'll be locked up, but there are dozens of more guys like that out there. They're a dime a dozen and you seem to keep meeting them." His lips formed a thin line, evidently stemming his anger.

"I can't keep doing this, Kara." Chase stared at her, his eyes flashing.

"Shit, Chase," Kara said and her voice cracked. A tear slipped down her cheek. "Please don't give up on me. You're all I've got."

Alex pressed her lips together. Here she was with more family than she could handle and poor Kara had only Chase. And Kara evidently wanted *her* family.

Chase's frown eased. "I'm not giving up on you. Christ, though, Kara, I *hate* when I can't reach you and I don't know where you are. We're getting you a backup battery for your phone and a portable charger. You have to communicate with me and your indefinite grounding is continued indefinitely. I don't care if you miss the rest of high school."

"Okay, I got it. Who needs a life anyway?" Kara said, though her lips curved into a semblance of a smile.

"You won't be completely cut off." Chase turned to Alex. "You'll still have Alex stopping by to tutor you, right, Alex?"

Alex nodded. "It does appear I'm sticking around for a little longer, so, yes, of course I'll continue to tutor her." She met Kara's gaze. "If you still want me to, that is."

"Yes," Kara said and wrapped her arms around Alex's

neck and hugged her hard before pulling back. "I always wanted a sister. I think you'll do."

Alex glanced at Chase, wide-eyed.

He shrugged. "I told you, she's stockpiling family and it doesn't matter to her if you're blood related or not."

CHAPTER TWENTY-ONE

"SHE WAS OUT as soon as her head hit the pillow," Chase said as he closed the door to Kara's room.

The girl *was* going to be the death of him. How he was going to get through the next week, let alone months or longer with her, was beyond him. He'd be a worn-out old man in no time.

Alex turned with him toward his living room. "What a trying night. I'm glad she's safe at home."

"Me, too."

"I'm not a parent or anything and I'm not exactly a people person, but I get why she did this. And I think she learned from it. Maybe you shouldn't go so hard on her. She did seem truly sorry."

"Right, until she does it again. I'm not letting up on her grounding until I feel better about who she's going to be hanging out with."

"Maybe you just need to meet some of her friends. Let her have a small dinner party or something, so you can check them all out and say yay or nay on each of them."

"I'll need background checks on all of them. That boy, Bruce, looked pretty much wholesome. Who knew he'd be an absolute dick? Hell, I can't tell her who she can and can't see. She's going to do what she wants. Why can't she just pick better friends?" He blew out a breath. "I'm going to have to block her phone from texting or get her a very limited package. I think that's what has her wearing out her battery all the time."

He stopped in the arched opening to his living room and turned to her. The soft lighting played across the angles and curves of her face and he clenched his hand into a fist to keep from stroking her cheek.

"Thanks so much for coming over tonight, and for bringing the Chinese food and then going with me to pick her up. I think it made a difference to her that you were there, but none of it was any fun and I know you had better things to do."

"Actually, with Robert in the hospital and my family not wanting me around, I'm pretty much a free agent, but you're welcome."

"So, how are you feeling about your family today?"

She shook her head. "I really don't know. I have so many siblings and both of my parents, even though my mom isn't so much like a mom to me anymore, and I do have a lot of history with them, obviously, and it's not all bad. They make me insane and they piss me off and I don't feel like they appreciate me all that much—since yesterday maybe not at all. But then I look at Kara and all she's been through and how all she really has is you and how she's holding on to you with both hands…"

She met his gaze. "I see how much she truly appreciates family, the concept, and her actual family, as limited and unconventional as it may be, and maybe, just maybe, it makes me appreciate it a little more, as well."

Hope stirred in him, but he tamped it down. He wasn't putting himself out there again for Alex to trample until she was a little more committed to her family ties. Maybe she just needed a little more time, or maybe she'd never be ready. One thing was for sure, though, he wasn't going to rush into taking a stand on this one again.

Not until *he* was sure.

He inhaled slowly and resisted the urge to reach out to her. He didn't want someone who was just a little appreciative of her family. He wanted the whole ball of wax.

Cocking his head, he asked, "What would it take for you to feel completely committed to your family?"

She closed her eyes for a moment, as if pained. When she opened them, her beautiful blue gaze was full of doubt. "I don't know," she said. "Maybe I'm just too different from them to ever feel like I can totally connect, but—" she let out a loud sigh "—I'm going to see what I can do. I may not always like them, but I do love them. I know it's late, but I think I'll stop by the hospital to see what's going on. Maybe tempers have cooled."

He placed his hands behind his back to keep from taking her hand in his. He said, "Good luck to you, Alex. I hope it all works out for you. Please give your brother my best."

"Thanks, Chase, I hope everything works out for you, as well. I know you have your work cut out for you with Kara and you have a lot you're dealing with at the university museum, as well as at school. I want you to know that you're completely off the hook for the gala. If you want to find someone else to go with, I completely understand. And you don't have to decide now, but if you still need me to go with you, I'm fine with that, as well. I think we can both be adults about this. We hadn't planned it to be a real date, anyway, so if you still want to go with that, then, by all means let me know."

Appreciation for this woman filled him, along with a dose of melancholy. He'd looked forward to showing her off in earnest to everyone there, not just Paula Dixon. He'd imagined Alex on his arm as his significant other in all ways. Settling for less than that held little appeal.

"Thanks," he said. "I'll let you know."

TRAFFIC WAS LIGHT on I-285 as Alex exited toward Northside Hospital. Hopefully, Robert was sleeping and the rest of her family had headed to their respective homes. If, however, her father was still at the hospital, she planned to send him home to sleep in his own bed.

She was too wired to sleep herself. She just needed to check in to see that her brother was all right. She pulled into the hospital parking lot. A cool mist wrapped around her as she exited her car and she shivered.

The night had been too trying. First, all the worry over Kara, and then afterward, during that conversation with Chase, it was all she could do to keep her composure. She was happy to not have hard feelings between them, but his congenial attitude was almost more than she could bear.

What would it take for you to feel completely committed to your family?

He was still standing on that soapbox, but after witnessing Kara's distress, part of her understood his need for family commitment. How could Kara have thought Chase would give up on her? He was just getting started in earnest with his sister and she had a lot of adjusting to do as far as settling into her family.

And Alex *wasn't* sure what it would take for her to commit to her family. She was admittedly gun-shy after they'd jumped on her for trying to find Robert's biological father and then kicked her out of his hospital room. She'd answered Chase as honestly as she could. As far as she could tell, her family had a whole different idea of what commitment was all about.

Still, she'd see what she could do.

The hospital was quiet, and since it was past time for visitors, Alex waited until the nurses at the cancer ward's nurses' station were busy before she crept by to her brother's room. The door stood slightly ajar. She pushed it open and entered to find Megan asleep in a chair beside the bed.

A low light over a side sink near the bathroom cast a bluish-white glow over the room. The heart monitor and blood pressure cuff maintained the same steady rhythms they'd kept when she was last here, but the hiss of the oxygen was missing. The mood was subdued, quiet.

Robert stirred, moaning softly. Alex moved to his bedside as he rolled to his back and opened his eyes. He fumbled for his water glass on the nightstand. She resisted the urge to help him, until his straw sucked air at the bottom.

"Here," she said as she refilled his glass from a pitcher on his bedside tray that was pushed off to one side.

He nodded and drank a little more before collapsing back on his pillows. "Hey."

"Hey. How are you feeling?"

"I've been worse. I think they're going to let me go home tomorrow."

"That's great, Robert. I'm sure Dad's happy about that." She gestured to Megan, asleep in the chair. "I'm glad to see he went home. I was going to boot him out if he was still here."

Robert squinted at the wall clock. "He just left maybe an hour ago."

She nodded again to Megan. "Maybe I should wake her up and send her to Dad's. She's going to be sore when she gets up. I know you don't need a babysitter, but I can stick around for a while, but only if you'd like."

"You and I seem to be on the same no-sleep schedule." He shifted over and patted the bed. "Sit down, so you aren't towering over me. I don't like having to crane my neck to look at you."

"Wow," she said as she took the offered seat. "I feel

honored. I've gone from family pariah to honored bed guest."

"Don't get your head all puffed up. Like I said, you were hurting my neck."

"So, you're still mad?"

"What would you have done if that guy had been alive?"

"Honestly, I don't know. I hadn't figured that part out." She was quiet for a moment. "Chase's aunt Rena showed me a picture of him, of him and Mom. They were in this nightclub and she was all dressed up and was holding this martini glass and she was looking at him with this expression of rapt adoration."

She shook her head. "I don't know how to explain it, but I hated seeing that picture. Like, who was that woman? It certainly wasn't Mom, not *our* mom. I think… I think if he'd been alive it would have been really hard to go to him after that. I don't know. I might have for you— for the chance of him being a donor."

Expecting an outburst from her brother, she paused.

"Go on," he said.

"Well, it's funny, because when I started I went solely for you, to find you a donor, even though you didn't want that particular donor." A short laugh escaped her. "I think if I'd actually found the guy, gotten him and you both somehow to agree to the transplant, your body would have rejected his stem cells. You didn't want him on a cellular level."

Robert chuckled with her. "You're probably right about that."

"Anyway, somewhere along the way it became more about Mom and more about me—about finding out how she could have done that. I just really wanted to understand who that woman in the photograph was, because she was some stranger to me."

She inhaled slowly. "And then I guess I started to question who I was. I mean my own mother wasn't who I thought she was and possibly my father was this Charles guy she loved in some way that didn't fit with the rest of her life. What if he was my father, too? Who did that make me?"

"It makes you a royal pain in the ass."

"Yeah, I guess so."

Megan stirred behind her, sitting forward and rubbing her eyes. "What time is it?"

"Almost midnight, past your bedtime," Robert said. "You should have gone with Dad. It freaks me out to have someone in here watching me sleep."

"You don't sleep," Alex said.

"Are you going to stick around?" Megan asked Alex.

"I don't know." She looked questioningly at Robert.

He shrugged. "Suit yourself. Do you have a tablet or laptop or something I can go online with?"

"I'm sorry," Alex said. "I have my laptop at Dad's."

"I have a tablet." Megan pulled the device out of her bag. "Here you go." She handed it to Robert. "I'm going to Dad's, if that's cool."

"Sure," Robert said. "You heading out tomorrow?"

She nodded. "I'll stop by on my way out if you're still here. My flight isn't until one. I'll be back for the tablet one way or another." She leaned over and gave him a hug. "You have a good one. Try to sleep."

"You, too," Robert said as he turned on the tablet.

Alex scooted over into the chair her sister had vacated.

"Where are you going?" He patted the bed again. "You can see better here."

"Oh? Okay," she said, curious about what he wanted

to show her. She settled again next to him as he logged into a website.

"I created this," he said, handing her the tablet. "I wanted to rant and be miserable and all these sites have all these stupid rules and they want everyone to be all fucking nice about the fact that they have cancer and life sucks."

She scrolled through his website. She'd thought he'd created a blog, but here he'd established an entire community of grouchy cancer patients just like him, where they could swear and spew all the anger they wanted and the other participants just cheered them on.

"Wow," she said. "This is really incredible, Robert. *Fight Club for Cancer Warriors*. 'It's not pretty and we don't sugarcoat it.'" She met his gaze. "This is what you've been spending all of your time on?"

He grinned. "Yeah, bitching online. I've had a lot to bitch about. I didn't think you'd approve. There's some pretty foul stuff on there."

"I like it and it looks like you're helping a lot of people on here."

"I didn't have a choice. I kept getting censored on these other forums and I got kicked out of a few. I just needed a place to vent and I wanted it to be to other people who felt the same way."

She covered her mouth to quiet her laughter.

"Why is that so funny?"

"The other night when I came up and you were working on this and I could tell you weren't feeling well. Probably because you'd caught a virus that morphed into pneumonia, so the next time I want to take your temperature, we're bloody well going to take your temperature, by the way.

"Anyway, Becky had recommended that I let you vent

to me and I was trying to give you that opportunity then, but all you cared about at the time was this website."

"I felt like shit and you were bugging the crap out of me. I was on a huge rant that night."

"Well, I can only imagine if you had actually vented to me the way you vent on that site. I would have been stunned. I mean, I totally get it, but I would have probably burst out crying and run away."

"See, that's why we need a safe place to get all that crap out where it can't hurt anyone." He touched a tab on the site. "Here's my favorite, The Hurl Pool."

She glanced over some of the posted topics. "Wow, you guys just really hurl it all out there."

"And girls. We've got some pretty pissed-off women on here, too."

"I'm so impressed. I can't believe you did this. And I'm really glad you didn't vent to me. In fact, I'm okay if you never vent to me. Why did I think just because Becky lives here, she'd be the one to ask for advice on how to deal with you?"

"Ah, Becky's okay, but I don't think I'll share this with her."

"Oh, but you felt compelled to expose *me* to that," she said, laughing. "Gee, thanks, I feel so honored."

"Honestly, I didn't think I was going to ever show that to you, especially not to you." He shrugged. "You know, you're always so clear on what's right and what's wrong. Everything is black-and-white with you. I didn't think you'd understand this." He gestured to the tablet.

"I understand that," she said. "I know that's the way I am—black-and-white—at least the way I was before the past couple of weeks. Everything's gotten so muddy since then. I'm starting to see gray in a lot of places I didn't before."

"So." He turned off the tablet and set it aside. "What the hell is going on with you and my buddy?"

Shit. Just when they were starting to get along. "Look, *he* broke things off with me this time." She shook her head. "We didn't even make it twenty-four hours. That must be some kind of world record for the shortest relationship."

"Let me guess, he got all bent out of shape when you walked out of here yesterday."

"Yes."

"He railed at you for not being here for your family."

"You guys kicked me out."

"I was going to vent, to spew out a whole lot of nastiness if you stayed, and that wouldn't have been good for anyone."

"Okay, I see that now."

"Look, Alex, I see that you were well intended, that in *your* eyes what you did was right. I don't want to argue and evidently, you got a lot more out of the experience, so we aren't going to harp on it, but in my eyes, what you did was a huge waste of time and money, because there was no way in hell I was going to use that guy as a donor."

"Okay, fine, I don't want to argue, either."

"See, you and I always know where we stand on things. But for Chase, he has to weigh things out. He's always been really cautious about that and for him the only thing that matters is family, which is kind of funny for a guy who doesn't really have much of a family of his own. I get that his dad is trying and that he has a problem he's working on and that he's a great guy when he's sober, but for Chase it's that he really values family. Mostly, that's because he hasn't had one outside of what he's had with us."

"I know, he's all about family and I haven't been so much, and it's a big issue between us."

"Look, he's a good guy. I know I don't need to tell you that. But it takes him forever to commit to something. Part of it is because he had a shitty childhood, but part of it is because once that guy commits it's really hard for him to break that commitment and it's really hard for him to see other people break their commitments."

"Right, I get all that about him."

"Did you know it took him a freaking entire year before he'd ask you out?"

"Really?" A sliver of joy washed through her. "I *knew* he was into me way back then."

"Yeah, but you were only fifteen and he was all freaked out, because it was *you* and he didn't want to screw anything up with the family. I kept telling him to ask you out, that it was totally cool."

"Well, he took his freaking time," she said.

"Exactly, and when that man committed to you, he *committed* to you and then you stomped all over his heart. So, yeah, I get that he freaked out about you being anti-family, because my guess is that's more important to him now than it ever was."

"Right, so what are you trying to tell me. *He* broke it off with me, remember?"

"But why?"

"Because you guys suck," she said, but she smiled.

He laughed softly. "Right, so what do you need to do to get him back?"

She cocked her head. "You're assuming I want to get him back. What about me heading back to Baltimore when all is said and done? Why get attached to him again, if I'm just going to leave?"

"Is staying here really not an option?" He held her gaze.

What *would* it be like if she stayed? "I don't know, maybe. I'll have to figure it out."

"So what are you going to do?"

"Make you guys not suck."

"I think he's going to have to settle with that."

She yawned. Robert frowned. "Are you getting ready to ditch me?"

"Oh, no, I'm good," she said. "I can plant myself in this chair if I need to."

"You'll get a sore neck. Why don't you head home? I think I might actually sleep."

"Okay, if you're sure."

"But, Alex, there's something you should know about before you walk out that door."

"What's that?" she asked.

"The first rule about *Fight Club for Cancer Warriors* is we don't talk about *Fight Club for Cancer Warriors*."

She grinned. "Got it."

CHAPTER TWENTY-TWO

THE ALARM SHOCKED Chase from sleep the following morning. He pried open his eyes and stumbled his way through getting dressed. Kara had already left for school, but on the breakfast bar he found a plate of scrambled eggs with cheese, toast and turkey bacon with a side of grapes. He dropped his briefcase and devoured the food without even sitting. How was it possible he was hungry after he'd eaten all that Chinese food last night?

How was it possible when he'd walked out on the love of his life the night before eating the Chinese? He closed his eyes and groaned. How had things gone from stellar to cellar so quickly with Alex? And now they were polite friends and she'd be happy to accompany him to the gala as his friend, if he wanted her to.

Well, of course he wanted her to, but not as his damn friend.

Nearly an hour later, thank you Atlanta rush hour traffic, he pulled into the museum parking lot. He had to get his head around work this morning. He stopped in the little downstairs bistro, dying for coffee. He'd just placed his order when a tap on his shoulder had him turning to face Paula Dixon.

"Mrs. Dixon," he said, schooling his features into a pleasant smile. "How are you this morning?"

"I'm doing well, Chase, thank you."

"What will you have?" he asked.

She leaned over him and ordered her skinny latte from the young barista, and then she turned to Chase. "Have you been avoiding me?"

"Now, why would I do that?"

She narrowed her eyes on him as the barista handed them their drinks. "Come sit with me then."

"Fine, but I can only stay for a minute."

"I've been thinking with all the requests we've gotten, instead of waiting for the existing exhibition to travel we should split the collection into smaller groupings to send out. We can cover more ground that way. With so many university museums out there that are interested, we shouldn't be stingy."

He hesitated for a very long moment. There was no way in hell he was going to agree to that, but he still needed to keep on his white kid gloves with Mrs. Dixon, even though her annual endowment was late in coming. Again, he pasted on his smile. "I will certainly take that under advisement and will look into it."

Her sculpted eyebrows arched. "Look into it? I expect you to make this happen, Chase. Think about it. How fun would that be? I've been thinking I should travel more. I have a granddaughter who will be starting college next year. We could accompany you on the exhibition installation trips and view the various campuses. We could all travel together. Doesn't that sound wonderful?"

It sounded as if he was going to lose that wonderful breakfast Kara had made him. "I'm not sure, Mrs. Dixon—"

She grabbed his hand. "Please call me Paula, Chase. I don't know why you insist on being so formal. I think we are closer in age than you realize."

"Mrs. Dixon, my schedule simply can't take the additional travel for the increase in exhibitions you're suggesting, let alone the museum budget or the rest of my workload."

Determination glinted in her eyes. She patted his hand. "You can manage anything you set your mind to, darling."

"As I said, I'll give it due consideration." Again, there was no way in hell he'd support this plan.

"I will, of course, go to the director with my suggestion. Agnes and I are having lunch tomorrow. I'm sure she'll be happy to consider the smaller exhibitions."

Damn it. He was going to have to find a way to limit her control. "I'm sure she'll be supportive. Now if you'll excuse me, I need to get to work."

"Wait, Chase, I think I understand. The travel is too much, isn't it?"

Thank God she was going to be reasonable. "Actually, yes, especially if you insist on my overseeing every installation and setup. Frankly, we don't have the budget for the additional travel."

Her gaze slipped away the way it did when she was up to trouble. "I could probably look at having you travel less."

Suspicion filled him. Was she being a considerate soul, or was she up to no good? "Thank you, that would make my life so much better."

"Maybe if I do that, you could do me a favor."

Uh-oh. She *was* up to no good. "What kind of favor are you talking about?"

"Oh, nothing major. As we discussed, I need a little help with appraising and finding a buyer for the new pieces." She pulled a manila folder out of her bag. "I brought you the provenance, as promised."

"Oh." He stared at the folder. He had a funny feeling about those artifacts. "And the provenance is good?"

"Oh, yes," she said and slid the folder to him. "Why don't you hold on to that and think about it?"

Well, I'll be damned. This felt too much like blackmail. Why was she wanting to sell and why did he have a bad feeling about all of this? Slowly, he picked up the folder. "Very well, let me review this and I'll get back to you."

"Thank you, Chase." She smiled that ruby-red smile. "Please make that sooner rather than later."

"I'll see what I can do," he said.

"I'm putting together some research on the pieces for you. I thought that might be helpful."

He shrugged. "I'll look at whatever you have. When I have the time, that is."

"I'll also update some of what you have on the original collection. I found some new sources you didn't include in your initial research. We can update some of the tagging."

"My research isn't all included in the tagging."

Frowning, she shook her head. "I couldn't very well start from scratch without seeing how you'd done the original research. I thought a little consistency would be good, even if the new pieces go elsewhere."

He frowned in confusion. "So, you read my research files? I never published that research."

Her eyes widened. "I didn't think you'd mind, since you were out of town. Finding the hard copies wasn't too difficult. Your filing system makes sense…somewhat. The electronic copies were a little difficult, but then I found your password list and was able to log in as you and find them. I'll email you the updated files when I'm finished."

He stared at her, stunned. Not only had she rifled through his desk, she'd stolen his log-in information and gone through his electronic files. This was too much.

The electronic notes of "Call Me Maybe" sounded

from within her purse. She pulled out her phone and smiled. "There's Agnes now."

"I'll let you get that, then," he said.

She nodded and moved away, already chatting to the director. Chase clenched his fists. The woman was out of control. He needed to put a stop to her meddling and he needed to do it now.

RESTLESSNESS DROVE ALEX from her bed after just a few short hours of sleep. To burn off the unwanted energy she went for a jog along the river. The trail was cool at the early hour and her legs felt strong. She ran until she thought she couldn't run any farther and then she pushed herself to keep going.

So what are you going to do?

Make you guys not suck.

And how, exactly, was she going to do that? Not that her family sucked. Well, sometimes they sucked, but sometimes *she* sucked, as well. Looking back, maybe going behind Robert's back to find his biological father hadn't been the smartest thing she'd ever done. Maybe she should have talked it out with him first.

When those roots have been torn from the ground, it's really hard to trust in them again.

Regardless of what had happened with their mother and Charles McMann, they had been a strong family once. Could they be again? Somehow, she had to find a way to replant her roots. Did that mean considering staying in Atlanta? Was her family worth her reestablishing herself here? They would likely continue to knock heads over issues like her unauthorized search for her brother's real father, or whatever else might come up as a result of them being people of differing opinions.

Regardless of the outcome, though, she was glad she'd

gone with Chase to see his aunt. The trip had definitely given Alex a new perspective on so many things. And she wouldn't have taken back that afternoon with Chase for anything. If he were truly out of her life in that respect going forward, then at least she had the memory of that perfect afternoon with him.

I'll do everything in my power to make this better for you, Alex.

If Chase could make an effort like that for her, couldn't she make one for him? All he wanted was for her to mend things with her family. But was it too late? And how was she going to fix things?

"THANKS SO MUCH for coming by," Chase said to Tony as he closed his office door and then cleared papers from a chair for his friend.

"I decided to meet a client up the street for lunch, so this was on my way. Do you have the contract?"

"I know this isn't your area of expertise and I have the opinion of the university's attorney, but I thought it wouldn't hurt to see what you thought, as well. It's a donor agreement form signed by the husband of one of our benefactors," Chase said as he handed the paper to Tony.

"Even though it was his collection and he donated it, he always deferred to his wife as far as any issues of control," Chase explained. "I believe that stems back to her family being among the original founders of the university. He did it as a wedding gift to her, as I understand."

Tony glanced at him, his eyebrows arched. "This gives the donor a sizable amount of control. Is that the norm?"

"Shit, no, thank God," Chase said. "I'd be pulling out my hair if that were the case. This was an unusual circumstance. The donation was made back in the late seventies and the collection was considered extremely valuable. The powers that be at the time were aching to get their hands on it and allowed these conditions. You'd never see anything like this today."

Tony leaned back and chuckled. "She's sending you all over to Timbuktu and back with this, isn't she?"

"She is and I've been very patient, thinking it was in the museum's best interest, but things need to change around here or I'm not going to make it."

"Well, rest assured, my friend, that this was binding to her late husband only. She isn't named in this document and it even has a clause about all rights reverting to the museum upon his death."

"Yes, I saw that," Chase said. "I wasn't sure if her being his wife and inheriting his worldly goods would change any of this."

"The good news is that in this instance it's clear-cut." Tony handed him back the paper. "It's up to you now to take back control. You have full legal rights to do so."

"Thanks. If I'm going to make any changes in the control over the collection there can't be any question about the interpretation of the agreement," Chase said and pulled out the manila folder with the provenance Paula Dixon had given him the other morning. "Again, I know this isn't your area of expertise, but I'm curious as to what you think."

Tony opened the folder and scanned the contents of the first page, glancing up at Chase and shaking his head on occasion. When he'd finished reviewing all of the pages, he set aside the folder. He steepled his fingers. "Is this from a trusted source?"

"I don't know where she got this. She says it was in a crate left by her late husband, but I don't believe it. I've had a funny feeling about it from the start."

"And what about the early ownership, prior to 1983? Were you able to validate the initial gallery?"

Chase shook his head. "I found no existing record of such a gallery."

"I think you have your answer, then, my friend."

"Yes, that's what I thought," Chase said. "I don't think she means anything underhanded by requesting to sell it. I think she just got a bum deal and is trying to make the best of it. She may not even know she was duped."

A chuckle escaped his friend. "I love how you see the best in others, Chase. That's why you make a better curator than an attorney."

"Ah, but that's why I have you to count on, my friend."

"That you do," Tony said as he stood and shook Chase's hand. "I'll see you at the hearing, then."

"I'll be there with bells on."

Chase relaxed back in his chair after his friend had left. Now that he had the upper hand with his beloved Mrs. Dixon, he wasn't quite sure where to start. The museum was her life, after all.

Surely, he could find a compromise and make a stand all at the same time.

THE MORNING WAS STILL YOUNG when Alex finished her run and headed to see her mother at the nursing home. She had a lot of ground to cover and starting with her mother seemed to make the most sense. She pushed through the main doors, near what used to be the receptionist's desk before the health-care cost reductions eliminated the receptionist.

The sound of tinkling silverware and murmured conversations drifted to her from the dining room. Smiling, she searched the early-morning diners for her mother's familiar gray-and-auburn hair. The nursing home seemed to have a lot of nonsleepers. She'd probably fit in well here.

The flash of a familiar smile caught her eye. Her mother sat on the far side of the dining room, sipping coffee with another woman. Alex wound her way through the tables, smiling at the other residents and exchanging a few morning greetings along the way. Her run had certainly improved her mood. She should probably take it up on a regular basis.

"Alex!" Her mother rose and extended her arms as Alex approached.

Happiness filled her as she hugged her mother back. Whether they were in the current decade or not, this was the mother she remembered. She drew back, smiling.

"Mom, it's so good to see you so clear-eyed today."

Her mother frowned. "I'm so sorry, sweetheart. I guess I'm hit or miss, aren't I?"

"It's okay," Alex said. She gestured to her mother's breakfast companion. "I don't want to interrupt. I was just out and about and felt the need to stop by."

"This is Peg." Her mother indicated her friend. "She actually works here in the front office, and when I come to, so to speak, I check in with her to see what's been going on. She's in that front office, and though she doesn't catch everyone, she has a good idea of the comings and goings around here."

Tears pricked Alex's eyes. Her mom was really her mom this morning, not the woman in the photograph or the one with early-onset Alzheimer's. She was *Mom*. Alex shook Peg's hand. "I'm Alex. It's nice to meet you."

The woman rose. "We don't know how much time she'll have for this round. I'll leave you two to visit."

Her mother frowned. "It's not that I'm not thrilled to

see you, but I understand you've been around a number of times recently. I'm just surprised you're here."

She gestured for Alex to sit and resumed her seat, as well. "Although, what excellent timing. Please, catch me up on everything. Without the receptionist, it isn't easy to keep track, but Peg says you and Becky are my only recent visitors. Oh, and she said Megan stopped by for a little bit yesterday, which was also a surprise."

She pulled a little photo album from her pocket and showed it to Alex. "She identified all of you from these."

Alex flipped through the pictures and laughed. "Those are from the late eighties, early nineties. I'm surprised she could still pick us out."

"Quickly, what are you and Megan doing here? What's going on with Robert and your father? She hadn't seen either one of them in a while and that's a little unusual."

"Dad comes by?" Alex asked, surprised.

Her mother nodded. "When Peg told me I'd been having a gentleman visitor, other than your brother, it took me a while to figure it out, but, yes, evidently he comes sometimes. I think it's kind of sweet."

"I know he still cares about you," Alex said. "He told me you were just about perfect."

"He said that?"

"Yes."

"And what's going on with you and with your brothers?" She waved her hand. "Just tell me, is everyone healthy and happy?"

Alex met her gaze, but she couldn't form the words. Should she tell her mother what was happening with Robert? Her throat burned and tears gathered in her eyes.

Her mother gripped her hand. "Oh, my God, who is it? Someone isn't well?" She bit her lip and her gaze darted away and then back. "It's Robert. That's why he hasn't been by."

Agony etched the lines of her mother's face. Alex closed her eyes. She shouldn't have come. She shook her head. "He's going to be okay. He has to be."

"If you thought that, you wouldn't be so upset." She squeezed Alex's hand. "What is it?"

"Hodgkin's lymphoma. He was nonresponsive to the original rounds of chemo, so he underwent a stem cell transplant, using his own stem cells." At her mother's confused look she added, "It's like a bone marrow transplant, though less invasive."

"So, he got some of his own blood stem cells?"

"Exactly."

"But he isn't okay?" her mother asked, her voice unsteady.

Alex shook her head. "The tumors started growing again shortly after the procedure. His oncologist wants him to undergo a second transplant, using donor cells this time." Alex dropped her gaze. She'd started it, nothing but the entire truth would do now. "We were all typed, or our blood was typed to see if any of us could be a match."

Her mother stared at her, unblinking. "And none of you matched?"

Alex shook her head.

"Oh, my God, then what can be done?"

"His doctor is continuing a search of the national donor bank. We're asking friends to get typed. We'll keep looking for a donor until we find one."

Her mother's eyes rounded. "What about me? I'm his mother. He got half his DNA from me. That's got to count for something. Can't I get typed?"

Alex again shook her head. "We talked about it and Robert won't allow it. Your lucid periods are so rare, even if you agree to it and signed some kind of document while you were lucid, which I highly doubt is legal, he wouldn't want to put you through the trauma. What are the chances you'd be lucid when it was time for the procedure?"

Tears gathered in her mother's eyes and rolled down her cheeks. "I understand. But what about your father? He got typed, too?"

"Yes," Alex said as the room blurred.

"And he didn't match, either?"

Alex met her mother's gaze. "No, Mom, Dad wasn't a match."

"At all? You'd think a parent would be a good option."

"In most cases, but not here."

"Not here? You mean not with your father?" A frown creased her brow.

"Normally a biological parent is a half match, but Dad wasn't."

Her mother's eyes widened. "Oh, my God, are you saying he isn't Robert's father?"

Alex nodded, unable to speak through the burning in her throat. "Why? Why, Mom? I went to see Chase's aunt Rena and she told me about Charles McMann."

"Oh, my God, Alex." Her mother covered her face with her hands and her shoulders shook. "I did this. I did this to Robert. That's why Jacob wasn't a match and none of you were matches." She pulled her hands away and straightened. "I didn't know. I swear I thought he was your dad's."

Alex gave her a pointed look. "*My* dad's?"

Her mother closed her eyes. "Oh, Jesus." She shook her head. "I don't know, honey, I'm so sorry, but I don't."

Alex squeezed her eyes shut. "I'm sorry, Mom. This isn't why I came here."

Her mother wiped her eyes with a napkin from the

table. She inhaled slowly. "I've screwed everything up for all of you and I'm guessing you want to know why."

Reaching across the table, Alex squeezed her mother's hand.

"It doesn't matter. I thought before that I wanted answers. I thought that I needed to understand why you did what you did and that I wanted to know if this Charles was my father, too, but I've realized something over the past week or so. I realized it doesn't matter."

"Oh, honey, I can't tell you enough how sorry I am."

"I don't think I realized until just this moment what unconditional love is. I'm not going to deny that I'm upset and that I've been angry with you over this, but I'm looking at you now and it's killing me that this is hurting you so badly, so I guess that means I still love you, even though you screwed up royally."

Her mother shook her head. "I did. I really screwed up, and I don't know what to do to fix it."

"It's okay, Mom." Alex stood and hugged her mother. "The important thing is that Robert isn't alone in this. The silver lining is that we've all come back together to rally around him. We'll keep searching for a donor and whether we find one or not, whatever is to come, we'll meet it head-on, in one united front."

Her mother cried and hugged her. Alex blew out a breath and patted her back. This was what she'd come for. She'd needed the feeling of her mother's arms around her. Whatever life had to throw at her now, she was ready.

CHAPTER TWENTY-THREE

CHASE STARED AT THE SHINE of his shoes as Tony took a seat beside him. Had he been too industrious with the shoe polish? Tony had said to just be himself, to look nice, but not to dress in a power suit, so Chase had gone for dress slacks and a blazer, but he'd been nervous and maybe his shoes had turned out as more of a pair of power shoes to go with the power suit he hadn't worn.

"Nice shoes," Tony said as he set his briefcase on the chair beside him.

"Shit. I knew I overshined them."

Tony raised his eyebrows. "Relax. I think everyone is on your side here."

Chase nodded, but his nerves remained on edge. This wasn't done until it was done and what if they decided that he didn't make a good guardian for Kara?

Justin Harris, Kara's caseworker who had come by to do Chase's home assessment, took a seat at the table across the aisle from them. Chase nodded to him, but the man simply stared back at him, his expression unreadable. A woman in a dark suit joined him, and Chase raised an eyebrow at Tony. Why did *she* get to wear a power suit?

As though reading his mind, Tony leaned in and whispered, "You look like a dad, not a CEO."

Chase nodded imperceptibly. His friend had better be right.

They all stood as the judge entered and took her seat at

the front of the courtroom. Chase surreptitiously wiped his palms on his slacks and tried to appear fatherly, per Tony's instruction.

The judge motioned them to sit. "This is a hearing to transfer legal custody of Kara Marie Anders to Chase Mitchell Carrolton until said minor reaches age eighteen. Is Mr. Carrolton present?"

"Here, Your Honor," Chase said and stood.

The judge consulted her papers. "And we have a Mr. Tony Abilene representing you." She peered over her reading glasses as Tony stood and responded.

She smiled at the man and woman at the other table. "And I see we have Mr. Justin Harris with the Department of Family and Child Services, and Ms. Greta Young as the court-appointed Special Advocate."

They both stood and nodded their greetings and returned the judge's smile. Chase's stomach knotted as they all resumed their seats. He inhaled slowly. Kara was already planning a celebratory dinner tonight. What if something went wrong?

"I see a motion to no longer provide reunification services to the parents was filed some time ago." Again, the judge peered over her glasses. "Are either of the girl's parents here?"

Chase held his breath and glanced around the small courtroom, but it appeared no one else was present. The judge put aside her paperwork.

"Okay, let's get to this. Mr. Carrolton, would you care to tell the court why you've requested custody of Miss Kara Anders?"

Chase nodded. "Yes, Your Honor. You see, Kara is my sister, actually my stepsister, but the 'step' part had never really mattered to us. In every sense of the word, she's my sister. Her mother married my father when Kara was three years old and I was seventeen, almost eighteen."

Pausing, he glanced at Tony, and his friend nodded for him to continue, so Chase went on. "My father had some challenges. He, unfortunately, liked the bottle a little too much, and Kara's mom couldn't take that. One day she split and we never heard from her again. Well, I think Kara got birthday cards for a couple of years, but then those stopped. You see, Kara didn't have much of a family after that, except for me. My dad was great about half the time when he was sober, but mostly I took care of her. I went to a community college so I could stay at home and look after her as much as I could, but then I transferred to McKinney University and I moved to the campus and got a job as a security guard. I went home as often as was possible, but I couldn't always be there.

"And then my dad got one too many DUIs and Kara ended up in the custody of the Department of Family and Child Services. I wasn't able to support her at the time, but I swear I have always been an emotional support to her. We talked on the phone or texted almost every day." He shrugged. "And now that I'm older and I'm stable, I want to take care of my sister. I'm just sorry I wasn't able to do so sooner."

Silence descended over the room. The judge sighed as she wrote something on a paper before her. Chase glanced at Tony, but his friend's expression was unreadable. Shit. Had he babbled too much? He shouldn't have mentioned his father's drinking.

"Mr. Harris, can you speak to the department's stand on this?"

"Yes, Your Honor," Mr. Harris said as he stood. "Our findings show that Mr. Carrolton meets satisfactory stan-

dards as far as maintaining a stable home and employ-
ment. He travels a good bit for work, but considering the
minor is seventeen and the number of days he travels per
trip are limited, we feel this isn't a reason to deny custody. My interview with Miss Anders corroborates Mr.
Carrolton's statements that he has maintained a close relationship with his stepsister, demonstrating a strong at-
tachment bond toward the child."

He paused and consulted with the woman beside him
for a moment and then said, "With the prerequisite that
Mr. Carrolton attend adequate parenting classes, the department recommends placement of the minor with Mr.
Carrolton."

Relief filled Chase as the judge nodded her agreement.
"This court hereby grants custody of Kara Marie Anders
to Chase Mitchell Carrolton until the minor reaches the
age of eighteen."

As they exited, Chase turned to Tony, smiling. "I can't
believe that's over. Thank you so much for all your help."

"No problem, though I still say you don't know what
you're getting yourself into." Tony pulled his phone from
his pocket and frowned. "Sorry, man, I have to take this.
I'll see you later, okay? Go celebrate."

Celebrate. Chase felt suddenly disappointed. It wasn't
as if he didn't look forward to celebrating with Kara. She
was going to be thrilled, even though she hadn't shown a
single sign of being concerned over the outcome.

But then she'd likely jump on her phone to text all her
friends and Chase would be left on his own. Celebrating
with Kara would be great, no doubt, but celebrating with
Alex would be so much better. What good were these
wonderful moments in his life if he couldn't share them
with her? Had he been too quick to break things off with

her when everything had gone south after their return from Indiana?

He'd made a stand for Kara. Was he ready to make a stand for Alex, as well?

ALEX SIGHED AS SHE ENTERED her father's house. She'd been on an emotional roller coaster since her early-morning run. The time she'd spent with her mother had been bittersweet, but she was glad she'd told her mother the truth and they'd had that connection.

She felt lighter now that she'd let go of all that anger.

The aroma of coffee reached her, and Megan called out to her as she hit the stairs, but she replied, "I need a quick shower and then I'll be down."

She raced through her shower, marveling at how her mother had tolerated hugging her after her run. She'd pushed herself on the trail and wasn't as fresh as she'd have liked to be. She'd been determined to see her mother, though, and was glad she'd gone when she had and had caught her mother in a clear state of mind.

Those moments were becoming so rare.

Fifteen minutes later, she descended the stairs to find Megan and her father in the kitchen. Megan's bag was by the door. They both greeted her as she entered.

"I'm so glad I caught you," Alex said, slipping into the seat beside her sister. "We haven't had a chance to catch up."

"Catch up?" Megan drew back to better see her. "When do we ever catch up? The only time I ever see you is when Carly insists you come over, and then you spend the time hanging with her and avoiding me as much as possible." She shook her finger. "Don't think I haven't noticed."

"I can't deny that. But you do know why, don't you, Megan?"

Her sister's eyebrows arched. "Because I'm always harping on the family. But family *is* important, Alex." She turned to their father. "Right, Dad?"

"That's true," he said.

"Yes, it is," Alex said.

"I'm so glad you agree," Megan said.

"I wasn't ready to hear it before," Alex said.

"Honey," her father said, "I think we've all done things in the past that might have given the impression we didn't think family was important. I know you've been hurt by the actions of—" he shrugged "—well, your mother and me, the two people you should have been able to count on the most."

"I saw Mom," Alex said. "Just now. I went for a run and then I had this compelling need to see her and she was *Mom*. She knew me and wasn't living in some delusion of the past. She was clear of mind and we talked."

"Oh, my God." Megan pressed her hand to her chest. "You told her about Robert."

"I really didn't mean to, but she has a woman there who helps her keep tabs on all of our comings and goings and she knew that Robert and Dad hadn't been by." She turned to her father. "I didn't know you visited her."

He nodded and fiddled with his coffee cup. "I haven't been able to get by there lately between your brother and the hardware store."

"Well, Mom figured that out," Alex said. "She figured something was wrong because you guys hadn't been by and when she asked me about it I bawled like a baby."

"Shit, Alex," Megan said.

"It was okay, though. She was upset, but I think she had a right to know."

"She did," her father said, nodding. "She had every right to know. If it were me, I'd want to know."

"Well, it *all* came out." Alex bit her lip. "About Charles McMann and everything."

Megan stared at her, her eyes rounded. "You couldn't spare her that?"

"The one thing your mother doesn't want is to be spared anything because of her illness," her father said. "Especially if it has to do with this family."

"It just all came out," Alex repeated. "I really just wanted to go there to see her, to see if I could get over being mad at her."

"And did you?" Megan asked.

"I did," Alex said, smiling. "We hugged and we were sad, but it was okay, because she was Mom today and that was what I needed more than anything."

Her father again bobbed his head. "I'm glad for you, Alexandra."

"And Robert and I had a kind of coming to terms last night, as well," Alex continued. "And one of the things I realized was that I kind of thought all of you sucked, I'm sorry to say, but part of that was because I also sucked, and I freely admit that. I know I haven't been an active participant in this family for years and that's been my choice, but in light of all these recent revelations, I've come to look at family in a different light.

"We aren't perfect in any way and we fit Aunt Ellis's nickname, the Broken Family, way too well, but no family is perfect. The perfect family that I thought existed all those years ago was really an illusion. We were so screwed up, but we didn't realize it. So I figure if I go into this now, knowing all that, not expecting us to be perfect, then when we fall to pieces again, as we inevitably will, then it will be okay. I think I've learned that I can love you all unconditionally."

Megan squeezed her hand. "I love you, too, Alex."

Her dad smiled, but made no further response. Alex reached for his hand and her throat tightened. "Dad, I've been the hardest of all on you, and I can't tell you how very sorry I am for that. I'm still not happy with what you did, but I know I don't understand what was going on with you and Mom at the time. I know we're all human, and I'm sure I'll do something totally stupid at some point to wreck everything, but you'll all be more understanding when that happens."

"So, speaking of which," Megan said, "what happened with you and Chase? I spoke with Robert this morning and he said your on-again status is officially off-again."

"It is," Alex said, her mood slipping. "It's so ironic. He broke it off with me the other day because I turned my back on all of you."

Megan looked shocked. "But you're making amends. You just said you love us. I for one am stunned. Aren't you stunned, Dad? We should call Chase and let him know how stunned we are."

Alex shook her head. "Please don't. I'm turning over a new leaf, and part of it may be because of what I went through with Chase. But let's give it some time to make sure I've got this whole 'being a part of the family again' thing down. If things are meant to work out with Chase, they will. I don't want anyone coercing him. Is that clear?" She glanced from Megan to her father, whose eyes were misty.

"Absolutely," Megan said.

"I think I need a hug," her father said, and for the second time that morning, Alex hugged it out with one of her parents.

THE SCENT OF GRILLED SALMON filled the air as Chase pushed through his front door. He inhaled deeply as Kara stepped hesitantly toward him.

"Well," she said, "are we official?"

Smiling, he spread his arms wide. "We're official."

With a squeal, she launched herself into his arms. He laughed and swung her around, then set her down again on her feet. "I wasn't so sure it was going to happen, but it actually went pretty smoothly."

"I told you not to sweat it. How could they say no to you?"

"I'm not exactly the saint you make me out to be, you know. I had a wild streak when I was younger."

She quirked her mouth to the side. "If you're referring to your little fireworks episode, I hardly call that wild."

Surprise filled him. "How do you know about that?"

"Alex may have mentioned it at our last tutoring session. You were upstairs with Robert and she was trying to make me feel better about my episode at the police station."

He shook his head. "You two talk too much. How come she knew about this Bruce guy and I didn't?"

Kara's shoulders shifted in an easy shrug. "She asked."

"She asked. That's it? So all I have to do is ask you who you're hanging with?"

Her eyes widened. "I have no secrets, Chase. If you want to know something, just ask me. I had a thing for Bruce, but obviously, that's over. Jerk." She grinned. "Him, not you." Her eyebrows drew together. "Except, what the hell is going on with you and Alex? It's all weird between you two now. You did something stupid, didn't you?"

Frustration filled him. "Can we not talk about that? Dinner smells incredible. Let's celebrate."

She planted her small blonde self in front of him. "I'm not dishing up a thing until you tell me what's going on. I let you off easy and didn't ply you with questions when you came to get me from Roy's and you were in that shitty mood. I'd been hoping you and Alex would have hooked up on your trip. But you've been so disgustingly polite to each other. You did something to screw things up."

"It's complicated, Kara."

Her eyebrows arched. "And you think I can't comprehend complicated?"

"No, of course I don't think that. The whole thing just makes me a little sick and this is supposed to be a happy time. We're supposed to be celebrating."

"And I was hoping to have Alex here celebrating with us, so why isn't she?"

He shook his head. "Dad's right, you are trouble. Maybe I should go back and tell the judge I changed my mind."

She socked him so hard in the arm he took a step back. "Ouch. Okay, truce. I'll talk." He gestured to the kitchen, where she'd already set the table. Dishes with amazing aromas dotted the surface. "Let's sit."

She planted herself in the chair across from him, her gaze intent. "Okay, spill it. Tell me what you did so I can help you fix it."

He shook his head. "She walked out on her family. Robert was in the hospital, in a bad place and none too happy that we'd gone looking for his real father. Tensions were high, but she just gave up. She washed her hands of them."

"So you washed your hands of her."

"It sounds horrible when you put it that way."

Kara let out a heavy sigh. "It *is* horrible. You were upset with her for turning her back on her family, which

I get. It's awful. People don't appreciate each other the way they should." Her gaze pinned him. "And then you turned around and did to her exactly what you were upset with her for doing."

"It was a matter of self-preservation. She'd gotten way under my skin again. You don't know what it was like before. I don't think I'd survive that again." He stopped and inhaled deeply. "You're right. I did to her what she did to her family."

Kara nodded but didn't comment.

Chase fisted his hand. "But she's the one who started this whole 'not a *date* date' thing. I mean, it worked before the trip, but…"

"I knew it. You *did* hook up." She groaned. "And then you blew her off. That's so much worse."

His frustration increased. "I guess you're right."

"So grow some balls and tell her it was to be a *date* date or forget about it."

"You mean, kind of like make a stand. That sounds familiar."

"Make a stand, grow some balls. Tomato, tomahto."

"You like to boil it down to the obvious, don't you?"

Her ponytail swung as she shook her head. "If we'd all keep it simple, the world would be a better place."

"I wish it were simple." He rose and moved toward his bedroom, saying over his shoulder, "Enough of this depressing stuff. I'm officially your guardian and we're celebrating."

He returned a moment later and handed her a big wrapped box. "It's heavy. Be careful."

Her eyes rounded as she accepted the weight of the gift. "And iron skillet?"

Laughter rose in his throat. "Open it and see."

She made short work of the wrapping and grinned happily at him as she hefted the skillet. "You do love me."

A heartfelt smile parted his lips. "Welcome home, Kara."

"DID YOU FINISH proofing the last round of promotion material for the new exhibition?" Chase peered over the assistant curator's shoulder as she sat working at her computer.

Donna jumped and turned to him. "Don't sneak up on me like that. I finished it this morning and let Marketing know we're okay with it."

"Excellent."

"Have you gotten a date for the gala yet?" she asked.

He shrugged. He hadn't been able to confirm anything with Alex yet. He'd taken Kara to the Petersons' house the other night so Alex could tutor her, but between Robert being home and needing help and Alex working with his sister, he hadn't had a moment alone with her.

"Chase, it's this Saturday. You've waited too long. You won't find a date with it just being a few days away."

"I have one lined up," he said. "I just need to confirm it."

"Well, you'd better get on the phone. You need to give a girl some time, you know. She might need to buy a dress, get her hair or nails done."

He smiled. "I don't think any of that will be an issue."

"Are you sure?" she asked.

He frowned. "Well, okay, maybe not."

"So call her."

"I will."

Donna's smile lit her face. "You're going to have a date, Chase, a real date. I'm so proud of you."

He opened his mouth to correct her, but then he closed

it again. Part of his issue in bringing up the subject with
Alex had been that she was so bloody ready for it *not* to
be a date. He wasn't sure if his ego could take having a
friend date with her. How would he even act?

"Who is she?" Donna swiveled her chair around to
face him. "Where did you meet? Online?"

"No," he said, shaking his head. "I've known her almost all of my life."

"Oh." She pursed her lips. "So she's more of a friend."

Again, he opened his mouth, but then closed it. How
was he supposed to explain his relationship with Alex?
"It's complicated."

"Oh." Her eyebrows arched. "That actually sounds
promising. Complicated in a good kind of way?"

"Um…yes, I think…I hope. Yes." He nodded. "Complicated in a good kind of way. We've sort of been on
again…and then off again."

"I can't wait to meet her."

"Right. It should be…interesting."

She held up her wrist, showing him her watch. "You
should totally go call her now."

Shit. She was right. He bid the assistant curator goodbye and then headed for his office. His heart thudded as
he called Alex and the ringing sounded across the line.
It rang four times and he was readying a voice mail reply
in his head when she picked up.

"Chase?"

"Hey," he said and then his mind went blank. She
sounded breathless. Why was she breathless?

"Hey, what's up? Are you bringing Kara by tonight, or
should I see if I can come over there?" she asked.

"Yes, either way would work. What's better for you?
Should we just come over there?"

"Why don't you two come by here? Robert is feeling

so much better. I'd bet he'd be willing to let you come up to say hello, let the two of you have some bonding time while I work with Kara. Dad is at the store and I'm not sure, but I think he'll be back early tonight. Business has picked up and he hired another full-time person, so he can start letting Becky take off more."

"She's getting close, isn't she?" he asked.

"She is, but she's got another month and a half still to go. I imagine it will pass fairly quickly, though. I'd better hurry and plan her baby shower."

He stared at the phone. She wanted to throw her sister a baby shower? That could be a very good thing.

"What have you been doing just now, when you answered the phone? You sounded out of breath."

"I was just running."

"Running? Do you mean *running* running or like running to catch the phone running?"

"*Running* running. I think I might find a group to join. You know, like a running group. There are a couple online that look good. One is the Atlanta Running Meetup and there's also Dunwoody Running. I may check them out. I think running makes me a nicer person."

"Really?" he asked. She wanted to join a running group? Here in Atlanta? Not that that meant she wanted to stay or anything. "I think you're already pretty nice."

She chuckled softly and the sound made his pulse quicken. "So, about the gala, I know we haven't talked any more about it, but it's this Saturday and I know it isn't a lot of notice, but do you think you would still be interested in going?"

Silence hummed along the connection. He checked the display to see if the call had dropped. "Alex?"

"I'm here. Sorry, I was just thinking about whether or not I needed to stick close to home Saturday night."

"And?" He gripped his phone, surprised at how badly he wanted her to say yes.

"And, yes, I can still make it."

Happiness filled him. "That's great, Alex. I'm glad. I'll pick you up at eight. Does that work?"

"Works for me."

CHAPTER TWENTY-FOUR

"You're coming back there with me, right?" Robert stared at Alex as soft music played on an overhead speaker.

She glanced around the empty waiting room and then back at him. "Seriously? You want me to come back with you while you have a massage?"

"And energy work. Who knows what mumbo-jumbo she's going to try on me after she gets me all relaxed and vulnerable."

"You realize you're going to be naked for this massage?"

"I'll have a sheet covering me. I've had massages before. I'm cool with you being there."

She cocked her head. "What about HIPAA regulations?"

"I don't think this qualifies. Besides, I don't give a damn about that." He glanced around. "I looked at the website, but I'm not sure exactly what this Reiki thing is going to be like. I'm slightly freaked out about it. Are you going to have my back or not?"

"You're so weird, but, yes, if you want me to go with you, I will. But just for the Reiki, not the massage."

Ten minutes later a side door opened and a tiny woman in yoga pants strolled over to them. "Robert Peterson? I'm Diana Erickson. I'll be working with you today."

Robert stood and shook her offered hand. "Yes, I'm

Robert, and this is my sister Alexandra. I want her to come back with me for the Reiki, if that's cool."

Diana Erickson's eyebrows arched in surprise, but she shrugged. "That's fine. I understand you've been undergoing chemotherapy, as well as radiation therapy."

"Yes, I have, but it's been a while since I've had the chemo, though it was that high-dose crap with the stem cell transplant."

She nodded. "Why don't you come with me and we'll do the massage first. Then when you're ready for the energy work I'll come back for your sister."

Alex nodded and resumed her seat as Robert left with the tiny massage therapist. She passed the time reading a running magazine she'd brought. Eventually, the woman returned. "It's very nice you're accompanying your brother."

Alex laughed. "I'm surprised he let me. He was feeling well enough to drive himself, but I think he's a little uneasy about the Reiki."

"I understand. I'll go easy on him. From the questionnaire he filled out I see that he's had a good bit of chemo and even though it's been a while since his last treatment, the toxins stay in the body a long time. The massage will help to loosen those toxins, so we'll have to do just a little at a time so it doesn't overwhelm his system to process it all.

"Are you familiar with Reiki?" she asked.

"Only what I've read online. Our other sister actually suggested he come for this. I think she knows a little more about it."

"Reiki is good for cancer patients. It's good for everyone, but it's good for cancer patients, as well. Reiki is a smart energy and it will move to where it is most needed."

She pressed her hands together and smiled. "I will know when he has had enough."

She gestured toward the back. "Shall we?"

Alex followed her down a short hall to a dimly lit room. Robert lay on his back on a massage table with a sheet draped over him. Soft music floated through the air.

Diana Erickson showed her to a chair on one side of the room. Robert's phone sat on a table beside the chair. As Alex took her seat, Robert rolled up on the table to see her. "Monitor my phone, please, Alex. Dr. Braden is supposed to be calling with the latest donor search results."

She nodded and her mellow spirits plummeted with his request. "Wait, what am I supposed to do when he calls? I can't interrupt."

He rolled his eyes. "Step out and take the call."

Take the call. Easy for him to say, but what if the good doctor had more bad news? Then Alex would have to break it to everyone. As the massage therapist/Reiki practitioner moved to the head of the massage table, Alex settled into her chair, praying that if Dr. Braden called it would be with good news.

CHASE EXHALED SOFTLY as Kara stood on tiptoe to straighten his bowtie. He pulled on his collar, which felt way too constricting. "What did they do, starch this shirt?"

"You know, you'd look way hotter if you didn't look so nervous," Kara said.

"I *am* nervous," he said, surprised he could so readily admit it. "I feel like it's prom all over again."

"Did you take Alex to prom?"

"I asked her, but she turned me down. Twice. Once for my prom and then again for her prom."

"Why did she turn you down?"

"She said they were too pretentious, with everyone putting on airs and that the music would suck."

"So, if you didn't go to prom, how is this the same?"

"She still wanted to get dressed up and go out to dinner and then we did our own dancing later, on our own."

"Where?" she asked, her eyes taking on a dreamy glaze.

He shrugged. "In her basement, but she had it fixed up and *she* picked the music. She said she didn't need a big party with tons of people. All she needed was me."

"Wow, that is so romantic," Kara said. "Did you just melt all over the place?"

He scrunched up his face. "I'm a dude. We don't melt. We're impervious to that crap."

Her lips curved into a delighted smile. "Okay, if you say so."

"Hey, are you okay that I'm taking her and not you?"

"Sure, I don't need all that hootie-tootie gala stuff. I've got Roy here to keep me company. We're going to have an *Aliens* marathon. Can you believe he's never watched that shit?"

"That *stuff* or *those movies*. We've got to clean up your language."

"Right, right, I'm sorry. He has never seen those fine films."

"Better," he said as he looked at his watch. "Shit, I'd better get going."

Kara giggled and waved to him as he rushed out the door. Twenty minutes later he stood on Alex's front doorstep, tugging again at his collar, sweltering in the tuxedo. Why did these events call for such formal dress?

"Calm down, it's just Alex," he coached himself under his breath.

A moment later, Alex herself answered the door. She

wore a long, gold evening gown that draped off one shoulder and then simultaneously hugged and draped over every curve of her body. She wore her hair pulled back on one side, and it had a shine and a more subtle wave than it normally did. She smiled and he stood for a moment, speechless.

"Hey," she said. "You look beautiful."

He laughed at that as he swept her into a quick hug. "*I* look beautiful? You are…stunning. I don't even have words to describe what you are."

She laughed and the sound tickled up his spine. "Okay," she said. "Are you sure you didn't start drinking?"

"I'm positive. You look amazing. I mean, you always look great, but this is over-the-top. I won't be able to look at any of the other women now."

"Well, I don't want to cramp your style," she said, "especially since this isn't a *date* date."

He opened his mouth to protest, but then stopped. So she really didn't want it to be a *date* date.

"Robert emerged from his room for a change. He and Dad are watching some *Aliens* marathon on TV. Do you want to come say hello before we head out?" Her smile spread all the way to her eyes. "Robert has news to share."

"Then, yes, absolutely I want to say hello and hear some good news, especially if it concerns my good buddy Robert."

Admiring the view from the back as much as he'd admired the view from the front, Chase followed Alex into the family room with its wide-screen TV mounted on the wall. Jacob turned to them as they entered and clicked the remote to pause the movie as a huge spacecraft soared through the darkness of the universe.

He rose to shake Chase's hand, greeting him with much gusto as Robert rose, moving a little more slowly than his father, but smiling just as wide. Chase shook his friend's hand, then pulled Robert into a back-patting hug, happy to see Robert was beginning to fill out a little.

"Robert, buddy, how are you? You're looking chipper."

"Yeah, he should be," Jacob said, smiling. "Tell him, son."

Robert spread his arms. "We have a donor."

"Oh, my God." Chase pulled him into another back-slapping hug. "That's incredible. That's actually the best news ever. Is it anyone you know?"

Alex shook her head. "Just some random donor from the national donor bank."

He grinned. "We should celebrate."

"We are," Robert said, gesturing toward the coffee table. "We've got a movie marathon, popcorn made from organic corn and popped right on the cob, and we have kelp smoothies."

"Oh, yum, except what the hell is kelp?" Chase asked.

"It's good for you," Alex said, frowning.

Robert gave Chase a look of reprimand. "Alex made the smoothies."

"Awesome." Chase turned to her, smiling. "Is there more? I'd love to try one. Maybe we should stay here and celebrate. This looks like fun."

Alex looked at him incredulously. Jacob and Robert retook their seats without further comment. Chase's gaze swung from the two men back to Alex, who stared at him with her hands on her hips.

"Or not," he said. "Are you ready to go?"

A slow smile curved her lips and she nodded. "Good night, guys. Don't wait up for me."

THE CLINKING OF WINEGLASSES and champagne flutes greeted Alex as Chase pulled her past a group of older women and men, laughing and toasting to some happiness that had them all smiling. Remembering the older woman on the plane who had traveled the world, Alex longed to stop and speak with this bunch. They looked as though they'd lived full and interesting lives.

But Chase seemed to have a destination in mind as he cut through the crowd, her hand firmly gripped in his. So she kept her smile in place, nodding to various revelers as she passed in Chase's wake.

It was a shame, really, that this wasn't a *date* date. Chase had taken her breath away when she'd opened the door to find him on her front doorstep, dressed in a tuxedo and looking good enough to devour. The man certainly cleaned up nice.

Several women stopped to take a second look at him as he passed by, and even though this wasn't a *date* date, Alex tempered the surge of jealousy each time by casting the women a smug smile. Yes, regardless of whatever her relationship with Chase was, hers was the hand he was holding.

"Here," he said, at last stopping by a set of French doors that opened, not to the outside, but to another exhibit area, from the looks of the displays evident through the glass.

"There's a little more space here, so maybe we can breathe," he said, his gaze sweeping over her in a way that warmed her skin.

"You are so very gorgeous, Alex," he said. "So, tell me about this baby shower for your sister. What's going on with that? I was a little surprised to hear you were planning something."

She nodded. "I know, I'm not the best at planning that kind of thing, but Megan said she would help me. She's such a research guru. She's the one who had me take Robert to his first Reiki session."

"Reiki? That's some kind of energy work, right?"

"Exactly. I'm not sure what difference it made, but Robert liked it. He's asked me to take him back again."

"Is he not up to driving himself? He looks a little stronger, but if you need help taking him places I can maybe work an appointment or two into my schedule so you don't have to do them all. I imagine things will start getting heated up once he gets started on the new transplant."

She touched his arm, grateful for all he was always willing to do for her family. "Oh, that's so good of you to offer, Chase. I'll check with him, to see if he might like that, but honestly, and this will change, but for now he *can* drive. He just prefers for me to go with him. He's made me promise to accompany him to all of his appointments." She smiled as pride filled her. "He prefers me to Dad these days. He says I take better notes. And I always have a list of questions, which of course Megan helps me put together beforehand."

"Really? That's wonderful, Alex. It sounds like you guys are all really getting along." His gaze warmed.

Did he have any idea how his every little move and glance seemed incredibly sexy to her tonight?

"We are." She smiled again, warming as his gaze lingered on her lips. She inhaled a slow breath and faced him. "Chase—"

"There you are." A pretty blonde swooped up to Chase in a stunning red strapless gown and hooked her arm through his. Her gaze swept over Alex. "And there *you* are."

"Alexandra Peterson, this is Donna Berry. Donna is the assistant curator here. Alex is my...date." Chase raised his eyebrows, looking like the kid who'd gotten caught with his hand in the cookie jar.

"Hello, Donna, it's good to meet you." Alex shook Donna's hand. Why was the woman arm in arm with Chase, and what was with that introduction? Why did he look so guilty?

"And this is my boyfriend, Max," Donna said, letting go of Chase and grabbing a handsome guy with a cropped, military-style haircut.

"It's a pleasure to meet you, Max." Alex shook the young man's hand with much gusto.

Max smiled broadly at her. "It's a pleasure to meet you." He turned to Chase and shook his hand, as well. "So you're Chase. I've been wanting to meet you. I understand you're usually Donna's date."

"That's right," Chase said. "Donna has done me the honor for the past three years."

Alex's gaze slipped again to the young woman. Had Chase dated her? Donna leaned forward and touched her arm, saying, "It's so nice to see Chase here with a *real* date."

Surprise filled her. Had Chase thought of this as a *date* date? She cast him a questioning look, which he returned with another heated glance at her lips.

"We're going to go get something to drink," Max said. "Can we bring you anything?"

"Oh, no, thanks, I'm fine and Chase doesn't drink," Alex said, placing her hand on Chase's arm.

He shifted, tucking her arm in his. "Donna knows."

"Right," Alex said. "She was your date for three years."

"Oh, not a *date* date," Donna said as they started to move away. "Watch out, Chase. Dragon Lady, ten o'clock."

"Who's Dragon Lady?"

"Just stay put, no matter what happens," Chase said,

but his hand clamped over hers, so she couldn't have slipped her arm from his if she tried.

An older woman with bleached hair teased up into an intricate French twist pushed her way through the crowd toward them. She had an elegant look to her, one that came from money and good breeding, and by the look of her designer gown and strings of diamonds, she had plenty of the former.

Before she could say one word, Chase began the introductions. "Alex, may I introduce Mrs. Paula Dixon. Paula, this is Alexandra Peterson, my *date*."

Alex swung her gaze to Chase. Had she imagined it, or had he emphasized the word *date*? Or was that merely her cue this was the docent he wanted to avoid?

"How do you do?" the woman asked and extended her hand to Alex.

For the briefest second, Alex thought the woman expected her to kiss her beringed hand, but she dismissed the notion and shook her hand instead. "Mrs. Dixon, what a pleasure to meet you."

"Dixon was the name my dear late husband, Albert, gave me, but my maiden name is McKinney."

"Oh, like the university?" Alex asked. So Mrs. Dixon had the good breeding to go with her money.

"Yes, like the university. My great-granduncle was one of the main founders." She frowned at Chase. "Why are you two hiding way back here? I had to circle three times before I found you."

"We're not hiding," Chase said with the sweetest smile. "We have a good view of everyone from here."

Did he always paste on that sweet smile for Mrs. Dixon? She was no doubt an important benefactor of the college and possibly the museum.

"You never got back to me." The woman's gaze slipped

to Alex and then back again to Chase. "About that matter we discussed the other day."

"Do you mean the matter of the newest artifacts you showed me?"

Her gaze slid to Alex again. "Maybe we should discuss this in private. We need to talk about your schedule for next month, as well. I was thinking you should look at some of the North Carolina university museums."

"We don't need to discuss this in private. I don't have any secrets from Alex. She's a very significant other in my life and I'd like to share everything with her."

Alex glanced at Chase. Though he kept his attention on the older woman, his fingers curled around hers.

The woman frowned. "But this is business—"

"That we don't need to discuss, not here or anywhere else, private or not."

"What do you mean?"

"I mean that as far as the artifacts go, I don't feel that the provenance is sound enough to prove the authenticity of those items."

Her eyes rounded. "Why, those artifacts are from West Africa, as sure as I'm standing here."

"Mrs. Dixon, I don't doubt they are authentic. I doubt that they were obtained legally. Prior to your involvement with them, that is. I'm guessing you didn't actually find those artifacts in a crate your husband left lying around, though. Did you?"

She opened her mouth, but then frowned and shook her head.

"It was an online auction, wasn't it?"

"Yes," she said, her voice barely audible above the crowd.

"And the seller gave you such a deal you bought the items without first seeing the provenance."

"Yes, but I did see the artifacts in a good webcast. As you could see they are very authentic."

"Which does you no good if you can't prove they weren't obtained via looting, after such actions were specifically outlawed." Chase placed his hand on the woman's shoulder. "I'm so sorry, Mrs. Dixon, I'd love to help you out, but I'm afraid I can't do anything for you."

"Balls," the woman said, pink tingeing her cheeks. "I can't believe I let myself get taken like that. I was hoping to use them as a sort of investment."

"If you want any kind of financial advice, Alex here is an expert. She was responsible for helping with the budget for her last company."

Warmth filled Alex's cheeks. "I'm not an expert on investing, but I do understand budgets and finance. Granted, I also put together a budget analysis that convinced my senior team and board they needed to lay off a bunch of people, myself included. It was kind of shortsighted of me, actually. I'm not sure that falls under the 'expert' category."

"So you don't currently have a job?" Mrs. Dixon turned to her. "If Chase vouches for you, that's good enough for me. I'm in a little bit of a pickle with my finances. I admit my Albert handled all of that and I haven't carried on his good work in that department since he's been gone. I tried talking to a financial planner, but I don't trust just anyone with my money." She straightened. "With my family's money."

"Alex, can you find some time to do a little consulting with Mrs. Dixon?" Chase asked.

Alex looked from him to the woman. "I suppose I could work something out, though my schedule is going to be very difficult starting next week."

"And she's not cheap," Chase said to Mrs. Dixon.

"Of course, I'd pay her top dollar." She turned to Alex. "I will work around whatever is best for you. Chase can give you my number and you just call when you find the time. I'll make myself available."

She turned then to Chase. "Thank you so much. The news on the artifacts is disappointing, but since you've found me such a better solution I'll let that slide."

She started to leave, and then stopped. "So, we'll talk schedules on Monday."

"No, I'm sorry, that was the other part of this," Chase said. "The donor agreement was made between the university museum and Albert. He always deferred to you as far as control over the collection and we've continued—*I've* continued—to honor that, but my schedule will no longer support the amount of travel required by recent requests, so, per the legally binding document your late husband signed, control of the collection now falls to the museum."

The woman drew back and stared at Chase for one long moment, before a slow smile spread across her lips. "Oh, my, you are very attractive when you assert yourself, young man." She turned to Alex. "You hold on to this one. He looks like a keeper to me."

"Yes, ma'am," Alex said. "I plan to."

And with that, Mrs. Dixon turned and faded into the crowd.

"Do you?" Chase asked, his smile warm.

"Do I what?"

"Plan to hold on to me?"

Heat again filled Alex's cheeks. "Yes. What was all that?"

"All what?"

She gestured with her hand. "That, with Mrs. Dixon. It was almost like watching a showdown."

"Yes, that was me taking back my life." He turned and pulled her into his arms. "Good. That was the rest of my plan. To take back the rest of my life. You said yes. Yes, you plan to hold on to me."

His body was warm and firm against hers. Her heart thudded. "Yes, I plan to do that, if you'd like me to, that is."

"You're like, happy with your family these days, aren't you? Running to appointments with Robert, planning a shower for Becky with Megan. You're just one big happy family, aren't you?"

"Oh, no, we're still pretty dysfunctional. I share a bathroom with Robert and he can't remember to put the toilet seat down."

"I'll put the seat down for you."

Happiness filled her. "That's pretty big, putting the toilet seat down. That's pretty enticing stuff."

He pressed his forehead to hers. "I've got other stuff. I can be pretty damn enticing."

"Really?" she asked, pulling back to look at him.

"Really."

She held his gaze, full of heat and promise. "Show me."

Without another word, he pulled out a key and unlocked the knob of the closest French door and then opened it just far enough for them to slip through. He led her through the second exhibit room, full of artifacts from the Holocaust, then down a short hall to another room, this one smaller than the last, with a padded circular bench at the center, looking out over the inset shelves of African artifacts that circled the room.

"This exhibit is still under construction," he said as he led her to the bench. "It hasn't been opened yet to the public."

She glanced around at the shelves of items. "It looks wonderful to me."

He pulled her close. "I didn't bring you here to look at the art."

Smiling, she moved away from him and then slowly hiked up her gown before straddling the bench. "That's right. You were going to show me your stuff."

He straddled the bench, as well, facing her. He again pulled her close. "Before I show you anything. I want to get something completely clear. This *is* a *date* date."

Again, she smiled, unable to contain her joy. "I think I got that."

"Good," he said and then he kissed her.

The kiss was at first soft and gentle, but then he urged her mouth open with his and his tongue found hers, swirling and stroking with a possessiveness that left her breathless. He kissed her long and deep, stroking his hands up her back, then down, kneading her bottom in a way that had her pressing against him, trying to get closer.

He drew back and started fumbling with his bowtie. She stilled his hand. "You should know if the tie comes off, the dress will have to go."

"Well, I don't know," he said. "I really like you in that dress."

"Really?" She stood and stripped off the dress so she stood wearing nothing but a thong and her shoes. "You don't like this any better?"

"Shit, woman," he said as he continued to fumble with his tie. "Help me get out of this damn penguin suit."

Laughing softly, she moved behind him and untied the tie while he unbuttoned his shirt. In mere seconds he spun toward her, bare-chested, and captured her mouth in another searing kiss, pressing her close, her breasts rubbing against him.

He groaned softly as he kissed his way down her neck and cupped her breast. "You are so beautiful," he murmured against her skin, right before he took her nipple into his mouth.

She sank her fingers in his hair and gasped with pleasure as he suckled hard, sending waves of heat through her. She bit her lip and moaned. His breath warmed her wet skin and then he moved back up and lifted her in his arms.

His gaze was dark and serious. "Be my family, Alex. I love you. I always have. I want you to be mine, truly mine."

Her throat burned and tears pricked her eyes. "Yes, I will, Chase. I'll be your family. I'm yours, truly yours. I love you so much."

He kissed her again and laid her on the bench, covering her with his body, taking her with a love and commitment she'd always dreamed of with him. She'd come home.

* * * * *

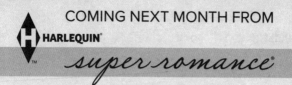

COMING NEXT MONTH FROM

HARLEQUIN®

super romance®

Available June 4, 2013

#1854 HIS UPTOWN GIRL by Liz Talley

For the first time since Hurricane Katrina, Dez Batiste is in New Orleans. But he's not here to play jazz—his music left him when the levees broke. Then he encounters Eleanor Theriot—a woman too rich for him—and suddenly his muse starts whispering in his ear again.

#1855 A TIME FOR US • *The Texas Firefighters*
by Amy Knupp

Grief is the cruelest form of guilt. Especially for Dr. Rachel Culver and her complicated feelings for her dead twin's fiancé. The attraction to Cale Jackson is wrong—she knows that—but he's also helping her cope. And the more they're together... Well, maybe they can heal each other.

#1856 THE FATHER OF HER SON
by Kathleen Pickering

Evan McKenna has never had to work this hard to get a woman to go out with him! The only guy Kelly Sullivan pays attention to is her young son. Lucky for Evan he's buddies with him and that friendship just might be the way to this single mom's heart.

#1857 ONCE A CHAMPION • *The Montana Way*
by Jeannie Watt

Matt Montoya longs to be a champion again. Not only has the tie-down roper suffered a crippling knee injury, he can't reclaim his former glory without his best rope horse. But Liv Bailey, who tutored Matt in high school, is Beckett's new owner—and she won't give him back!

#1858 A WALK DOWN THE AISLE
A Valley Ridge Wedding • by Holly Jacobs

Sophie Johnston and Colton McCray are about to say "I do" when chaos erupts. Take two people who are perfect for each other, add one shocking guest with a wild objection, mix with a pack of well-meaning friends and there's no way they can't find their way back to love!

#1859 JUST FOR TODAY... by Emmie Dark

Jess Alexander won't see him again, so what's the harm in spending one night with Sean Patterson? After all, she deserves some fun after the hurt caused by her ex. But when Sean shows up at her door offering a temporary dating deal, she can't resist his one-day-at-a-time offer....

YOU CAN FIND MORE INFORMATION ON UPCOMING HARLEQUIN® TITLES, FREE EXCERPTS AND MORE AT WWW.HARLEQUIN.COM.

HSRCNM0513

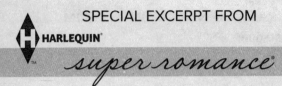
His Uptown Girl
By Liz Talley

It's time for Eleanor Theriot to get back into the
dating scene. And now a friend has dared her
to chat up the gorgeous guy who's standing
across the street! How can she resist that dare?
Read on for an exciting excerpt
of the upcoming book

She could do this. Taking a deep breath, Eleanor Theriot
stepped out of her shop onto Magazine Street. She shut the
door behind her, gave it a little tug, then slapped a hand to her
forehead and patted her pockets.

Damn, she was a good actress. Anyone watching would
definitely think she'd locked herself out.

Hopefully that included Mr. Hunky Painter Dude, whom
she intended to ask out. Like on a date.

She started toward him. The closer she got, the hotter—and
younger—the guy looked.

This was stupid. He was out of her league.

Too hot for her.

Too young for her.

She needed to abandon this whole ruse. It was dumb to

pretend to be locked out simply to talk to the man. Then he lifted his head and caught her gaze.

Oh, dear Lord. Eyes the color of smoke swept over her. That look wasn't casual or dismissive. Oddly enough, his gaze felt…profound.

Or maybe she needed to drink less coffee. She had to be imagining a connection between them.

Now that she was standing in front of him, though, she had to see this ridiculous plan through. She licked her lips, wishing she'd put on the lip gloss. Not only did she feel stupid, but her lips were bare. Eleanor the Daring was appalled by Eleanor the Unprepared who had shown up in her stead.

"Hey, I'm Dez. Can I help you?" he asked.

You can if you toss me over your shoulder, and…

She didn't say that, of course.

"I'm looking for a screw." Eleanor cringed at what she did say. *So* much worse! "I mean, a *screwdriver.*" *Please let this nightmare end.* "I'm locked out."

Turns out Dez is *not* just a random guy and there's more than attraction pulling these two together! Find out what those connections are in HIS UPTOWN GIRL by Liz Talley, available June 2013 from Harlequin® Superromance®.

REQUEST YOUR FREE BOOKS!
2 FREE NOVELS PLUS 2 FREE GIFTS!

HARLEQUIN®

super romance®

More Story...More Romance

YES! Please send me 2 FREE Harlequin® Superromance® novels and my 2 FREE gifts (gifts are worth about $10). After receiving them, if I don't wish to receive any more books, I can return the shipping statement marked "cancel." If I don't cancel, I will receive 6 brand-new novels every month and be billed just $4.94 per book in the U.S. or $5.24 per book in Canada. That's a savings of at least 14% off the cover price! It's quite a bargain! Shipping and handling is just 50¢ per book in the U.S. and 75¢ per book in Canada.* I understand that accepting the 2 free books and gifts places me under no obligation to buy anything. I can always return a shipment and cancel at any time. Even if I never buy another book, the two free books and gifts are mine to keep forever.

135/336 HDN F46N

Name	(PLEASE PRINT)	
Address		Apt. #
City	State/Prov.	Zip/Postal Code

Signature (if under 18, a parent or guardian must sign)

Mail to the **Harlequin®** Reader Service:
IN U.S.A.: P.O. Box 1867, Buffalo, NY 14240-1867
IN CANADA: P.O. Box 609, Fort Erie, Ontario L2A 5X3

**Are you a current subscriber to Harlequin Superromance books and want to receive the larger-print edition?
Call 1-800-873-8635 or visit www.ReaderService.com.**

* Terms and prices subject to change without notice. Prices do not include applicable taxes. Sales tax applicable in N.Y. Canadian residents will be charged applicable taxes. Offer not valid in Quebec. This offer is limited to one order per household. Not valid for current subscribers to Harlequin Superromance books. All orders subject to credit approval. Credit or debit balances in a customer's account(s) may be offset by any other outstanding balance owed by or to the customer. Please allow 4 to 6 weeks for delivery. Offer available while quantities last.

Your Privacy—The Harlequin® Reader Service is committed to protecting your privacy. Our Privacy Policy is available online at www.ReaderService.com or upon request from the Harlequin Reader Service.

We make a portion of our mailing list available to reputable third parties that offer products we believe may interest you. If you prefer that we not exchange your name with third parties, or if you wish to clarify or modify your communication preferences, please visit us at www.ReaderService.com/consumerchoice or write to us at Harlequin Reader Service Preference Service, P.O. Box 9062, Buffalo, NY 14269. Include your complete name and address.

HSR13R

Wild hearts are hard to tame....

Matt Montoya longs to be a champion again.
Not only has the tie-down roper suffered a
crippling knee injury, he can't reclaim his former
glory without his best rope horse. But Liv Bailey,
who tutored Matt in high school, is Beckett's new
owner—and when their tempers clash over who
stakes claim, sparks fly in more ways than one!

Enjoy the latest story in The Montana Way series!

Once a Champion
by Jeannie Watt

AVAILABLE IN JUNE

It all starts with a kiss

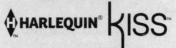